Ian McKinley

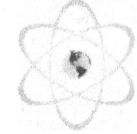

2015, TWB Press

www.twbpress.com

Extremophile
Copyright © 2015 by Ian McKinley

Edited by Terry Wright

Cover Art by Terry Wright

ISBN: 978-1-9440451-01-2

Extremophile (ik strēm' ō fīl), *n.* 1. a microbe or 'bug' that thrives under extreme conditions, e.g. of temperature or radiation; and due to slow metabolism, often very long-lived. 2. someone who is attracted to extreme lifestyles involving wild sex, designer drugs, and physical combat; life expectancy very short.

Extremophile

Day 1 ...take a walk on the wild side

As usual in greenhouse Glasgow, it was hot and extremely humid. There were only two types of weather in Glasgow these days: about to rain and raining. Dr. Bruce Roberts reckoned that it was just about to progress from the former to the latter, giving him another reason to regret his decision to walk through the Combat Zone, the CZ as the locals called it, rather than simply take the metro from the docks to his hotel.

It was about nine-thirty in the evening, he estimated. In mid-May, it should still have been fairly light outside. However, the overcast sky reflected only a faint reddish glow from some of the smarter parts of the waterlogged city that still boasted streetlights. Here, in Partick, the only lights were the signs for bars, pachinko parlors and brothels, which huddled together as if for mutual protection around the bases of the few relatively intact blocks of flats. These islands of garish neon and raucous karaoke only emphasized the deep gloom of the bombsites that separated them. *Bloody typical!* he mused. *Shortage of accommodation causes continual conflict between the original residents and environmental refugees, so what do the fuckwits do – blow each other up, which just makes water-tight digs even rarer!*

It would probably have been okay if he had just walked straight through at seven-thirty, but the temptation to stop for a beer had been too strong. A Guinness in the Glasgow Hilton would certainly cost as much as it did back home in Switzerland. This contrasted with the CZ, where drinks were cheaper by a factor of ten or more. Also, the bar entertainment was definitely a consideration. Many of the strippers and pole dancers were stunningly beautiful, reflecting the ethnic mixing pot that the West of Scotland had become.

Despite buying a number of colorful cocktails for the bar girls while they hooked their wares, it had been a very cheap evening. Indeed, one of them had not only been incredibly cute, but had made him a proposal that he had seriously considered. Only when he noticed the time on a small watch, which hung from her left nipple ring like a micro taximeter, did he decide that it was past time to make tracks.

On balance, it's probably just as well. He grinned wryly. *Although almost all the viral diseases that I might encounter in Scotland are readily curable, some of the new fungal VDs in the CZ could really fuck up my love life for a while.*

There used to be a police control point at the bottom of Byres Road, but now he discerned only a burnt-out shell in the gloom. *SFA* was scrawled on the wall in two-meter high luminous letters—whether a comment on life or a claim of responsibility for the attack, he wasn't sure.

He had left the bars behind and now saw the lights from the wall around the Uni compound and began to relax. Once through the access gate, he'd be safe in a controlled area the entire way to the Gilmore hotel complex. Unfortunately, this bit of no-man's land between the red-light district and civilization was particularly desolate, and nobody else was in sight.

A rustling noise from the ruins of the control point caught his attention. In Glasgow, natural sounds reflected the constant dampness: drips, splashes and squelches. The rustling noise came again. There was a sharp click, and then light flared from the doorway as a piece of paper caught fire. The flame revealed two kids, one still chewing whatever the burning paper bag had previously contained. Without breaking step, Bruce continued walking as if he had noticed nothing out of the ordinary. The burning paper was thrown into the back of the ruined building, landing with a hiss as the flames expired. Now the kids were only grey shapes against a black background.

"Hey, Jim, got any Blues?" The voice was hoarse, probably due to the detergents, polishes and cosmetics that had been drunk or inhaled in the search for nirvana. Despite this, the kid sounded only to be in his early teens.

"Old boring farts don't do Blues," the other shadow contributed in a throaty stage whisper. "Let's just roll the fucker."

Why fucking now? Why fucking here? Even more to the point, why fucking me?

Bruce crossed the street, turned his back to the wall of a long-abandoned tenement block and, still trying to betray no external sign of concern, chose his spot to make a stand. He kicked a space clear of the largest pieces of sodden rubbish that cluttered the pavement.

The two shadows emerged from the doorway and took on more substance as they stalked across the potholed street. Although it was too dim to make out their features, the yobs were typical street shit: thin with spiked hair and dressed in ragged shorts, stained vests and heavy boots. The taller of the two pulled something from his belly-bag while the other detached a chain that he wore like a belt around his shorts.

"Ho, you, cunt-features," called the ned with the chain. "Drop the fuckin' jaekit and the shorts and we'll no bother carvin' yeh." Even his wrecked voice couldn't hide the insincerity of this offer.

This pair of psychopaths would pulp their baby sisters for the sheer fun of it. Drop my shorts here and I'd well deserve the serious buggering that I would certainly get. Before, or while, they sliced me up.

He stood still. Sweat ran down his face, trickled down his back, and pooled under his armpits. Chains were bad enough, but please don't let this other fucker be carrying a malky. The cutthroat razors that had always been popular with Weegie muggers scared him shitless. Something to do with not feeling the cut—just the rush of blood and the slack feeling as part of his anatomy was sliced off.

Life's too short to worry about the cost. It's time to even up the odds with some chemical help. He carefully extracted a tab of SLOWDOWN from the pouch under his left jacket lapel and slipped the pill into his mouth.

A sharp click and then the taller thug lunged at Bruce with a long knife.

Not much chance here to surrender quietly.

He didn't like knives either, but at least the stabbing and slashing moves made it clear where the weapon was going. The SLOWDOWN kicked in, making the psycho's jab appear slow, as if the air had turned to treacle.

I may be an old fart... He grinned. *...but I am definitely not boring. These poor bastards are just about to find out what state-of-the-art designer drugs are all about.*

He swept the blade aside, took his assailant's wrist in his left hand and punched him hard in the groin with his right. As Bruce moved under the punk's lifted arm, his high-pitched scream became even higher when the twisting wristlock brought the would-be mugger to his toes. Continuing to spin, he swung the frantically struggling punk round to use as a shield against the whistling chain.

So far, everything felt like a standard workout in the dojo, but a smooth tatami mat was a world away from the slimy morass of a Glasgow CZ street. As he turned, his foot slipped on something unknown and probably unmentionable. He dropped heavily to one knee and heard a wet smacking noise before the screams from his captive cut-off with a choking gurgle.

Regardless of the fact that his buddy was in the way, the chain-wielding nutcase had let loose, and it was a very long chain. The knife fighter fell to his knees, the chain looped once round his shoulders and several times round his neck. Before the chain could be worked free, Bruce lunged over the struggling figure and head-butted his other attacker in the stomach while pulling at the back of the kid's knees. He fell heavily onto his arse with a grunt of pain. Giving his opponent no chance to recover, Bruce dropped on top of him, grabbed his ears and smashed his skull repeatedly off the wet macadam.

SLOWDOWN was widely advertised to be at the cutting edge of combat pharmaceuticals. It not only sped up reflexes to the point that attacks appeared to come in slow motion, but also enhanced all other senses. If not for this, he couldn't have heard the intake of breath behind him, which caused him to flatten himself heavily on top of his luckless assailant. The incoming kick was close enough to his head to brush the ends of his closely cropped hair. Rolling forward under the kicking leg, which seemed to be moving fast even in slowtime, he pistoned both feet into the crotch of his new attacker. As the small body flew into the air, with a scream indicating more rage than pain, Bruce shoulder-flipped himself onto his feet.

In the faint, ruddy light, he could make out little detail of the compact form crouched before him. As it feinted to the left and then let loose with a back-roundhouse kick that arched towards his head, he countered with a low sweep that should have taken out the figure's supporting leg. Despite his chemically enhanced reactions, he was not even close to making contact. In a move reminiscent of the levitation practiced by top ballet dancers, the attacking kick had transmogrified into a floating aerial twist that touched down as lightly and silently as a feather. Whether due to an enhancement of some chemical or biophysical sort—or just plain natural ability—it was evident that he was completely outmatched in terms of nitty-gritty street-fighting skill.

Without conscious thought, he instinctively threw himself at the crouched form, arms spread wide. This unconventional move clearly confused his aggressor, and as the body started a backwards flip, Bruce's hand caught hold of an ankle. While rolling over his shoulder and onto his feet, he grabbed a small bare foot with his other hand and twisted hard.

Extremophile

A scream, definitely of pain this time, quickly cut off as Bruce swung round, which lifted his attacker clear of the ground. The flailing body, which couldn't have weighed more than half his hundred kilos, accelerated through the air before smashing hard against a wall. He pulled the leg between his calves, twisted round to establish a lock on the vulnerable knee and dropped heavily on top of the squirming body. Reaching forward to grab the spiked hair, he became suddenly aware that he was lying on a slim girl who appeared to be wearing nothing other than a leather bodice.

Taking advantage of his momentary distraction, the girl arched her back and managed to smash her head against his chest, painfully bumping his chin on the return movement.

Chivalry is all very well, but there's a time and a place for everything. I was taught never to raise a hand against a woman, but I guess there are exceptions to every rule.

He dropped his weight forward, simultaneously putting full pressure on the girl's knee joint and pushing her face into a soggy pile of rubbish. The mixture of muffled screams and curses quickly turned to choking noises, as her nose and mouth were forced deeper into the slimy filth. He slipped his hand round her neck, found the carotid artery, and gradually applied pressure until the writhing ceased and slumping relaxation replaced the tension in her small body.

The fight had probably lasted about thirty seconds clock-time, although his sped-up metabolism made it seem much longer. One Blue-head had suffered a minimum of a very severe concussion. Bruce had no inclination to find out what state the one with the chain round his neck was in, but he didn't seem to be breathing, which might indicate that the simple chain was not all it seemed.

He pressed on the luminous panel on the pocket of his jacket and turned over the girl's body. In the light, he could now see that she was wearing more than he thought, although the leather thong couldn't have an area of more than a few square centimeters, so he hadn't been far wrong.

Unlike the neds, the girl's features did not have the wrecked look seen on the posters warning of the consequences of substance abuse. Her bare feet showed the patterns of emplaced carbon fiber inserts and, when he looked closer, he also saw traces of armored points on her hands, knees and elbows. If she had managed to make contact with any of her attacking moves, he would have been in very bad shape. Under the layer of muck, which might have been mud but was probably dog shit, her face seemed to indicate an age in her mid-teens, although her figure indicated that she might be older. Given that she could afford combat implants, however, it was clear that physical appearance couldn't be considered a reliable indicator of her age.

Something's not kosher here.

The feeling of wrongness was palpable, but he couldn't quite pin it down. Nothing else for it, time to bite the bullet. He pulled out his wallet and selected a blue rhomboid of CLEARUP from the selection of pills in its back section. He grimaced in anticipation before placing it on his tongue, swallowing and walking quickly along the road.

He did not get more than five meters before his stomach cramped and he lost the three pints of Guinness from the CZ bar. The retching felt as if it extended from his stomach to the back of his head, dredging the deepest sources of bile from his duodenum and ripping neurons loose from his hindbrain. All the gains from a minute of slowtime were compensated by several minutes of the worst possible hangover, which lasted for at least a century of perceived time.

Wiping his mouth on the sleeve of his jacket, he looked round but saw no sign of movement from the punks on the ground, who had again become shadows. His attention was drawn to the smallest of the forms and the previous vague aura of uncertainty crystallized into the clear incongruity presented by the girl.

Lowlifes with cheap and nasty weapons were the natural denizens of this area. Odd idiots like myself, who'd been too long away from the city or had abandoned what little common sense they once possessed in the CZ bars and brothels, were the typical prey of such predators. But what the hell was a high-grade martial artist dressed like a hooker doing here? It didn't make any sense at all.

The obvious course of action was clear, get into a secure zone asap and forget about the entire episode. Nevertheless, he walked back and checked out the slim girl. She was breathing regularly, but showed no signs of coming to. Rustling noises in the gloom caused him to look around. He could make out gliding shapes in the deepest shadows: hyenas and other scavengers drawn by the noise of the fight.

The chances of this semi-naked female waking up in time to get herself together before these fuckers pounce are negligible. But, if I wake her up, there's a distinct risk that she'll kick seven shades of shit out of me, regardless of my Good Samaritan gesture.

"This is not a good idea," he said, as if speaking

aloud would stop something stupid from happening.

Completely ignoring his own good advice, however, he carefully took a patch of LIGHTSOUT derm from his wallet and slapped it against her left buttock. He then removed the drawstring from his jacket and cut it in two with the largest blade of his Swiss army knife, using the smaller piece to tie the girl's thumbs together and the larger to bind her ankles. Then, with a grunt, he heaved her over his shoulder in a fireman's hoist. After a first staggering step, he started to march steadily up Byres Road towards his hotel, which lay within the Gilmour Hill campus of Glasgow University.

The wall around the Uni compound was a stark contrast to the rubble behind him. It seemed to grow from the ground with the appearance of fine porcelain, whiter than white in the light of the high-power globe lamps that protruded from the wall at fifty-meter intervals. A flash of his ID card at the holo-reader caused the outer gate to unlock with a loud click. In the security check cubical, Bruce looked towards the retinal scanner so that he could be identified as the owner of the card.

It's very easy to steal a card, but a lot more difficult to present the appropriate retinal pattern. Not a very sophisticated system, but enough to keep the scruff out.

To Bruce's surprise, but considerable relief, the security software seemed to be unbothered by the unconscious body slumped over his shoulder. He guessed this was not an eventuality considered when the designers were training the system's neural network. The inside gate drew back and he emerged into something more like his expectation of twenty-first century civilization: clean, bright and safe. However, being Glasgow, still hot and humid.

***

The old university buildings lay off to Bruce's left. Some of them were still used by mega-rich faculties such as Technolaw and Cosmetic Engineering, but many now comprised an up-market annex to the main hotel. The hotel itself had originally been the main university library. It had a secondary security control at the entrance, but this was so subtle that he hardly noticed it. Scanning during his approach was enough to confirm his identity. As he entered, a disembodied voice with a mid-Atlantic accent informed him that his luggage had already been received and sent up to his room.

Bruce was momentarily distracted by wondering, *does the smoothness of the check-in under such strange conditions reflect only the growing automation of Hiltons or has it something to do with the amount of my time that I spend in the bloody places? It just seems unreasonably easy to wander in with an unconscious, semi-naked girl over my shoulder. Everything is certainly picked up and logged by security cameras, but what anomaly would it take before a human ever looked at the video recording?*

The lift opened as he approached and the voice enquired, "Your room, Mister Roberts?" A grunt and a nod seemed to satisfy the lift's expert system. His ears popped within the few moments between the closing and opening of the door. The muzak in the lift was some kind of carved-up sequence of antique Smiths tracks. "Just what I need," he murmured as he headed towards his room, "music to slit my wrists to."

Twenty meters along the corridor, the door of room 812 opened to a shoulder push, the disembodied Smiths following him into the room. The lights went on, the door double locked and the air conditioning switched on to full blast. In order of priority, he cancelled the music and, with a grunt of relief, threw his burden onto the king-size bed. She landed with a dull thud on a mattress set to tatami-mat hardness.

First things first. He ordered a twelve-year-old

Bowmore from the microbar, brought vidnews headlines up on the main wall in place of a somewhat surreal, sunny view of Ben Lomond, and dropped the air conditioning from arctic to merely chilly. He then stripped off his clothes, took items out of various pockets and piled them on a coffee table before chucking the sweaty garments into the refresher.

As the peaty whisky cleared the sour aftertaste of regurgitated Guinness from his mouth, the warmth in his stomach began to build up, releasing tensions that only became evident as they started to ease out. He also became aware of a throbbing pain in his left leg and a rather suspect mark on his knee.

So much for taking things easy before starting on my new contract. He grimaced. *My original plan for a quick pint in the CZ before checking in at the hotel and then hitting a couple of the clubs in Curry Valley has now gone completely out the window.*

He remembered being talked into sharing a haggis supper with the very cute hostess in the bar, greatly amused by her imagination as she described the pleasures awaiting him if he would only venture upstairs with her for an hour or two. Despite having lost his dinner along with the other contents of his stomach, he was not at all hungry. He could order something from room service, but it seemed a waste of money.

On the topic of money, he was trying to avoid thinking about the cost of the three designer drugs that he had used. He could have gotten himself into some serious mischief in Zurich's Niederdorf for a fraction of the price. Always a believer of speak softly and carry a big stick, he was not one to skimp on carrying a full range of defensive chemware. However, deep in his Scottish soul, he hoped never to have to actually pay the replacement costs of using it.

Well, I don't seem to be making things any easier for myself, picking up bloody stray ninjas. Dragging a wheeled office chair from the work desk, he settled down to more closely examine his attacker while he finished his drink. Even without setting up closer physiological interrogation, it was clear that the girl was now faking unconsciousness, despite the powerful drug that he had used. Either hypermetabolism or pharm defenses, he guessed, which could be equally probable in this case.

No doubt about it, very trim and somehow not the kind of woman to be found roaming Glasgow's CZ, despite her exotic choice of clothes. "Well then," he said aloud. "I'm just about to hit a hot, refreshing shower."

On the way to the shower he noted that the mail light was flashing. Whatever it was, it certainly could not be worth postponing a wash for, so he hit the hard-copy dump.

Under the massage jets, everything seemed very much better. After the blow-dry, laser shave/trim and an aerosol deodorant, he left the shower feeling human again. The Uni hotel was not cheap, even by Swiss standards, but at least the facilities were top of the range. Despite his technical background, it had taken years to learn to relax under even Jap or EC shower lasers, while the thought of the scanning errors that could occur with a cheap Lithuanian or Bolivian kit had often resulted in a neo-hippie look developing on some of his trips to more exotic locations.

Back in the main bedroom, the killer nymphet was still pretending to be out cold. He scowled at a heap of paper now piled under the com unit. The top sheet was clearly a job offer from a headhunting agency, so Bruce immediately realized that he had forgotten to set the filter on the hard copy dump.

Shit, there must be at least a hundred pages of output here, of which at least ninety-nine percent is certain to be garbage. The battle against spam seems to be a bloody Red Queen's race: any gain in filter technology is immediately balanced by developments that allow it to be bypassed.

He lifted the pile and threw it onto the desk on

his way towards the bar. After some hesitation, discretion got the better of valor; he replaced the tube of draft Guinness and, in its stead, slipped an alcohol-free pale ale into the flash cooler.

Twenty seconds later, he flipped the cap off the beer bottle and took a long swig while walking over to the bed. He placed the frosted glass against a rather comely buttock and noted the involuntary intake of breath with considerable satisfaction. His smile quickly vanished as he saw that the woman had almost managed to work off the cord binding her thumbs, both of which were now bruised and bleeding.

He grimaced. *Shit, that must really hurt. How can she do that without making a sound?*

He scampered over to the funbox and opened the lid.

Good Grief, this hotel really caters for all tastes. He smiled while flipping past trays of dildos, lubricants and plastic underwear until he found the ropes, chains and handcuffs. *Just the very dab for a bit of BDSM fun.*

He extracted a set of red silk cords from their compartment, wincing as a flashing display recorded that fifty ecs had been charged to his account. *Fuck, that's dear. I could have had one of the CZ bar girls for less.*

Fetching his Swiss army knife from the pile on the coffee table, he walked back to the bed.

After very carefully placing a noose round the girl's neck, he secured the ends of the cords to the rings conveniently situated on the heavy posts at either side of the headboard. During this maneuver, a pair of stunning blue eyes opened and stared directly into his.

The girl appeared completely unbothered by this little bondage number, her calm was only broken by the slightest wince of pain as he gently cut the thong binding her thumbs. Very slowly, she rolled onto her back and held her arms towards him. Without taking her eyes off his face, she cautiously sucked first one bloody thumb and then the other. As he held out his hand, she meekly allowed him to bind her wrists and secure them to the posts.

"I realize that I'm not quite the perfect host..." he double-checked the knots, "...but I wonder if maybe you'd like to tell me what the fucking hell that was all about. The idiot muggers I deserved, but what led you to have such a good go at kicking my fuckin' head in?"

"Cool it, Jim!" The girl answered in a lilting voice, which indicated Irish roots buried under a strong Glasgow accent. "There's no point makin' a big fuckin' deal about this. It was just a fuckin' contract job. Broken bones for dosh sort of thing. Absolutely nowt personal."

"Yeh, so you carry out hits of some sort. I'm hardly an expert, but wearing a bimbette kit while strolling through the CZ doesn't sound very professional to me."

"Okay, smart arse! So the entire fuckin' show was cocked up. The profile I got on you was right on the button, with the visit to a knocking-shop on your way back from the docks rated at over ninety percent. The offer from your little hoor friend, the one with the clock on her tit, was the key. Sorting you out with a bit of triple fun with her AC/DC friend should have had a ninety-five percent chance of success. I was the friend, which would've allowed us to sort things out in the comfort of the upstairs bedroom. Then you fuckin' upped and took off. What was that all about, by the way? Anyhow, I was following you when the geeks decided to have a go at you. The chance to make up for the miss was just too good to pass up. Christ, but you are one truly jammy bastard."

Am I really so predictable? I could imagine someone being able to hack my travel plans, but where the fuck are these percentages coming from? It's true, I'd been extremely close to taking up that hooker's offer. Then the feeling of incongruity surfaced again. *If the girl's straight, someone's gone to a lot of effort and expense to take me out. Why?*

The woman was silently staring at him, expecting a response.

"This is all very flattering, but there's no way that anybody's going to pay the kind of serious cash that you're talking about just to have you give me a kicking."

"Well then, Bruce-son, you'd better just wake up and smell the fuckin' Starbucks."

The familiar way she dropped in his name shook him to his core, making the entire story somehow more believable. He drank another mouthful of his alcohol-free and worried about the implications of the intimate knowledge she had about his behavior patterns.

"Okay, somebody's certainly done their homework on me. So who the fuck are you and what the hell am I going to do with you now?"

"You can call me Engel for a start—"

"Engel...that's Angel in German," he interrupted with a grin. "Cute in a kind of Hello Kittyish way."

"Short for Totesengel, fuckhead," she growled.

"Angel of Death, so not quite as cute then."

"Will you just shut the fuck up and listen? As

you must have worked out by now, I'm just a freelance. Look, mate, I don't have anything against you personally. I fucked up, so you're off the hook, and I can forget about the contract. I was just doing a job but, right enough, trying to take you down is hardly friendly. I do really appreciate that you brought me here rather than leave me to be shagged to bits on the street. But come on, I've provided some information that's got to be very valuable to you. You could decide to fuck me over in revenge, but we're not in the CZ now. The hotels here are pretty accommodating of their clients' peccadilloes, but you'll end up in deep shit if you try to get all mega sado on me. I'm not one of the great fuckin' unwashed out there in Partick. I'm a fuckin' registered citizen, I'll have you know."

"There's certainly a rather fine line here. I could give you a seriously good shagging and nobody'd give a flying fuck. As long as you're not significantly damaged, someone in your line of mischief would do yourself more harm than good by making a fuss."

"We could surely come to some sort of agreement on that," Engel murmured, looking straight into his eyes. "You could, for example, get a quick in-out as compensation for your troubles and then I could fuck off." She slowly ground her pelvis and her voice deepened. "What about it, Big Boy?"

Just then he became conscious of the fact that, since his shower, he had been wandering about buck-naked. Although not in the least body shy, the throbbing sensation of a growing erection made his situation particularly noticeable.

"That certainly sounds like the best offer that I've had all night," he replied, thoughtfully. "I'd want to take a few precautions, all the same."

After Engel's nod, Bruce set about tying her ankles to the rings on the posts at either side of the footboard. After cutting the thong that bound them together, he pulled her legs wide apart and secured the silk cords tightly to the posts. Going over to the luggage rack where his baggage had been stacked, he pulled a small black pouch out of a side pocket of his massive kit bag and held it out of Engel's sight when he returned to the bed.

Sitting on the side of the bed, he carefully checked the silk ties binding her ankles and wrists. He thought that those should do on their own, so he slackened the noose around her neck. "Don't want you strangling yourself in the height of your passion," he explained.

Her leather bodice was fastened by a series of six straps with quick-release buckles. As each button was pressed, the belts snapped open as if they had been under considerable tension. Releasing the last strap was sufficient for the front of the bodice to jump apart, revealing a pair of medium sized, but extremely well-formed breasts. Slowly, Bruce rubbed the side of his fingernail against one of the pink nipples and then started to roll it between thumb and forefinger.

He was watching Engel carefully and spotted a small smile flicker over her lips, just before she shut her eyes and started to gently rock from side to side. The beautiful breasts seemed to be out of place when the muddy face, hands and feet were considered, but such incongruity was not influencing his hormonal levels at all.

My hard-on would choke a donkey, Bruce thought proudly as he inspected his state of arousal. *I should obviously tie up young girls more regularly.*

Taking up the knife again, he carefully cut the two sides of the g-string and peeled off the postage-stamp of leather. He could not avoid an obvious intake of breath at the sight of her smooth, hairless quim. Again, out the corner of his eye, he noticed a trace of a smile on Engel's lips and a slight wrinkling of her closed eyes.

The combination of hairless mons and muddy

urchin's face reinforced the impression of youth, but the way in which she pushed against his finger as he stroked her outer labia was anything but innocent. Either she was really turned on by this sort of thing or was well lubricated in advance; he very strongly suspected the latter.

Surreptitiously, he reached into his black pouch and drew on one of his ABC gloves. While holding her lower lips apart with his right hand, he slowly thrust the gloved index finger of his left hand deep inside her.

Even through the heavily reinforced material, he could feel the trap clamp onto his finger. As he withdrew it, Engel's eyes opened, but now she looked much less amused. The device was a ring of memory plastic, which must have been set for touch-activated contraction. The evil-looking spikes lining the inner rim would have easily penetrated any normal condom, even the heavy-duty jobs which were de rigueur in the CZ.

Walking to the toilet, he noticed, without much surprise, that his once proud erection had shrunk to a fraction of its former size. *Narrowly missing putting my willy in a bear-trap certainly works like a cold shower.*

Selecting a pair of surgical scissors from his black pouch, he carefully cut off the plastic ring and, holding it in his gloved hand, peered at it closely. The inner spikes seemed to be hollow and the contraction of the ring acted to inject its contents through these needles. Drops of a white fluid coated the points. He selected a sterile needle from a pack in the cabinet and allowed capillary suction to draw one of the milky drops into it.

Throwing the glove and the plastic trap into the recycler as he passed, he strolled over to the work desk where his laptop had been placed. "Not many people have the kit to do this just lying around their bedrooms," he said aloud while he pulled the micro-analyzer out from a pocket of the shoulder bag lying next to the desk. He plugged it and the laptop into sockets on the worktop. Opening a small hatch on the top of the analyzer, he dropped the needle in and pushed the lid closed.

Using the laptop touchscreen, he quickly skimmed through a nest of windows until he found his analysis package and started the sequence running. He jumped over a full metallurgical characterization of the needle itself and focused on the trickier pharmo-chemistry of the fluid. Screening out all other options, he focused the interpretation on the likely physiological consequences of injecting a few hundred microliters of the mixture present. Even with this top-of-the-range software and the number-crunching power of the hotel network, the analysis would take a bit of time. He strolled back to the bed.

"Well, a girl has got to try," Engel said, looking markedly less cool. "It's nothing personally, just a job, you know."

"You said that before. I must say that I'd really hate to be the type that you do take exception to on a personal level. What do you do that's nastier than GBH and lacerating a bloke's dick? Anyway, I'm extremely glad that I don't seriously piss you off."

Surprisingly, this little outburst seemed to embolden Engel. "I'm just cannon fodder here, just do what the fuckin' client pays for. If you go around sticking your fuckin' prick into strange girls tied up on beds, then hell fuckin' mend you. You've dropped into deep shit that's beyond your wildest nightmares of an outbreak of diarrhea on an elephant farm."

She looked at him thoughtfully. "If you were to make it worth my time, I could help you move your fuckin' arse from under a roadtrain of grief that's bearing down on you at a great rate of knots. I'm fuckin' sure that you need me more than I fuckin' need you. Look at your fuckin' analysis of the knock-out juice, if you don't believe me."

Somehow the rough language spoken in the soft,

lilting tones seemed to make her points more strongly than any screaming tirade would have done. He meekly walked over to the laptop and threw the results of the interpretation onto the main wall screen.

Completely non-toxic. That wasn't at all what he expected. *A very strong cocktail of soporifics and suggestibility enhancers, but all top-end, biodegradable stuff. For a day or two I'd have been wandering around like a zombie. Filled with this stuff, I'd have happily taken a cheese grater to my private parts if someone ordered me to. But the drug would later self-destruct, without leaving the smallest chemical hangover. This wasn't a hit by some rich bastard that I'd managed to offend as part of my working or social life. This was state-of-the-art kidnapping. It made absolutely no sense, so Engel could well be right in her assessment of their relative need for each other.*

Following the execsumm of the analysis, the screen was now scrolling through technical detail, holograms of active substance molecular structures and such. Although not aware even that he was reading it, he murmured "pause" to freeze the screen. The exact mixture in this cocktail was registered as ENSLAVE and was produced exclusively for the use of military and paramilitary groups. It was almost certainly available on the black market, but was officially used in Europe only by specialist police units in Catalonia and army units in Scotland, Wales and Eire. Bruce looked at the nymphet tied to his bed.

Well, if that's your average squaddie, I am going to really regret buying my way out of national service. But army makes even less sense than the freelance that she claims to be. So, maybe freelance, but with a lot of resources behind her.

Turning back to the girl, he noted that she had twisted round so that she could read at least part of the screen.

"What are you going to give me now: name, rank and serial number?"

"Engel is all you're getting, mate. Even someone as fuckin' green as you should know you're completely out of your depth. If you'd be good enough to give me a drink of water first, I'll give you enough info to let you see the depth and density of the shit you are in."

He walked into the bathroom and filled a glass with water. Thinking proactively, he removed a tab of OUTCOLD *(eight hour strength)* from the open cabinet, hardly noticing the credit record of five ecs. The pill dissolved instantly in the water, leaving only a very faint hint of lemon in the air.

Back in the bedroom and cupping her head, he helped Engel drink from the glass. She finished it greedily, which was not at all a surprise considering what she had been through and the dehydrating effects of the knockout derm. "Another glass please," she murmured, but she was snoring softly by the time he returned with a refill.

Okay, what the fuck do I do now? For lack of any better idea, he started leafing through the mail sheets as he sipped the last of his pseudo-beer. He was almost halfway through the pile without finding anything relevant when one of the job offers caught his eye just as he was about to drop it into the mail recycle chute.

Multidis. Engineer / Scientist wanted for immediate placement: 6 month contract: grade 5 risks / pay / compensation: specialties - C5;E7;M5;m3;GC9: reply Swaz 8307 qscsq

03823:05:45 :: 16.00

In itself, not a very special offer although it matched his own specialty profile very well, but the palindromic mail address in Swaziland caught his attention. Calling up his notebook on the wall screen, he displayed the advertisement that he had answered to obtain his present contract.

Multidis. Engineer / Scientist wanted asap: 6 month contract: grade 5 risks / pay / compensation: specialties - C5;E7;M5-6;>m2;GC9: reply Swaz 8307 qscsq 7038

Ian Mckinley

22:04:45 :: 09.00

Very strange!

No, not even ultra-strange, truly fucking weird. What on earth could anybody in Africa want with two contractors with military security clearances who specialize in analytical work in highly contaminated nuclear sites?

Bruce dragged the leather bodice from under the sleeping girl and tossed it into the recycler. He then threw himself onto the bed, resting his head between the sleeping girl's tits. *Very, very nice!* He ordered the room system to provide a gentle background of original, unadulterated Smiths and the main wall screen to Ben Lomond by moonlight.

He slowly drifted off into a light doze, but the worry wouldn't go away.

If this was a job in Africa, why conduct the interview in Glasgow, of all bloody places? And, much more to the point, how is it linked to someone sending this Todesengel to kidnap me or, given our first encounter, beat me into a bloody pulp. I've worked in some dodgy places in my time, but maybe this contract is just too dangerous.

I could refuse it, I guess, but still have to ensure that I can defend myself long enough to do so.

Day 2 ...I wanna die before I get old

A crash of heavily sampled Stravinsky blasted Bruce from his bed like a scalded cat. Alarm bells or buzzers he could sleep through, but this was like a Belfast battlefield on a busy day. Using his carefully chosen code phrase, "Shut the fuck up!" he cancelled the wake-up call and limped towards the shower. His tit-pillow of the night hadn't reacted at all to the commotion, which might indicate that her superwoman performance of the previous evening was pharmaceutically based.

Up your performance on bottom range drugs and you get totally fucked up when they fade. Go for top range, however, and you're merely knackered, possibly sleeping for days until your body fully recovers.

His fuzzy recollection of the previous night was focused by the bright blue-black bruise on his left knee, a twinge of pain balanced by Schadenfreude as he realized that the two thugs responsible probably felt a hell of a lot worse.

That is, of course, if they are still capable of feeling anything at all! And, as for Sleeping Beauty...well, she really is a beauty, even if she's caked in shit and will probably feel as if she has been gargling it when she finally comes to.

On the positive side, the sun was almost shining. Between banks of showers, bits and pieces of various rainbows could be seen in the distance. Bruce had opted for full transparency and enjoyed the view as he showered, easing out the crick in his neck from his ergonomically-unsound, even if very pleasant, sleeping position. The panorama was great as long as he didn't get too close to the wall. Not only was it a bit vertiginous, but it also allowed a view onto the ugly sprawl of slums and ruins scattered round the Uni compound.

While he wandered aimlessly about the room, scratching his bum and dithering about whether to have breakfast in the room or to wander downstairs to the restaurant, his eye caught the strange job offer again. It still seemed bizarre, but he assumed that it would become clearer when he finally met the enigmatic Dr. Flynn, his contact in Glasgow for the contract interview. This diversion helped him to make up his mind. He ordered a large mug of black coffee and a couple of whole-corn croissants from the service terminal. While he was at it, he chose some background Hildegard of Bingen to aid digestion and called up the contract link from his notebook onto the room video system. Looking at it now from a more critical viewpoint, it was amazing how little the job spec really revealed about the work involved.

He sipped coffee that tasted of tar but, nevertheless, provided a solid caffeine kick, emphasized by an associated warning of the dangers of this stimulant in red text on the side of the mug. Skimming through the background bumf that had been provided on the job, he became aware that he was not retaining anything. Ten seconds after reading a block of text, his eyes would drift over to the bed and details of penalty clauses were submerged by questions like whether this enigmatic girl had shaved her naughty bits, used a depilatory cream, or simply had the follicles removed.

The appointment with Flynn was set for 10am in the nuclear bioengineering department. It was now eight thirty, giving him at least an hour to work out what to do with the psychopathic nymphet. *Jumping on top of her and shagging her within an inch of her life seems like an eminently good option, especially as her vaginal booby-trap had been removed*. His growing hard-on wilted quickly as he realized that, while the obvious trap was gone, this did not mean, by any stretch of the imagination, that she was defenseless. If he wanted to live dangerously, he would be much better off with a CZ hooker; messing around with this *Angel* would be suicidal.

Well, with bonking to bits out of the question, what can I do with this bloody girl? Terminal drug overdose or crippling physical damage are both logical options, but if I'd been any way logical, I'd have left her in the sodding CZ in the first place.

He moved over and sat beside his nubile captive. He forced himself to concentrate on her face, rather than the more distracting parts of her anatomy, noticing a distinct twitch of her nose as he leaned towards her. The smell of coffee seemed to achieve more than the cacophonous alarm had done.

"What the fuck do I do now?" he mumbled to himself and was immediately nailed by her stunning blue eyes.

"A cup of coffee and a glass of San Pelegrino would be a fuckin' good start," she mumbled back at him.

Bruce confirmed the order and, putting his own mug down, walked over to the delivery hatch where the coffee was already waiting. As he watched, the bottle of mineral water slid into place beside it. Ripping the cap off the bottle, he poured it into a beer glass from the rack above the minibar and turned back towards the bed with glass in one hand and mug in the other.

He almost dropped both. Engel was sitting up, neatly coiling the cords that had previously restrained her wrists. Adding insult to injury, her ankles were still tied, which for some perverse reason, made her look even more naked than she did before.

Jesus, this bloody woman knows how to make me look like a complete dork. I've got cold water splashing over one hand, hot coffee over the other, with a slowly rising erection just to add to my discomfort.

Engel was clearly amused. "Give me the coffee before you spill it over your fuckin' willy." She leant towards him to take the cup from his hand and place it on a bedside table. Without a further word, she also took the glass from him and downed the water in a single swallow, followed by a very loud burp. "Rollmops!" she murmured as some kind of an apology.

Swapping the empty glass for the coffee, she took a slow sip and smiled. "You were about to explain what the fuck you were going to do with me."

Painfully aware of his rather exposed position, Bruce thought about grabbing a dressing gown from the wardrobe but, somehow, it seemed a bit late for that. "I don't suppose you would consider fucking off and promising never to come within a hundred kay of me ever again? Even better, can you think of a good way of convincing me that I could believe such a promise?"

"Actually, I might be able to solve this little problem for us," she replied, slurping coffee noisily. "First of all, though, can I get rid of these fuckin' ropes around my ankles or do you want to continue staring into my cunt?"

He ripped his eyes back to her face and felt his ears warm.

How the fuck did this happen? I have this naked, muddy nymph tied to my bed and yet I'm the one who is embarrassed.

Aloud, he gave in. "I suppose you might as well, as I doubt that I could stop you in any case, if you really put your mind to it. Also, while you're at it, would you like to tell me how you managed to get those other bloody ropes off?"

"Professional secret." She smiled as she put the now empty cup on the table, bending double at the waist to quickly untie the last two cords. These she again coiled neatly and placed beside the others. With athletic grace she rolled off the bed and stretched on her tiptoes. Bruce was amazed that she could move at all, considering the beating she had received and the position she had lain in all night.

"Now for a shower and a pee...not necessarily in that order. Christ, but I'm bursting! If you're worried about me getting up to any mischief, you're welcome to watch." With another quirky smile, she turned and walked into the bathroom, leaving the door ajar.

Totally demoralized, Bruce headed for the wardrobe, much though he would have rather taken up Engel's offer. Thinking of his interview, he dragged some semi-formal clothes from his kitbag, choosing leather shorts and sandals and a crushed silk shirt. He did not mind a bit of formality, but there was no way that he was going to wear long trousers in this climate. He grabbed a pair of his usual tanga briefs and crammed himself into them, not easy in his present state of arousal, which was not helped by the tinkling sounds emanating from the loo. For the first time ever, he wished that his taste ran to baggy boxers.

A flush and then the sound of the shower. He topped up his cup and sat on the chair beside his selected clothes. As he worked his way through his coffee, he tried to imagine what possible option to sort this mess out Engel could have in mind. *If, of course, she really did have some kind of plan and wasn't just messing me about, looking for another chance to pounce and bring my body in for whatever bounty is on offer.*

The shower died and a few seconds later Engel drifted back, vigorously rubbing her short hair with a large bath towel. The black hair of last night was now fair with a distinct ruddy tinge.

Now, would the pubes have been a giveaway, if she had actually had any? Better not take this thought further, he decided, noting that his underwear was becoming even more uncomfortable.

"Well then, what sort of devious ninja plan do you have in mind?" he asked as Engel casually slid past him and started sorting through his kitbag, piling discarded items on the floor.

"For a start, some underwear." She slipped into a white pair of his generally tight briefs. "A bit baggy, but these'll do. They should, at least, decrease the pressure on yours."

Bruce was acutely aware of the fact that it did not at all.

Engel completed her dressing by putting on one of his best white shirts, with only about three buttons closed. The net result should have been relatively modest if Engel had done a serious job of drying herself after her shower. As it was, both shirt and knickers became completely transparent at all points of contact with her body. She now looked even more naked than before.

Christ on a bike, if this doesn't stop I'm either going to jump her bones and to hell with the consequences or I'll have to excuse myself and go into the toilet for a wank.

As if reading his mind, Engel continued. "You know, apart from the obvious priapism problem, you're really not such a bad guy. I really didn't believe your profile: very much into young girls and the usual lesbo fun package, but basically a softy. All letching and no action. Don't say anything." She blocked his apoplectic outburst. "This isn't a fuckin' slag-off, you're just abnormal in that you're not as much of a shite as most men of your type. Actually," she blocked him again, "I should really say not as much of a shite as most of the men slumming in CZ brothels. Mind you, the women are often worse."

"Okay, so I'm a fucking wimp for not taking a broken bottle to you after I took you down. Anyway, I'm not letting you get me riled up so that we come to blows while you're fully awake, as a serious kicking is just what I don't need to start my day. So, back to

the key point: just how do I get out of this mess and
rid of you pronto?" Bruce suddenly stopped in mid
flow and looked at Engel quizzically. "And, bye the
bye, what is all this *my type* shit? You're definitely not
some kind of new-morality nutter or ultra-militant
God-botherer are you? If so, you're certainly hiding it
well."

Engel's smile broadened. "I could really get to
like you, even if your boner vanishes when you get
angry. But, get a grip. Do I really look like a prude or
a religious fundamentalist? I'm clearly not a hooker."
A hard stare dared him to challenge this assertion.
"But I have worked with some of the girls before and
I know what they have to put up with. Bottom line is
I'm just a special ops contractor, a fuckin' good one I
may add. Mainly government stuff that's too subtle
for the fuckin' special forces. My specialty is pick-up,
soft and more-or-less gentle. I bring in the targets
breathing and, usually, with a full set of functioning
soft bits. The typical Rambos doing this stuff think
they have done a good job when they return enough
of the subject for unambiguous DNA identification.
What a bunch of wankers!"

For the first time, Bruce felt he was really hearing
something from the soul of this exotic woman.

"So, what do we do? I could take you in and,

with this option, at least one of your wishes will be granted. You will never see me ever again. Of course, should you survive the encounter with my clients, it's very unlikely that you will be able to remember anything about this entire fuckin' episode anyway. But don't get your hopes up." She looked straight into his eyes. "You probably also wouldn't remember how to zip up your fly and would spend the rest of your days with the mad old dossers in the Saint Enoch Centre." She referred to the half-flooded ghetto where the down-and-outs ended up when they finally reached the end of the road to nowhere. A real zoo!

"Assuming that you don't want to take up this dead cert chance to get me out of your hair, there's a possible alternative. You don't get your fuckin' neurons nuked, however, you don't get rid of me immediately either."

"Of the two options, I'm not sure that the neurons nuked isn't the lesser of the evils. Anyway, assuming that I'm open to any suggestion, I definitely need more background on what's going on. What the fuck is the whole thing about? Why would anyone want to pick me up, for fuck's sake? I'm a bloody techie, not a soddin' politico or spy or something." He couldn't help feeling that the entire situation was becoming increasingly surreal.

"Ah! Now we come to the crux of the matter. You're clearly a pawn in this entire game. And don't get your knickers in a twist." She blocked his interruption again. "I don't mean that as personal criticism. It's just that you're caught up in a very, very big game. I don't know all the details, but you're supposed to be kept away from Flynn at all costs. Whatever Flynn is up to, the good professor has been trying to get hold of a techie just like you for, at least, the last six months. You're number four that I know of and, so far, the first to make it into Glasgow, much less the Uni compound. Your hotel reservation and baggage delivery was spotted, of course, but why the fuck did you fly to Belfast and take the skimmer to Glasgow?"

Bruce said nothing, realizing that his professional interest in the constant changes to the West Coast of Scotland as a result of global warming would seem morbid to most locals. These poor sods had to live on a daily basis with the consequences of sea-level rise and frequent storm-surges, for him it was just short visits every few years.

"You really gave my clients a tough time," she continued. "I think the main heavy teams were already set up somewhere else. This pick-up was organized on very short notice. Not really my preferred modus operandi, but you know the Golden Rule..."

Funny, as she gets more into the details of what's going on, the accent gets smoother and the colorful swearing vanishes. Strange indeed.

"Say this is all kosher," he said, with the job description that puzzled him so much on the previous evening coming to mind. "So what? How does this help me get shot of you?"

"Obvious to anyone of the meanest intellectual capacity," she replied, smugly. "Nobody ever thought you had a hope in hell of getting this far. With the type of heavyweights involved, I play the game to plan, but also try to ensure that I know as much as possible about what's going on. In the greater scheme of things, I'm not a pawn, although certainly nothing more than a rook." She smiled. "It's clear to me that you've buggered up the entire system by getting into Glasgow, through the CZ and, in a matter of minutes, into contact with Flynn. Whatever the payoff is, it's got to be really fuckin' ginormous to justify this level of effort. So why not break out of the system and go for the devil we don't know?"

"What's this we, white woman? I don't see where a *we* comes into the picture at all?"

Engel stretched again on tiptoes with fingers

aimed at the ceiling. "Ain't it obvious, Bruce, we're partners. Look..." she blurred into a twisting motion and a back roundhouse kick stopped about one millimeter from his temple, "...your options are rather limited at present." Keeping her supporting leg and body almost immobile, her upper leg cocked back, blurred forward and materialized again below his nose followed by a playful tickle from her big toe. "Either I take your bleeding body in for the specified bounty or we're fuckin' partners. That's it. Your choice."

"Let's say we're fuckin' partners then." Bruce attempted, unsuccessfully, to mimic her accent. "What's all this shit about Flynn? I'm supposed to be meeting him for the first time in about..." he glanced at the corner of the screen, "...an hour."

"You certainly don't know much about our enigmatic Professor Flynn, that's obvious," Engel said with a smug smile. "In truth, though, I don't know a lot myself. In any case, the best option would be to play things by ear and see what we find out at the meeting. Talking of which, you may want to think about putting something else on, your present rig-out is a bit minimalist for a meeting with some top-level boffin."

Taking the path of least resistance, Bruce started

to put on the clothes that he had already selected. Engel limited herself to doing up a couple more buttons of the shirt and adding one of his belts that, he noted, she managed to loop twice around herself. While she had been mentally pushing him around the place, he had forgotten just how small she was. From behind, she looked a bit like a kid dressed up in her father's clothes. However, face on, she managed to look like an elegant woman in some kind of exotic designer kit, even with bare feet.

Let's just go with the flow and find out what Flynn's all about. He started getting his comm junk stuffed into his shoulder bag.

***

The nuclear bioengineering department was no more than five minutes' walk from the hotel. Nevertheless, even at this relatively early hour, the heat and humidity were enough to start trickles of sweat running the instant Bruce left the air-conditioned lobby. He vaguely remembered days from his childhood when Glasgow was cold and wet. He even remembered when, during his teens, the first major Global Warming monsoons began to hit the UK. At that time, most concern was about perturbation of the Gulf Stream leading to a polar climate for Scotland. *Some bloody chance! There're now two well-entrenched groups of experts: one predicting further warming and the other that the present weather is simply a transient on the way to a return to the original or colder conditions. Arthur C. was certainly right. For every expert there's an equal and opposite expert! The one thing they all agreed about, though, that whatever the temperature would be, it was going to be wet.*

During the daytime, there weren't a lot of students to be seen around the university. Undergraduates generally attended classes only in the very early morning and late evening sessions; this allowed time for most of them to have a full-time job to earn the dosh needed to pay the high fees charged by any of the real faculties. Ultra-rich kids did dot around the place on their way to private tutorials and cramming sessions, which should ensure that they could move into the exulted exec classes and thereby earn enough money to pay for the same sort of treatment for their own kids. *The Masons may have been wiped out, but their legacy lingered on in the UK.*

The *NB Department* had its own internal security fence and entry cubical. Bruce and Engel entered together, and she stood behind him as he presented his face to the identification screen. "Doctor Roberts plus one for Professor Flynn." Bruce almost never used his academic title, but the one realm where it did seem to have some kind of benefit was academia.

"Elevator right; floor twenty-three; right; room three," instructed the machine which, perversely enough, seemed to have been programmed with an Edith Piaf rip-off voice. Scottish rolling Rs were all very well in Glasgow, but the super-sexy French intonation seemed completely out of place. Well, at least, it seemed that getting Engel into the meeting planned for him alone was not going to be anything like as hard as he had imagined.

During the walk through the connecting corridor to the main lobby, through the lobby to the elevators and from the elevator to room three, Bruce and Engel saw only one very wasted-looking individual. He had shaved his head, pierced rings through ears, nose and upper lip, and wore a lab coat so off-white that it was almost green. *Either a post-doc or a maintenance tech,* Bruce guessed. CCTVs were, however, ubiquitous, and there was no doubt that the security here was extensive, even if not particularly obtrusive.

This was especially clear as he reached forward to knock on door three, which opened while his knuckle was only a quarter way to its goal. "Please enter and go to the meeting room to your left," the cyber-Piaf instructed.

The meeting room was smart and expensive-looking without being overly ostentatious. A U-table with five leather chairs curved round a central holo presentation cube that seemed to be completely state-of-the-art. "Please be seated. Professor Flynn will join you in a few moments," Edith continued as they entered the room.

Engel and Bruce sat on opposite sides of the table. Hardly had Bruce's buttocks touched the soft leather when Professor Flynn entered. Engel's face lit up with a Cheshire Cat grin at Bruce's reaction. The good professor was a breathtaking brunette, who was at least two meters tall and somewhere between statuesque and Rubenesque. Stunning, in any case, even if she hadn't been poured into a black-smoke tube that clothed her about as completely as a coat of paint. She did, admittedly, complete the ensemble with a dazzling white lab coat. However, as this was unbuttoned and flapped behind her, it only made the net effect more erotic, if that was possible.

"Let me introduce myself...Angela Flynn...and you must be Doctor Roberts and Miss Maiden."

Bruce was able, out the corner of his eye, to note that Engel's grin immediately vanished as she was identified by their host.

"I can't say how glad I am to meet you both. I

was beginning to think that the Network had things in the outside world sealed so tightly that nobody would ever get through."

Although she couldn't have been more than about thirty-five, Professor Flynn spoke with confidence and an air of what could only be termed *world-weariness*, which seemed more appropriate to someone very much older. "We're going to have a long chat," she continued. "Would you like a coffee or something?"

Dragging his scattered wits together, Bruce grabbed the opportunity to break into Flynn's flow. "Very nice to meet you, Professor Flynn. I think a coffee would be great." He glanced at Engel, who nodded. "Before you go further, though, maybe you could just let me know how you manage to be so well informed about my companion, who only opted to join me on this visit about half an hour ago."

"First, coffee...*for three.*" At this command, a girl immediately entered the room carrying a tray with four cups: two large black coffees for Bruce and Flynn and a cappuccino for Engel, who accepted it without comment. Bruce wasn't sure what impressed him more, Flynn's obvious intimate familiarity with their tastes or her choice of serving staff. The girl was a tall, slim blonde who could have easily been a model. The young woman, who was wearing a fully buttoned white lab coat, sat beside Engel and laid the tray with the remaining small espresso cup in front of her.

Flynn settled herself at the head of the table. "Let me introduce Doctor Drndarski, a postdoc who is working with me."

The blonde nodded at Bruce. "Please call me Eva."

Bruce faced the women around the table. *Jesus, my life is getting totally out of control. First the outlandish encounter with Engel, and now I'm in a room with what must be the three most stunning women I've seen in the last decade. Maybe it's the contrast in physical appearance that makes each seem even more dramatic than she would in isolation. Anyway, it still feels simply too good to be true.*

He dragged his attention back to Professor Flynn.

After a rather noisy slurp of coffee, she continued. "I'm not sure how much you both know, so first I should give you a bit of background."

As Flynn switched into what was clearly a lecturing mode, Bruce settled back so that he could monitor any responses on Engel's face to the unfolding story.

Angela Flynn evidently liked the sound of her

own voice, but the key points of the narrative were very clearly made. Flynn was funded by a grant from an unnamed Pharm multinational for curiosity-driven *blue-sky* research. The anomaly of someone so young managing to swing such a cushy number passed unmentioned.

In any case, her work involved some rather exotic microbiology, and she needed assistance with some external sample collection. The particular project she was working on had, serendipitously, turned out to have major commercial implications. Although classified with top security ratings, some details of the work had leaked and hence was now a focus for intensive industrial espionage activity. The NB department was now about as secure as it was possible for her sponsor to make it, which was probably pretty damn tight, Bruce guessed. The external work was, however, being blocked by some kind of opposition that she vaguely referred to as *the Network*.

Following first attempts to recruit someone suitable via the Pharm's headquarters in Basel, efforts had been moved to a production center in Africa. Despite this subterfuge, until now, the search had been characterized by a complete lack of success.

That explains Swaziland, a typical choice for

industries when lax environmental management regulations were more important than pre-existing technological infrastructure and transport distances to major markets.

Despite all measures implemented to bring someone with the desired experience to Glasgow Uni, the cards seemed to be stacked on the side of this Network in the information warfare involved. Bruce had slipped through by a series of coincidences. One key factor was living in Switzerland, which has one of the tightest internal electronic communications systems in the world to support its gigantic financial services sector. Almost as important was the fact that, although a free contractor, Bruce did not advertise his services, picking up work by personal contacts or e-recruiting. Finally, as an ex-pat native to Glasgow, his trip from Switzerland would not ring any bells in a travel monitoring system. In fact, the Network identified him only when he was in transit to the Glasgow Docklands Aeromarine Centre, which might account for their rather messy attempted pickup.

Engel scowled a little at this last comment.

In any case, not only did Bruce manage to make it to his destination, he also managed to bring his interception agent with him. Flynn's supporters had been working to subvert members of their various major opponents but had not bothered with the small independent contractors. Clearly that had been a mistake.

Taking advantage of a break while Flynn slurped the last dregs of her coffee, Engel broke in. "This is a bit more than fuckin' commercial espionage, it's a fuckin' battlefield out there. Your Network's got military right through it. Either your opposition can buy influence in some Mickey Mouse government, like fuckin' Wales, or there's a national component to your Network. Whatever you're up to has got to be more than another fuckin' cure for baldness."

He was amused to note that Engel had switched back to the rough, foul-mouthed Ninja-warrior archetype. Nonetheless, she raised a point that was also foremost on his mind.

Angela Flynn was completely unflustered by this outburst. "Yes, Maria, the stakes in this game are pretty huge."

Bruce's smirk at the revelation of Miss Maiden's actual name was returned by a glare from Engel.

"You'll surely understand, in this case, that I need to be sure of a commitment from your side before I can go into details."

Flynn looked at Bruce. "In particular, I need confirmation from Doctor Roberts that he'll accept the project. Thereafter, it's really up to him to decide if he wants your support and the level of information that you need in order to provide any services required. If you feel that you're getting in too deep for comfort you can, of course, choose to leave now."

Flynn's attention returned to Engel who immediately responded, "Me, I'm in for sure. I may not have burned my boats completely, but I certainly didn't carry out my contracted job. Doctor Roberts and I have already agreed on a partnership for this work." Engel's hard stare at Bruce dared him to contradict her.

"Well, sort of," he added. "In any case, disagreement with Miss Maiden is likely to result in blood all over your beautiful furniture."

"Your partnership is not a problem on our side." Flynn exchanged some kind of meaningful glance with Eva Drndarski. "The main thing is your confirmation of acceptance of the contract. Of course, the basics were specified in our original advertisement but the boundary conditions are a bit more complicated than was originally implied. As such, the salary would be triple that specified and a very much more valuable bonus is included."

He raised his eyebrows. *The original salary range indicated was already extremely generous, but nothing completely out of the ordinary. I guess that's why the true payment had been kept secret, though. Any job so extremely well paid would have set off alarm bells ringing everywhere, even if the Network didn't possess the very proficient information-mining operation that they clearly had on tap.*

"I'm certainly interested," he replied, "even if the risks involved also seem to be a lot more than was suggested. But you need to fill in a few more technical details. I have military security clearance, as you know, so I can commit to holding all information you supply hereafter confidential. In the event that I can't accept the contract for any reason, I'm sure that you have FORGET or some equivalent short-term memory eraser. You can give both of us the initiator now and then either the igniter or a scrubber, depending on our final decision. I'd certainly recommend that Miss Maiden here is given a full blood test to ensure no counter-pharm is present." Engel's glare should have killed him stone dead. "And I'd happily submit to the same treatment."

Angela Flynn smiled warmly at him. "How very reasonable for you to take this approach. We did, I'm afraid, rather jump the gun on this one." She looked meaningfully at the coffee cups in front of them. "The advantage of having a major Pharm guardian angel is that I have access to the very latest beta-test versions of espionage chemware. You have sampled an amnesia initiator that's active for up to ten hours. Tasteless, stable to a hundred-twenty C and, as yet, without a prophylactic. It won't go on general release until we have a counter for internal use, but the designers of this critter have been working on that for more than two years without success."

He was not especially surprised, but Engel looked extremely pissed off. *I'd have bet serious money that her body was saturated with a cocktail of blockers, which would cost a significant portion of her income to maintain. Now the entire effort had been completely sidestepped. Maybe even Engel is beginning to realize that she's playing out of her league here. Rook indeed, she's as much of a pawn as I am!*

"Okay, no problem with *us* there," Bruce answered, stressing the word *us*. "Now we can get to the root of the problem and you can tell us what your earth-shaking discovery was. I would guess something like a generic cure for cancer."

"Not so far off the mark." Flynn was lecturing again. "But I really have to start at the beginning to put the whole thing into perspective. My original specialty is extremophile microbiology, an area of considerable interest to the pharmochem industry..."

Extremophile

Again the flowing prose contained an admirable summary of the main points of Flynn's work. Extremophiles are microbes especially adapted to flourish under conditions that would be lethal to most life: very high or very low temperatures, strongly acidic or alkaline waters, high concentrations of heavy metals, high radiation fields and the like. Most syntheses of fine chemicals and pharmaceuticals — and even much production of bulk chemicals — depended on catalysis by gene-tailored microbes. Such *Frankenbugs*, as they were referred to by the gutter press, had the fantastic advantage of being able to synthesize complex products of incredibly high purity. They did, however, suffer from the limitation that all life was heir to: the tendency to evolve by random mutation or via promiscuous exchange of genetic material with any other organisms that might be encountered.

"Yes..." She paused for emphasis, looking straight into Bruce's eyes and raising an eyebrow. "Sex can be an especially difficult problem." She continued to explain that one way to limit both the extent of survival of mutants and the possibility of contamination involved carrying out production activities under very extreme environmental conditions. In the early days, work had focused on simple extremophile groups, such as hyper-thermophiles or extreme acidophiles. More recently, emphasis had moved to the more select groups adapted to combinations of such tolerances. Angela's own research focused on hyper-alkalophilic thermophiles with high resistance to both heavy metals and high radiation dose rates.

Piling one stress after another on generations of already very tough microbes weeded out all but the most robust survivors. High radiation exposures, in particular, caused high mutation rates in an environment where almost all such mutations were lethal. This was all much as expected, until one of the cultures under a particularly savage combination of abuse stopped growing. It didn't die or change in any obvious way, except that the individual cells stopped reproducing. They continued to metabolize nutrients and produce normal by-products, but stayed exactly the same size.

Rather than simply chuck the culture out and start again, as a more goal-oriented researcher would have done, Flynn focused her subsequent efforts entirely on this anomalous organism. The details of her studies were obscured by some particularly opaque jargon, but the upshot seemed to be that the bugs had adapted so well to their stressful living conditions as a result of developing an astoundingly efficient internal repair mechanism. Several generations after the original mutation, reproduction had stopped and all the genetically identical clones maintained a dynamic steady-state, remaining in prime condition except for the absence of cell division.

The absence of growth greatly limited the options for study available in the microbiologists' grimoires, but a crucial observation was that cultures of a wide range of organisms grown in contact with the static cells gradually also passed into a similar, non-reproducing state. An essential component of the transformation process must have been one or more mobile molecules that could penetrate the cell wall. Limited greatly by the small size of the production culture, Flynn set up a circulation extractor and a generic protein amplification cascade to concentrate possible transformation factors. Trial and error led to isolation of a group of prion-like proteins that, in combination, could produce the same transformation on test cultures.

The protein isolate was passing through another amplification cascade when the possible significance of the work finally dawned on Angela. The original community was now almost five weeks old despite the fact that the normal lifetime of an isolated, non-reproducing cell was in the order of days, at most. Life expectancy was a tricky thing to define for such simple mono-cellular bugs. Nevertheless, in many ways, such non-reproducing communities could be considered effectively immortal.

As often happens with such lab-based academics, rather than think further of the theoretical implications, Flynn carried out a simple experiment by injecting the protein concentrate into a couple of specially bred, short-lived fruit flies borrowed from a lab next door. Despite an expected lifetime of less than a day, the flies still seemed in perfect health one week later, when the next batch of amplified concentrate was ready.

At this point, Angela finally got round to emailing a summary of her results to date to her sponsors and preparing a protein concentrate sub-sample for detailed structural analysis. She sealed the rest of the concentrate produced in a micro-injector, in preparation for a more extensive set of animal tests, assuming her sponsors would organize the required authorizations. To keep this valuable sample safe in what was, as she freely admitted, a less than perfectly organized lab, she took it into her office and locked it in a desk drawer.

Extremophile

Security was not very tight at that time. Flynn returned to her office after dinner at about 10pm, as she usually did on Fridays in order to clear up admin and documentation. Just as she entered, she noticed a movement through the glass door leading to the lab. Luckily, the glass was semi-one-way, being completely transparent from her side but almost opaque from the lab. A tall black-clad figure was videoing all equipment and sheets of notes with a camera the size of a cigarette lighter. A computer screen, just visible at the end of a bench, flickered with cyber-graffiti, indicating that some hackware was doing its job.

Although not firing on all cylinders, which she blamed on the bottle of wine that had accompanied dinner, Angela set the dead lock on the connecting door before hitting the voice contact to security. She had only started with a whispered summary of the situation when the dark figure looked straight in her direction and pulled a gun. Obviously the line had been tapped.

Sirens went off as the figure walked quickly to the door and tried to push it open. Angela dropped behind her desk. A series of deafening shots rang out. Without thinking about it, she unlocked the desk and removed the micro-injector. As required by the strict regulations for working with genetically altered organisms, the door was pretty solid but not intended to take such punishment. The intruder had knocked a number of holes in the weakened glass with the butt of his gun and was now trying to widen them with a small gas cylinder ripped off a rack on the wall. As soon as the hole was wide enough, the dark shape started to push his way through.

Although frozen in place by fear of the gun, Angela boiled with rage at the audacity of someone trying to steal her work. Feeling in some way remote from the din of crashes and sirens, she slowly lifted the injector to her wrist, injected the full charge, and then hurled the empty machine at her attacker. Clearly taken by surprise, the masked shape attempted to duck out of the way and fell awkwardly back into the lab. At that point, two armed security guards crashed into the office. The guards were in the process of scanning the situation when a blinding flash and simultaneous explosion blasted out the remnants of the door in a sheet of flame.

Protected by the desk, Angela suffered only minor cuts and burns. The guards were less lucky, both suffering major blast injuries and burns, especially of the face and hands. The lab was totally written off and the thermite charge had reduced the intruder to charcoal. Not only was the original immortal culture gone, so too was the protein concentrate sample for analysis, which had also been lying in the lab, waiting to be sent off for characterization.

"This was all more than five years ago," Angela continued, "and since then I've been trying to recreate that culture without success. We've also been running an extensive analytical project on my blood, to search for the proteins responsible. This really is a needle in a haystack job, though. Do you have any idea of the number of distinct chemicals in your body? For security reasons, all work on this project is now concentrated in these new labs in Glasgow. Apart from Eva, however, the rest of my staff here provide only tech support and don't have any kind of detailed understanding of the project. Given our lack of progress here, I've been trying a little lateral thinking to identify alternative approaches that could cut this particular Gordian Knot."

Taking advantage of a sigh from Angela that broke the monologue, Engel quietly interjected, "Sorry for being dumb, but I still don't understand the vast importance of this work. Sure, better bugs for making pharms must be worth a bob or two, but I can't see it being enough to justify a campaign on this scale."

"I guess that I didn't emphasize the key point," Flynn responded. "My original speculation, which seemed to spark the original attack, was that any longevity factor that worked for both unicellular organisms and fruit flies might well also work in higher organisms. Since then, I've confirmed not only that this is the case, but also that the factor has a rejuvenating effect. A veritable potion of everlasting youth!" She looked a bit sheepish following the last bit of hyperbole.

Now Bruce could not hold back his curiosity. "But how could you do any further work on the extract if the lab was destroyed along with all samples? You said that you haven't been able to produce another immortal colony. Were your fruit flies in another lab?"

"No, all of the experimental work was carried out in the one laboratory. But I did have an experimental subject: myself. I injected the serum without any conscious thought. I guess it was maybe to avoid this thug getting hold of it, but probably irrational panic as I'd never been shot at before. Whatever the reason, and against any reasonable expectations, this simple procedure was sufficient to demonstrate that my original assumption was correct.

Extremophile

My name isn't really Flynn, although Angela is quite correct. You may even recognize my surname. White. In which case, you will know that I headed a large research group in Oxford before I retired about ten years ago." She spread her arms wide, showing off her large, firm breasts. "You are looking at the best preserved seventy-five-year-old that biological science can produce!"

Bruce and Engel looked into each other's eyes. He was so surprised that his jaw sagged while he tried to work through the implications of this outrageous claim. "You have got to be joking." He gasped as his eyes involuntarily returned to Angela's fine breasts. Just then he realized that he remembered a Professor White of Oxford. She was not only a Nobel laureate, but also a bit of a vid celebrity. In fact, he very vaguely recalled a v-lecture series during his degree course, in which some of the life science stuff was presented by White. That was almost twenty years ago, but, at a pinch, he could imagine Angela as a younger version of the tall microbiology professor whose upright posture made her a formidable figure, at that time set off by her grey streaked hair and wrinkled face.

"As you can imagine," Angela responded, "I have complete documentation of the rejuvenation process. This was quite sufficient for my sponsors to put me on an unlimited R&D budget and set up enhanced security to properly protect my work."

"Wait a minute, I seem to remember something about Professor White having a stroke, being in a care home somewhere," Bruce interjected.

"Yes, we think the original break-in to my lab was initiated by a competing Pharm but, despite all precautions, rumors of my work have spread more widely, and some kind of Network of Pharms and government agencies has formed a loose partnership against us. I reckoned that it would be best if White disappeared from the scene and was replaced by the young, dynamic Flynn. Our hope is that she looks much less of a threat than the original discoverer of the serum and this reduces the risk of her being targeted for further industrial espionage."

"Could you really build up a profile of Flynn that would stand up to serious investigation?" he inquired.

"We hope that we don't need to. Our staff records have the highest level of security in this organization. The key thing is that our opponents don't really know how far we've progressed and what our chances are of success. In any case, they're spending a fortune trying to spy on our work.

They've also set up a number of research teams to attempt to reproduce the original study. Fortunately for us, such a loose organization is inherently easier to infiltrate than we are, so we've a better idea of their progress than they have of ours. With the limited information they have so far on my project, they seem only to be heading up a number of very costly blind alleys."

Despite the clear advantage possessed by Flynn and her allies, five years of work with no joy was leading to concern that the original result was an irreproducible fluke. Statistics was a dangerous game to play as far as random mutations were concerned but, depending on the assumptions made, Flynn might just need eternal youth in order to have a chance of hitting again the combination of specific genetic changes required to produce another immortal culture.

"This is where you come in." She looked at Bruce expectantly.

"Your job description was specific enough that I can now guess where you're going to with this." He remembered his concerns of the previous night. "You're looking for someone with general academic training but extensive experience in toxic waste disposal and contaminated site remediation. Military-type ABC background, operational intelligence and infiltration were included as desirable extras. I suspect you might have some very special field sampling in mind."

"Very good, Doctor Roberts. I told you his CV was right on the button." The last remark she'd addressed to Eva. "Please go on."

"You were working with cultures adapted to hyperalkaline conditions and displaying high tolerance to heavy metals and radiation. I guess you'd like to have a look at some places where microbes have been living under such conditions for tens or hundreds of years."

Angela nodded.

Engel looked skeptical. "There surely can't be many places like that."

"You'd be surprised," Bruce responded. "I can think of dozens offhand. Nuclear waste dumps, atomic weapons test sites, contaminated research areas, terrorist nuke hits, an odd melted-down reactor or two..." He looked at Angela. "...is that what you were thinking of?"

"That sort of thing, but I'm really not an expert here. This is what we wanted you for. Of course, making a list of options is only a first stage. We then need to set up a sampling plan. As you may imagine, this work is rather sensitive and implementing the field work won't be a trivial job."

"Not trivial," Engel interjected. "I should fuckin' think not! You're not just proposing that we swan into some of the most restricted access areas on the planet, but you'll inevitably be facing up to a very heavy team looking to take your arse out with maximum prejudice." The last words rang in a rather convincing video-Yankee accent.

"If it was going to be easy we wouldn't need someone of Doctor Roberts' caliber." Angela leaned forward. "In fact, Miss Maiden, your own skills could certainly fit well into such a project."

Engel smiled, indicating that she had picked up on Angela's hint.

Over the next hour Bruce quizzed her on the aims of the project and the resources at their disposal. His concerns about the ambitiousness of the former were, to some extent, soothed by the sheer magnitude of the latter.

These Pharm folk don't mess about when megabucks are involved.

Normally, he had a very low opinion of the capability of large organizations to get their acts together for projects needing imagination, flexibility and dynamism, but this was certainly the exception that proved the rule.

Or maybe the driving force is elsewhere. This Flynn, or White, is a woman who seems to expect to always run things her way.

She casually dismissed Engel's question about travel restrictions by assuring them that a Pharm *diplomatic passport* would get them to ninety percent of their target locations easier than Bruce's Swiss ID. "And, if more is needed, we sponsor a lot of work at the pharmo-genetics lab in the Vatican City, and a Vatican passport will get you to most other places. Anywhere beyond the reach of that combination, you don't want to go to anyway."

Gradually, the technical details drifted into more practical aspects of the roles and responsibilities of the sampling team, should Bruce and Engel decide to take up the offer.

"As is clear with a project of this magnitude, there may be attempts made to buy you out." Engel looked ready to break in, but Angela held the floor. "I know you are professionals and would not normally jump ship, but the stakes here are extremely high."

Bruce grinned as an eyebrow raised in Engel's direction reminded her that this was what she had just done.

"The contract salaries are well above the going

rate, but there is an additional bonus of a million ecs paid tax-free to accounts of your choice on successful completion of your goal. It's true that even one million might seem like small beans compared to the potential of the product involved. So I'll personally make you an offer that will, I think, be hard to refuse. If I can get another culture established, you'll get a dose from the first batch of elixir that I produce. I can't think of a better incentive than a chance of eternal youth."

Bruce and Engel looked directly into each other's eyes. Bruce then turned to Angela. "You've made a very convincing case. I think I can speak for my partner and confirm that you've got yourself an extremophile sampling team."

"Excellent. Why don't we confirm our contract with a glass of Champagne?"

Eva was already moving towards a hatch, which opened to reveal four tall glasses coated in heavy condensation. She distributed the glasses and Angela toasted, "To long life and happiness."

"I would guess that this meeting was recorded and that no further admin is needed to confirm the contract," Bruce said.

Angela nodded in confirmation.

"I would also hazard a guess that the original

amnesiac was failsafe and that, in the absence of a destructor of some sort, it will kick in anyway. Now that we're working together, you can dose us up."

"You're dead right again, Bruce. You don't mind if I call you Bruce now, do you? In any case, I'm ahead of you yet again." Angela looked at his glass. "It's even vintage Veuve Clicquot proof."

***

At about twelve thirty the team decided to break for lunch and took the elevator to the basement, which contained a couple of restaurants and a pub. Angela led them to the pub. It was decorated in a conventional but unconvincing Irish tavern style. Without discussion, she ordered three pints of Guinness, a half pint of dry cider, three oyster platters and an NB burger. The food was actually available before the Guinness had finished settling, and they took their lunches to a booth in the far corner of the busy bar. "The oysters are really fantastic here. We have an international center for improvement of cultured shellfish and I consider these to be their *piece de resistance*. Eva, however, tends to overdose on them, so she is now limited to two portions a week. More tends to drive her hormones wild." Angela smiled at her younger colleague.

Extremophile

Over lunch, Angela remained mainly quiet and Eva took the lead in keeping small talk going. Almost incidentally, the drift of conversation showed how well her researchers had done in providing background on them both. She asked Bruce how he liked his new house in Hasliberg and how conditions for the last ski season had been there.

With the trend over the last few decades for central Europe to have hot summers and very cold winters with massive blizzards, snow could be assured in the higher Alpine resorts between late November and early May. Switzerland had the transport infrastructure to assure resort access under almost any conditions, but continuous heavy snow resulted in miserable pistes and made off-piste skiing rather dangerous. Eva seemed well informed about Bruce's interest in ski-touring but did not seem to have heard about his latest experimentation with avalanche skiing. She was very interested to hear more about this increasingly popular x-sport, but she was clearly of the opinion that anyone attempting it must be borderline certifiable.

Remembering how shit-scared he had been on the last occasion, he could not disagree with her on that. On the other hand, the adrenalin rush was like no pharmochem he had ever tried.

Eva's information on Engel was a bit sparser, but it was clearly enough to cause Miss Maiden some discomfort when asked about how climate changes had altered life in Lisdoonvarna, if she managed to spend much time in her cottage at Fanad Head, and if her sister was still teaching English in Taipei.

After this light lunch, the team returned from the normality of the social chat within the pub to the esoterica of the search for immortal bugs within the high-tech meeting room. The hubris of their final goal tended to recede from sight as they moved into a more standard work-definition mode. The central holo-unit started to build up a project hyper-plan, which Bruce peered at as it developed.

This is a map of the key steps on the way to our final goal, broken down by all the ifs, buts and maybes which need to be considered if we really want to put together a project that'll involve stepping very heavily on the toes of some extremely powerful government organizations.

Bruce was in his element. Using his laptop he could access all the essential details needed to fill in secondary, tertiary and higher hyper-plan levels. However, the critical primary stuff he had in his head.

Electronic accessibility of almost infinite volumes of data produces its own weakness. When you know where to look and you can distinguish the point one per mil of gems from the ninety-nine point nine-nine percent of total crap, the system comes into its own. Otherwise, the sheer volume of information makes the Web almost useless as a data-mining source.

A plot mapping the project goals onto possible sites was worked over a couple of times using a fairly standard MAA-AI package. This gradually reformulated their unstructured discussion into a quantitative site ranking. During these first couple of passes, Engel and Eva were generally quiet and left the technical stuff to the academics. In the third iteration, practicality came to the fore, and Engel increasingly took over Bruce's side of the discussion. Eva still said little, but it was noticeable that Angela increasingly looked to her for a small nod of support.

It was six o'clock before they could scan through a 3-D presentation of the complete sampling plan, which was color-coded to indicate optimum paths for specific boundary conditions.

You don't need a hologram to show this. The suitability of sites is inversely proportional to their accessibility. Not very surprising, really. It would, actually, be more worrying if it was easy to get into some of the places on this list.

"I guess it's now up to the client to make the final priority definition," he said to Angela. "Do you start with the very promising sites that will be a real bugger to sample, or do you go for the relatively..." he drawled the word for emphasis, "...simple sites which may not provide you with what you want but could set the opposition onto tracks that you'd rather keep them away from. Assuming that your Network isn't completely useless, your job-advert will already have given a lot of hints."

Surprisingly, Eva responded, "We have been able to keep the water pretty muddy in that regard. As far as NB is concerned, Angela has eleven individual research projects here, and all are presently looking for exotic specialists. In addition, the Pharm headquarters in Basel has a wide range of closely related work, all of which has some kind of formal link to Angela and most of which have been heading off in weird directions over the last six months. Our disinformation output is so large that there is little of what we do that is ever taken at face value. Despite their vast resources, the Network is now following so many diverse leads that it was inevitable that someone like yourself would slip through the net, sooner or later. Not that I'm trying to play down your own role, Maria," she added apologetically, in response to Engel's scowl.

"Okay, but down to nitty-gritty," Bruce

responded. "How do you want to rank this list? Why do I get the feeling that you're trying to lighten me up for some bad news?"

Angela was back on the ball. "I told you, Eva, Bruce is too sharp for this kind of game. I guess you won't be surprised that we want you to go for the most promising source, regardless of the risk involved." She looked directly into Bruce's eyes in an extremely disconcerting manner. "Building up a path that would allow the opposition to jump ahead of us is just not on, especially as some of the government organizations involved would have fewer problems getting into these sampling areas than we would. So what do we have in the top ten ranked by technical suitability?"

Bruce reconfigured the holo display. "Well, for high radiation doses, temperature and hyperalkalinity, it's hard to beat concrete components in reactors. To maximize the time aspect, you might go for some old beasts that have been run for component ageing studies or those that have been entombed for decades awaiting decommissioning. If you really want to have a microbiological zoo to start with, then the meltdowns come to the fore. Chernobyl is certainly the front-runner, but there's an even older military core meltdown in a cavern in Russia. It is quite a bit younger, but Fukushima also offers some interesting options. For lower dose rates, there are quite a few high-level waste repository options, and you might even want to consider the very long times available in high grade uranium ores."

"Oklo is a possibility," he continued, referring to the famous pre-Cambrian *natural reactor*, "but it doesn't fall into the hyperalkaline category, even if it is a good two billion years old. Weapons tests and the couple of nuclear attacks don't give enough long-term dose. All in all, I reckon that the melt-downs are your best bet, with the repositories a reasonable back-up. Not the kind of places that you breeze into with a drilling rig and get stuck-in sampling, I'm afraid. What do you think, partner?" he asked Engel.

"Not a hope in hell," she responded. "It might be more difficult getting into a bioweapons plant, but there's not a lot in it."

"I wouldn't say that it's quite as bad as that, but it would certainly need all the support that your backers can provide. How does this fit in with your expectations, Professor Flynn? Oh, sorry, Professor White."

"Call me Angela, for goodness sake. Anyway, we had already started getting together support for a repository sampling option. Believe it or not, we'd forgotten about Chernobyl and weren't aware that there was much potential at the other accidents you mentioned. I thought Fukushima was already cleaned up."

Incredible how a bit of global warming can change the viewpoint of the general public. Nowadays, inherently safe reactors are buried in the remote caverns of gigantic power parks, which produce electricity, hydrogen for transportation fuel, and desalinated water, even more critical for many regions of an overpopulated, increasingly warm world. The Chernobyl disaster is now as remote as the sinking of the Titanic and about as relevant to normal life.

"Chernobyl would be ideal in many ways. The remnants of the core were left in place and all possible void spaces filled with concrete or cement. It's not very warm thermally, although it's screaming hot from the radiation point of view. It's designated as a world scientific heritage site, so it's certainly not impossible to get into. It's more difficult to ensure that you don't go round the bend while jumping through all the admin hoops required to sample from the site. Formally, all samples taken have to be halved with the IAEA site archive and the results of all research carried out must also to be recorded with them. You can get round a lot of this red tape, but carrying out sampling on the quiet would be just about impossible. Maybe suitable samples already exist in some Uni somewhere, but if they don't appear on the IAEA records, they'd probably be from last century, so I'd guess they're unlikely to be of any use. I've set up a worm to chase such leads anyway, but don't hold your breath."

"How about unauthorized sampling," Engel asked. "Is that really out of the question?"

"Given enough dosh and the right political contacts in Vienna and Kiev, anything is possible. You wouldn't be able to just sneak into the active area with a rig one night and snaffle a load of samples, though. Hide the sampling in some kind of cover project and it'd be doable. Setting everything up would definitely take a lot of time. I'd guess six months at an absolute minimum."

"What about those others then, the other meltdowns?"

"Most have been cleaned up by now although there's a lot less known about the Russian one, which could be a good or a bad sign. It's situated in the middle of one of the last three Russian military reservations, so it's not very easy to get into either."

"And Fukushima?" Engel asked.

"That's an interesting one." Bruce noted that he

was now starting to sound as much like a lecturer as Angela. "That was the accident that really put pressure on a move towards inherently safe reactor designs. It's now largely forgotten because the clean-up was carried out so quickly and, due to acceleration of climate change impacts caused by clathrate destabilization, anti-nuclear coverage by the media died away after about a decade or so."

He caught sight of Engel rolling her eyes and decided to abbreviate technical detail as much as possible. "Anyway, three old reactors melted down in 2011, following a huge earthquake, but mainly as a result of the subsequent tsunami. The reactor control team did an incredible job under hellish conditions so that, although they had three melt-downs, most radioactivity was contained within the reactor buildings."

"But the reactors exploded, the whole area was evacuated, like Chernobyl," Angela put in, scanning through hyperlinked summaries and old 2D video clips that had opened on the holo display.

"Those were just hydrogen gas explosions, linked to venting of the reactor pressure vessels. This released some volatile radionuclides, which resulted in the immediate evacuation. Due to a combination of radioactive decay, self-cleaning and regional decontamination, evacuees were able to return within a few years. As you noted, even the Ichi-effu site was rapidly decommissioned and is now the Japanese national center for nuclear material recycling."

"Ichi-effu? What the fuck's that?" Engel asked.

"Sorry, that's the Japanese term used for Fukushima Dai-ichi. It's just equivalent to 1F. Anyway, all the old reactors are now gone."

"So what are you wittering on about? If they're gone, they're bugger-all use to us. I may not be a techie, but that's clear enough to me."

Bruce smiled at his pint-sized partner, pleased that she had inadvertently highlighted the benefit of his specific nuclear experience, which allowed him to see links otherwise obscured by the immensity of the information base available to them. "Yes, but the political pressure to demolish the damaged reactors as quickly as possible led to a rather unconventional approach being adopted. The entire RPVs...sorry, Reactor Pressure Vessels, from units one to three were removed as units and disposed of in caverns under the site, along with casks containing melt-through corium from the primary containment."

Angela used a wave of her hands to zoom in on a linked waste inventory from 1F decommissioning. "But all the waste was disposed of in the geological repository at...seems to be somewhere called Rokkasho? And I don't see anything about RPVs or corium."

"The vaults under 1F site weren't actually intended for disposal, it was just a temporary storage solution until a long-term disposal option could be developed. The thing is that there's now no incentive to do anything more with this facility. It's an expensive can of worms that nobody wants to open."

"And these caverns would be hyperalkaline and hot?"

"Both the RPVs and the corium casks are filled with a cement grout, while the caverns are backfilled with concrete and sealed to assure mechanical stability. Decommissioning was carried out while the thermal output of the corium was still significant. Prior to that, temperatures would have been significantly higher. Radioactivity will certainly be very high, especially near corium surfaces."

"Would sampling there be possible?" Engel asked.

"Just about anything is possible in Japan, but the logistics are a complete pain in the arse. Tokyo is the biggest building site on the planet, while most places outside the metropolis are rather shambolic. I've got a few good contacts at Tokai-mura though, so I could have a look at what could be done."

"Tokai? What's there?" Angela inquired as she searched for a link in the complex argumentation model.

"That's the base of the technical team supporting most waste management projects in Japan. I have a friend there who works on monitoring systems, so he'll certainly know what is happening under Ichieffu, even if the work is otherwise kept well buried."

"If that doesn't work out, what about the repositories?" Angela asked. "We had actually identified them as the most likely candidates."

"We have certainly a lot of options. There are thirteen regional repositories for high-level wastes that're presently in operation, plus a number of smaller national repositories, most of which are either decommissioned or non-operational but under active institutional control. There's some kind of IAEA safeguards supervision in all cases, but this is probably quite ropy in places like South America or South Africa that contain only reprocessing wastes and no spent fuel. A general limitation is that most repositories keep the highest activity wastes well away from any cement or concrete that would cause hyperalkaline conditions. I've set up a worm again here to look for options where suitable conditions might be found. Full hacks into the relevant repository layouts and inventories will take a bit of time, though."

"You'll notice that all that kind of data is already in the project database for a lot of repositories," Angela pointed out.

"Yes, but that's the openly available data for Europe and North America. I'm more interested in the repositories in more exotic locations. And also the data on the western sites that didn't find its way into the public domain."

Angela raised an eyebrow in a rather provocative manner, which almost broke Bruce's thread of thought. "Well," he scrabbled for the question implied, "not all the early sites were optimally selected for high-level waste disposal. In quite a few cases, a bit of remedial action was needed before, during, or after operation. Often this was played down in open publications or well buried. It is just like the Ichi-effu vaults. There'll be some kind of documentation somewhere, but you have to know where it is before you can find it. I'm sure you know all about invisibilizing data. The Pharms do it all the time."

Angela nodded with a wry smile. "Okay, it looks like we're starting to get somewhere, but we need to wait for the remaining data mining results to appear. I suggest we break here and call it a day for now. I've got some other things to attend to, so I'll leave Eva to sort you out. I'll see you for dinner tonight." With this, Angela nodded at Bruce and left the room.

***

Eva cancelled the holo display and then continued. "As you can imagine, we now need to keep you two under maximum security coverage. You'll be put up in the accommodation level of the NB building until you leave Glasgow. We're a bit restricted in terms of sleeping facilities of a suitable standard, so Angela has offered to put you up in her place. I assume that's okay with you?"

Bruce nodded. "I guess you can arrange to have my stuff brought over. Or have you done that already?" He noted the glimmer in Eva's eyes.

She smiled. "The prof thinks of everything, doesn't she? She already had a release drafted for the hotel, which was concocted from this morning's recording. Normally the hotel would need something a bit more solid but, as the NB department provided payment authorization for the original booking, there was no problem from their end. Come on. We can go up to your room and you can freshen up before dinner. As Angela said, we'd like to eat together, assuming that you don't mind."

"What about me?" Engel asked. "Have you also picked up my stuff?"

"Only anything that was lying about in Bruce's room, which would be included with his luggage," Eva answered as they walked towards the lift. "We didn't want to risk breaking into your flat in Milngavie. A range of basic stuff is in the room, however, including some clothes which should fit."

"I'm sure that they will. Your crowd seems to have done their homework."

"Top!" Eva commanded as they entered the open lift that awaited them. "Twenty-eighth floor," Edith Piaf confirmed as the door reopened a few seconds later.

The double door into Prof White's suite faced the lift directly. It opened silently at their approach and led into a very large living room that was sparsely furnished with a couple of black leather sofas and a massive glass-topped coffee table. Directly facing them was a wall of glass leading onto a terrace with a view of the old Gilmore Hill university building, now taken over by the Finance and Banking department. It was raining hard, but a certain brightness in the clouds suggested that the weather might clear up soon. To the left was an open-plan kitchen and dining room and to the right a white-painted wall displaying a couple of Escher and Dali prints, which turned into glass for about a third of its length. These windows gave a view into a well-equipped training room with a dojo area of tatami matting and a number of high-tech exercise machines along the two walls that opened out onto the terrace.

"Very, very nice," Engel commented. "They certainly look after Professor White in style."

"You are staying in there." Eva pointed to a door between *Christ of Saint John of the Cross* and *House of Stairs*. "I assume that you don't object to spending another night together," she added with a smile.

She would smile even more if she knew exactly how we had spent last night. He looked at Engel, who merely shrugged. "No problem for us," he replied cheerfully. "What time do you want to go out for dinner?"

"Actually, I was going to knock-up something for us here. Angela should be up about quarter to eight, so how about eight?"

"Brilliant! That'd give me time to work up an appetite."

Eva glanced at Engel and raised her eyebrows.

"I suppose it'd be okay to use the exercise room,"

Bruce continued quickly, much to Engel's obvious amusement.

"No probs, just go ahead. I'll actually have a little run on the treadmill before I get started with the food."

As Bruce and Engel entered the bedroom, the door slid closed behind them. An enormous bed, which was larger than an American king-size, dominated the spacious bedroom. Sliding mirrors led into a walk-in wardrobe, which seemed to contain all of Bruce's clothes from his hotel room. *Not only luggage pick-up but full valet service.* Generally he tended to live out of his bag while travelling, bothering to unpack only when staying somewhere for a week or more.

The wardrobe also contained a small but exclusive-looking set of new clothes that were obviously intended for Engel. An open door led into a bathroom with a toilet, bidet, a large bath and a shower.

"What now?" Bruce asked Engel. "Everything going to plan?"

"Well, partly. The two options were either to jump ship or just pretend to and rely on my amnesia inhibitors to give me a big info package for my previous clients. The second is probably out, I guess. I bet there's more to this amnesiac than we've been told so far. Anyway, the prof is right, nobody could compete with her offer. I think we're an extremophile sampling team."

"You'd say that anyway, as you'd assume that this room is wired for sound and vision."

"But the prof knows that we know. She also knows her offer is unbeatable in any case."

"Okay, let's go with the flow for the moment. I could certainly do with some exercise. My poor old body is beginning to stiffen up a bit after my exertions of last night."

"It seems a shame to miss out on that nice tatami next door. Do you fancy a chuck about?" Engel asked with a smile.

"Without being speeded up on the best pharms available, you'd undoubtedly kick the living shit out of me."

"No, honestly, just a gentle throw about. You're into Aiki-stuff I noticed, so all very soft." She looked straight into his eyes. "Trust me, little man-cub."

Ninja warrior dropping in Jungle Book references, what a wonderful combination. "All right, let's go do it. Just remember, I'm the techie they need for this work, so it won't make things any easier if I'm in traction. I must say, they really have thought of everything." He pointed to the gis on Engel's side of the wardrobe.

Bruce selected a heavy judo gi and started peeling off clothes. Engel passed over a similar but much smaller gi and selected a colorful pajama suit from some form of kung fu discipline. She turned towards him as she unbuttoned her shirt and replaced it with the kung-fu top. This was long enough to come to the top of her thighs. She didn't bother with the trousers.

Bruce thought about replacing his briefs with a padded jock strap but decided to take Engel at her word. As he tied the belt round his jacket, he realized that he was now committed. "Ready when you are." He sighed with a feeling of foreboding.

From the living room, they could see that Eva was already on the running machine. Looking more closely as they entered the exercise room, he noted that the machine was set at a gradient of about ten percent, but Eva was doing four-minute kilometers. *Assuming that she wasn't showing off, this was pretty serious for a little run.*

Bruce worked through some warm-up exercises while admiring the movements of Eva's buttocks, very nicely presented in tight little shorts, until Engel called to him. "That'll make you go blind! Here, something to even the odds." She tossed him a bokken – the wooden practice sword used in many Japanese martial arts.

"Why don't you attack me? Pretend you really mean it." Engel grinned.

Bruce didn't need to be asked twice. With a shout of "Ai!" used to concentrate force, he ran at Engel, cutting the bokken at her neck with all his might. He was well prepared for the twisting move that transformed his attack into a throw, covering several meters in the air before he hit the tatami mat in a break-fall that brought him back to his feet and already starting his second attack. During the next couple of minutes, he attacked at least a dozen times—in each case being thrown to a far corner of the mat.

Already beginning to tire from this frantic pace, he changed tactics and, instead of a swinging cut, charged straight towards Engel with the bokken pointed at her stomach. It looked for a second as if she had been confused by this move, but just before the point of the wooden sword touched her, her hands blurred as she pushed the blade aside and twisted under him to throw him over her back. He immediately realized that she was not giving an easy throw this time and just managed to get his feet and shoulders in position to take a slam into the mat and thus protect his kidneys. He didn't get a chance to breathe a sigh of relief before he had been forced onto his face with his right arm, still holding the bokken, locked in an excruciatingly painful position. His left hand slapped the mat frantically to acknowledge surrender, and the lock was instantly released. While he slowly got to his feet he noticed that Eva was watching them with evident amusement, even though her running pace seemed undiminished.

I need to slow this down a bit. Bruce walked over to a weapons rack, replaced the bokken, and substituted it with a wooden tanto, a kind of dagger. Without comment, he walked up to Engel and made a short stabbing move towards her chest. The move was rather slow, so that as he'd hoped, she grabbed his right wrist and moved aside, ready for a throw. Immediately, he slapped his left hand on top of hers to keep it in place while his right dropped the knife and curled over her arm to establish the wristlock. She dropped to her knees to minimize the force on her wrist, but the lock was solid. For the first time, she seemed to be caught out.

"Give up?" Bruce asked, increasing the pressure and moving her body to block a punch that looked to be aimed at his balls.

"Fuck off!" she replied succinctly through gritted

teeth while she attempted to worm her way out of the lock.

She may be small, but she's bloody tough. He slowly increased the pressure further. *That must really hurt.*

Suddenly her head snaked forward and she bit him hard on the back of his hand. Although not enough to make him let go, his grip loosened enough for Engel to pull her hand partially free. Taking advantage of the loss of the full force of the lock, she pulled him forward while she twisted her body through the air in a way that Bruce couldn't follow. The next thing he knew, he was falling backwards with Engel's thighs locked round his neck. His ears rang as they hit the mat and he grabbed the inside of her thighs as the headlock tightened like a vice. His shoulders popped as he strained with all his might to resist the pressure. Even in this situation, he was aware that his nose was only a couple of centimeters away from a sweaty g-string that was just about transparent. *What a way to die. Or, maybe, I just need a bit of lateral thinking.* He pushed his head forward and grabbed the thinly cloaked labia in front of him with his teeth.

The pressure on his head dropped off instantly. "You wouldn't fuckin' dare," Engel growled.

Bruce only nodded slightly without loosening his

teeth.

"Okay then." Engel opened her legs.

He twisted backwards when he released his very tasty grip, continuing a roll that just cleared a kick that scraped his ear. He sprang from his shoulders onto his feet just in time to twist under the slashing tanto and throw his attacker a good three meters to the furthest corner of the mat. Rather than a conventional breakfall, she twisted in mid-air and landed lightly on her feet, like one of the adolescent gymnasts who seem to come off a production line in eastern Asian countries in time for every Olympic competition.

She stopped and glared at him. "That was askin' for a good kickin'"

"Well, it serves you right. You bit me first."

Eva's laughter broke off any further exchanges. "Was that fighting or foreplay?" She giggled.

Both Bruce and Engel were forced to grin.

"Anyway, I think I'll call it a day with this kind of foreplay while my goolies are still intact," Bruce conceded. "A bit of kata and then I'm off for a shower."

He walked over to the weapons rack, selected a sheathed katana sword, and slid it through his belt. Kneeling on one corner of the mat in the seiza position, he started a series of breathing exercises to prepare himself for iaido. While his concentration focused more on his breathing and the feeling of inner calmness, he was aware of Engel in the center of the mat, twisting through a complex kata of kicks and punches. As a series of repeated high kicks in his direction revealed again the little panties that he had tasted so recently, he realized that this would indeed be a challenging training session. If he could concentrate in the presence of a distraction like that, he could concentrate anywhere.

Achieving the desired feeling of inner confidence, he started the series of exercises where the sword flashed into attack, eliminated his imaginary attackers with maximum efficiency, and was returned to its scabbard after being cleansed of equally imaginary blood.

After about twenty minutes, his mind returned to the reality of the dojo. He stood up, bowed formally to the mat, which still contained the whirling dervish clad in a yellow jacket, returned the sword to the rack, and walked to the door of the dojo. He was now aware that Eva had left and remembered that he had actually seen her go during his iaido session.

Just as he was about to leave, a foot flashed between his thighs and ended up, none too gently, against his balls.

"I'll be finished in a minute," a voice said behind him.

He looked round as the foot vanished, only to see a blurred small figure doing a series of back flip-flops towards the far corner of the room. *I guess I got off pretty lightly there. She may be small but, by Christ, she's bloody fast.* He returned to the bedroom, chucked his sweat-soaked kit into the recycler, and headed for the shower.

The shower was very large and fitted with every possible bolt-on goody. Bruce stood in the center with his eyes closed and savored a 4-pi pummeling by jets coming from every direction. He could feel a slight stinging from his hand in the soapy water. Engel's teeth had broken the skin and he now had an oval bruise that was seeping blood from several places. Maybe he should have given her more of a nip. He felt his erection begin to build up as his tongue ran over his teeth, searching for the traces of the salty taste.

"Thinking about me, are you?"

His fantasy was shattered by the voice from behind him. As he turned, a small naked body joined him in the shower and slapped him playfully on the buttocks.

"No way," he responded, more than a little flustered. "I was actually thinking about the luscious Eva. I think she's got a fancy for me."

Before he could waffle further, Engel burst into laughter. "Eva? You have got to be fuckin' joking!" Noting his puzzled look she continued. "Fuckin' men, you're all totally fuckin' blind. Eva's obviously the prof's little bed-warmer. I'm sure I could score with her, with them both for that matter, but you're certainly not quoted."

Engel playfully slapped his wilting erection and then turned her back to him. "Never mind, look at the bright side, you're now in a shower with the best looking woman on the premises. All you have to do is give me a good back-rub and I'll forgive you for biting my pussy. If you're good, then you never know, you might even get the chance to nibble it again under more comfortable conditions."

With this reference to his original fantasy, his erection started to recover. Engel giggled as it touched her buttocks when he began to message her neck.

Engel was so small that it was easier for him to massage her lower back from a kneeling position. It also minimized his embarrassment from continually poking her with a prick that stuck out like a poker.

She growled quietly as he squeezed her small, tight buttocks, which made the hair on the back of his neck stand up.

After a couple of very pleasant minutes he stood up. *If I keep this up I'm going to explode.* "How's that, partner? Am I forgiven?"

"Not at all bad. I think you may actually have your uses. Let's see if I can sort you out a bit so that you're presentable for dinner." With that she moved up to him, took his prick in one hand and his balls in the other and started to squeeze. As she did this, her blue eyes looked up straight into his. Without looking away, she began to lick his left nipple and rub her teeth against it.

My God, she looks about twelve. But what an extremely experienced twelve-year-old! He closed his eyes and arched his neck backwards. Almost instantaneously, it seemed, he was racked by paroxysms of pleasure coupled with a feeling of long-awaited release. He looked down to see the small hand that was now covered with spunk, but was continuing to caress his dick and he shot another wad that reached her breasts. "Jesus Fuckin' Christ!" he muttered under his breath.

"I take it that was a note of approval rather than a prayer." Engel grinned, washing sticky white fluid from their bodies in a completely unselfconscious manner.

"One very serious shortcoming..." Bruce sighed, "...just didn't last long enough." He bent and kissed her gently on the forehead. "We'll maybe have to cut down on the foreplay next time." He grinned as she nipped his nipple with her teeth.

"I should really have a shave." He rubbed his chin. "Don't want to be scraping skin off your inner thigh."

"No probs, we can shave together." She smiled mischievously and rapidly hit a couple of controls on a panel that would not have looked out of place on the Starship Enterprise. "Confirm!" she acknowledged and Bruce automatically froze as the lasers scanned his face and then vaporized stubble with nanometer accuracy. Engel displayed no such technofear, confidently moving about to expose her lower parts and armpits to the scan.

I didn't know the shaving lasers would do that. He tried to make out what setting she had selected. *How does she get clear-cut from the neck down while I'm untouched?* His musing was interrupted when a blast of warm, scented spray eliminated the haze of singed hair from the air. *This has certainly been a most educational shower.*

Extremophile

Emerging from the stall before the automatic blow-dry cycle, they dried each other with large towels then moved back into the bedroom to get dressed. Bruce selected a pair of white linen trousers and a loose silk shirt, opting for bare feet instead of sandals. Engel wrinkled her nose at the selection of dresses, but eventually chose a light blue tube that was so ephemeral that it could not have weighed more than ten grams.

"This seems to be the thing that the good professor goes for," Engel commented. "I'll have the fuckin' old bitch panting." Posing before the mirror, she very deliberately rubbed her nipples through the thin fabric until they stood up like acorns.

I don't know about the old bitch, but it's certainly working for me. There's nothing of the teen about her appearance now. This is a scorching-hot 100% woman.

They left the bedroom together and walked over to the dining area, where Eva was setting out long-stemmed wine glasses. She looked up with a grin. "You seem to have taken a weight off your mind."

Bruce hoped that he wasn't blushing. *How do these women do it? They seem to be bloody telepathic. On the other hand,* he consoled himself, *maybe Eva had access to the monitoring system that certainly existed in the bedroom and most probably covered the bathroom also.*

As he thought further about it, he wasn't really sure if such voyeurism on Eva's part was reassuring or not.

Eva walked round the table. She also wore one of the translucent tubes. Black and a bit more substantial than Engel's, by two or three grams maybe. "Come on, sit down," she encouraged them, drawing Engel towards one of the chairs at the glass-topped dining table. "That dress really suits you." She stroked her fingers up Engel's spine as she sat. "You look good enough to eat."

"Thanks," Engel responded. "We should have a workout in the dojo sometime and maybe you'll get a taste." The girls laughed, looking deeply into each other's eyes. Eva then removed her fingers from Engel's neck with evident reluctance and walked round the table to seat Bruce.

He quickly seated himself before she reached him, aware that thoughts of Eva with Engel's thighs round her neck began to have a visual effect on the front of his trousers.

Engel was obviously extremely amused, with a grin that said *I told you so* stretching from ear to ear.

The door opened and Professor White exploded into the room. "Sorry I'm late. I'll be with you in two ticks. Have a glass of wine or something." She shot through the door of the room next to Bruce's assigned bedroom.

"A glass of white?" Eva suggested, proffering a moisture-dewed bottle to Bruce.

"British Columbia Sauvignon Blanc..." he observed, "...just goes to show you, it's an ill climate change that does nobody any good. I believe some of this is as good as the classic New Zealand vintages of the nineties and zeros."

"Try it and find out." She poured him a glass. She didn't say anything to Engel, merely looked at her and raised her eyebrows. Following Engel's nod, she walked to her side and poured her a glass, again taking the opportunity to gently touch the back of her neck while she filled the glass. She then sat beside Engel and poured herself a glass. "Cheers!"

The wine was excellent, with the classic grassy smell and grapefruit flavor of the cool climate Sauvignon Blancs. Conversation naturally led on to wine and the changing provinces of production as a result of climate changes. Although agricultural science was constantly bringing out new cultivars to attempt to minimize the impact of such changes, it was inevitably a Sisyphean job, responding to the coupled impacts of climbing temperatures, evolving pests and diseases, changed rainfall patterns, and increasingly frequent conflicts over access to groundwater resources. In the long-term, the only practical option was to follow moving climatic optima and relocate production. To illustrate the point, Eva brought out the red she had selected to accompany the meal: a ten-year-old Cabernet-Shiraz *grand cru classe* from Yorkshire.

While Eva was topping up their glasses, Angela emerged from her bedroom. *Now there is a really competitive woman.* Bruce stared at the white tube she was wearing. It must have had half the mass of Engel's—and Angela was a very much bigger woman, to boot. Insubstantial didn't describe it; he had seen thicker body paint. He kept trying to think of this as a woman who should be living on a pension by now. It did not do any good at all; he still had problems tearing his eyes from her large breasts with their prominent nipples. With an effort of will that wrenched his neck muscles, he turned back to Engel, who appeared to be much amused by the ageing professor's effect on him.

"White, yes, I'll have a glass of that," Angela decided, apparently unaware of the impact her apparel had caused. She dropped down on the chair next to Bruce, toasted them all with the glass that Eva had filled for her, before inelegantly quaffing at least two thirds of the contents. "A BC sauv blanc I'd guess," she commented.

Bruce was impressed. He was prepared to concede that expert tasters could identify a sip of wine after a lot of pretentious sniffing and spitting-out. However, before seeing her in action, he would have doubted that Angela could even identify the color of the wine with her eyes closed, based on her particular drinking style. *Indeed a woman of many talents.*

Angela settled down with a refilled glass of wine, while Eva served some antipasto-type nibbles and the conversation returned to wine. Angela obviously knew her stuff and increasingly dominated the discussion as it drifted onto the subtleties of the merits of the last remnants of the old great vineyards as compared to the leading edge of the new. When Eva served the veal Carpaccio as a starter, Angela sorted out an additional set of fish-bowl dimensioned glasses so that they could do a cross-comparison of the York cab shiraz with a '25 Chateau Mouton Rothschild, which she'd managed to drag out of an NB reserve cellar. The discussion of the pros and cons of the last real wine to be produced in Bordeaux, before the blizzard of '27 finished off its *grand cru* classification for good, as compared to the top end of English heavy reds continued into the main course of

Tournedos Rossini, served very rare with a fresh side-salad.

Bruce sat back after he finished his steak. *I couldn't have had better in The Chip, or any other of Glasgow's top range restaurants. In fact, I couldn't have done much better in Zurich, where the average level of culinary skills dwarfed Glasgow by far.* "That was absolutely fantastic!" he complemented Eva. "Not only superb food but also amazing wine." He nodded to Angela.

"The night is yet young," she responded. "How about dessert, cheese, coffee, liqueurs?"

"Much though I'd like to see what kind of dessert could follow this, I think discretion is the better part of valor and I'll stick to a coffee. An espresso...or even a double-espresso, if you have it."

Eva nodded. "Coming up. And what about you, Engel?" Only at this point did Bruce notice that he could clearly see through the glass table that Eva had pushed Engel's hem up to the level of her crotch and that her hand was well ensconced between the petite ninja's thighs. Engel was totally unfazed and proceeded to discuss various fruit options without any hint of what was going on below waist level.

Bruce wondered if he dared change his order into a single espresso with double bromide on the side when Angela turned to him. "What do you think our chances are here?"

He started to feel relieved that things were moving to a more manageable technical level and began a speculative breakdown of the risks and benefits of the different options, when he felt Angela's hand slide up his inner thigh and start fondling his dick.

He could feel his eyes opening like a rabbit in headlights, while the two girls opposite simultaneously broke into laughter. "Be gentle, prof." Eva giggled. "He's no good to us if he has a coronary." Engel looked straight into his eyes, while at the same time pulling up Eva's hem to display a bush of golden hair. The slim scientist was evidently a true blonde.

Angela was now holding an erection that threatened to burst the velcro of Bruce's trousers. "I'll also have a double espresso," she ordered in a completely natural manner and smiled as Eva stood, only then pulling down her hem in a minimal concession to modesty. The effect was then completely ruined when she bent down to pick up a napkin, which had slid off her lap as she stood. *Now I know that not only is she a genuine blonde, but that she is very excited about what has been going on with Engel. I wonder if it would be acceptable to leave the table for a cold shower before the coffee arrives.*

Eva served coffee and placed a veritable cornucopia of a fruit-bowl on the table. Angela's hand drew away, returning the meal to a semblance of normalcy. Engel, who had been very quiet during the meal, then came to the fore and started asking questions about logistical details of the project. In particular, how could they move about to visit all these sites if the NB department was the center of such scrutiny by the opposition? Eva and Angela shared the task of responding, making it clear that a lot of thought had already gone into these matters.

The first step would be a move to Switzerland, which would then be the base for their future operations. The Pharm could readily provide any infrastructure they might need there. For possible operations in Africa, they could relocate to Swaziland. However, despite massive production facilities there, conditions were a bit on the primitive side. For North America, a Pharm-daughter in Bend, Oregon, was available to provide support, while for South America, contacts had been established at a Pharm-owned coffee plantation just outside the town of Poços de Caldas in Brazil.

Engel was particularly interested in the last of

these options. Eva explained that, despite advances in synthetic organic chemistry, it was simply cheaper to utilize natural products in many preparations, especially if the plants themselves were gene-tailored to maximize the output of the chemicals of interest. Hence the large number of Pharm subsidiaries running plantations that grew a diverse range of exotic crops. Angela had actually selected Poços because it was near Morro do Ferro, claimed to be one of the most naturally radioactive places on earth.

"Poços would be great to visit," Bruce commented, "but I think the chemistry and temperature there are all wrong. Low priority, at best."

"What about the Far East?" Engel asked. "That seems to be firming up as a likely top priority."

"I'm afraid, Maria, that's where we are weakest," Angela answered. "The Pharm has extensive interests throughout the Far East and Australasia, but all are run as joint ventures with some Japanese multinational, one of the Mitsubishis I think it is. We had hoped we could stay away from that part of the world."

"Murphy's Law in action again." Bruce sighed. "I'm fairly sure that 1F will emerge as front-runner from the technical multi-attribute analysis. I've got some contacts who can provide the technical support that we might need, but they're not at the hierarchical level that could give us the okay for a big sampling program. You really need someone *above the clouds* in the Japanese system. I'd guess a Tokyo University professor with connections or an AEC commissioner."

"How about a pharmo-genetics prof from Tokyo who was a runner-up at the Nobels last year? Would that work?" Angela asked. "There's a certain Japanese professor who has carried a torch for me for the last twenty years. Strange people, the Japanese. He was clearly besotted, although I was nearly thirty years his senior. I would guess that a forty-year younger me could wind him round my little finger. It'd complicate things to increase the number of people who know about my rejuvenation, but he seems to be a power in Japan. I probably wouldn't even need to get physical with him. He once offered a crate of champagne for a single used pair of my knickers."

Angela looked a little abashed at this revelation about her private life, but she recovered quickly. "I know he's not a nuke prof, but he might be of some use."

"Actually, someone like that might be ideal." Bruce began to see a cutting line through the Gordian Knot of 1F sampling. "I'd only been thinking about the nuke community, but they're extremely conservative in Japan and not likely to go for anything outside of the ordinary...especially at a facility that they would like to forget about. If there is a major national weakness of Japanese scientists, apart from their inherent inability to understand the western scientific method, it's undoubtedly their insecurity in the face of high-level experts in specialties outside their own. This might just move our problems down from impossible to only extremely difficult and outrageously dangerous. Could you set up your prof to support us in a sampling trip, if I could provide him with sufficient techno-babble justification?"

"Ah, there's the crunch. I think I could promise that he'd do anything for me...given the proper incentive." Angela wrinkled her nose. "You know how the Japanese are with long-distance requests, though. There are a million ways in which he'd be able to talk himself out of doing anything too outrageous if I wasn't there to keep him under control." With this she reached under the table and repossessed his wedding tackle.

"I don't suppose your sponsors are going to fancy you sloping off to Nippon, so maybe this isn't really going anywhere. Anyway, things elsewhere don't look as bleak as Engel likes to paint them." Bruce smiled at his partner, who glared back.

Angela stretched, leaning back on her chair and displaying her large breasts to maximum effect. "Well, I guess it's time for bed...said Zebedee," she added, cryptically. "If I can tear you girls away from each other, that is." She slid her foot up the inside of Eva's thigh.

Bruce was very aware that this move was obvious to everyone through the glass table, as was the fact that Angela was still stroking his unmistakable erection.

Ménage à trois is one of every lad's fondest fantasies. Bruce grinned as the options played out in his mind. *But à quatre with this line up. Life couldn't get much better.*

His thoughts must have been completely transparent to Engel. "I think that's a good idea. My partner and I have had a rather heavy time over the last twenty-four hours and he, at least, is in drastic need of his beauty sleep. We'll say nighty-night, then. And, by the by, what time do we get together for breakfast?"

Engel stood up and pulled Bruce to his feet before Angela could respond. "How about eight o'clock, would that suit you?"

"Brilliant, Angela, just perfect. Goodnight!" She leaned over the table and kissed the startled professor on the lips. The simple kiss drew out as their mouths opened slightly. Engel pulled back as Angela started to reach for her. "Night, Eva!" She turned and repeated the procedure with the younger scientist. "See you in the morning." Engel smiled as she dragged her bemused partner towards the bedroom.

"Night!" Bruce managed before he was dragged into the bedroom and the door closed behind them. "Well," he continued to Engel, "that was certainly one of the most pleasant dinners I've ever had, even if I could have done with a cold shower by half-time."

"What's so special about getting your poor little willy groped by an old, chunky woman?" Engel moved closer and took possession of the aforementioned bodily part. "At least it was the young, pretty one who was touching me up."

"I certainly noticed that. Why the hell did you drag us off so suddenly? It looked like the evening was going to get even better."

"Fuckin' blokes! Don't you ever think with your brains instead of your fuckin' dick? You're supposed to be a professional of some sort. Don't you know that it's bad business to shag the clients? Unless, of course, that's what you're being paid to do."

"I don't know what you're on about. In any case, you didn't seem to be holding back with Eva and were even sticking your tongue down the throat of the *old, chunky one* only a few moments ago."

"Yeah, okay, but that's different. Teasing punters is all part of the game, but we don't want to get into any sort of emotional commitment...at least not before we know a hell of a lot more about that pair. I've seen your profile, remember. You're a real bloody softy at heart. One good in-out and the chubby prof'd be able to wrap you round her little finger even more than she does now."

"So what was all that about with us in the shower. Not even a little bit un-professional?"

"Not in the slightest." She smirked. "I was just trying to make you presentable for dinner. You looked daft enough at the end, getting groped by your gran, without starting off with a hard-on that you couldn't get under the table. Anyway, you're not a client, you're a partner," she continued as his cheery look faded a bit while the implications of her manipulation became clear to him. "Anyway, I'll make it up to you as soon as you get your bare arse into that bed."

Not wishing to risk her changing her mind, Bruce shed clothing onto the floor as he headed to the bathroom to perform his evening ablutions. While he was standing to pee, he heard her enter behind him and start rinsing her mouth at the sink behind him. Just as he finished and shook off, she squeezed past him and sat down before the toilet had a chance to flush. "Is this helping you to get in the mood?" she asked, sitting with her thighs well apart.

Considering my present state of undress, this's clearly a rhetorical question.

Quickly throwing some water at his face and rinsing his mouth with a cleanser, Bruce scurried out of the bathroom and jumped into the bed. He lay under the cream-colored silk sheet, trying to ignore his tent-pole impersonation while he listened to the toilet flush and the sound of the shower. *Another shower: maybe I should join her.* Before he could decide anything, however, Engel flew into the bedroom and threw herself onto the bed.

Pulling back the sheet, she examined his erection. "That'll do." She sat on top of him and slowly started to draw his penis into her well-lubricated vagina.

Bruce groaned while she slowly pushed him deeper and deeper when, suddenly, he felt a crushing pressure clamp on his dick. Thoughts of horrendous booby-traps flashed through his mind as he screamed and threw her off, pulling his penis free and grabbing it protectively with his hands. It was a couple of seconds before his shock wore off sufficiently for him to register Engel's peals of laughter while she rolled around on the carpet at the side of the bed. She looked ready to literally split her sides.

Bruce slo-mo'd through his memory of the event, quickly realizing what had happened. When he had penetrated deep enough, the minx had squeezed his prick with her inner muscles, which was certainly intended to produce the resultant effect. "You fucking wee bitch!" He threw a pillow that hit her full in the face. "If there is one thing I cannot fuckin' stand, it's women who only get a sense of humor when they're on the job." His flash of anger, inspired by shock, was beginning to wane, and he could, reluctantly, see the funny side of the whole thing. "I just hope the walls are soundproof."

This set Engel off again. "Soundproof? Soundproof? I'll bet the place is not only cabled for sound and full holo vision, but could register the smells and thermal profile of you having a wank under those sheets with the lights out. Matter of fact, the lesbo lovers are probably curled up next door watching all of this in real time." She blew a kiss towards a blank wall and, with a last giggle at his discomfited expression, got off the floor and crawled back into bed.

Ignoring his lack of response, she slid her body against his and settled her cheek against his chest. Almost of its own volition, his hand slid up her back and started gently kneading the muscles at the back of her neck. She growled gently in appreciation, rubbing the damp, hairless patch between her thighs against his hipbone as she slowly slid her hand down his chest.

I don't believe it. Engel's actions were rapidly causing the desired physiological effect. *Considering the amount of time I've been erect over the last twenty-four hours, my brain must be suffering from lack of blood. Maybe that's an explanation for how I managed to get myself into this crazy situation.* Such thoughts quickly merged into a more animal surge of emotion from the older structures of the brain as Engel's ministrations brought him to a shuddering orgasm.

Feeling the small frame nuzzling his rather sweaty chest, Bruce thought he should try to see what he could do for his diminutive partner. Before the thought had actually transformed into action, however, he had drifted into a light doze.

Despite the pleasures of the evening, his sleep was restless. Now that the mystery of the contract had been solved, it was clear that he was taking on a job that was much more dangerous than anything he'd attempted in the past. Longevity was a fantastic reward for success but had to be balanced against the serious risk of getting killed if he made even the smallest error.

Day 3 ...a true story from the land of cows

Bruce awoke to the sound of snoring. *Engel may be small, but she's certainly bloody loud.* He flicked his wrist and read the time. *Seven forty-five; just about perfect.* He gently eased a rather stiff shoulder from under the short-cropped head and slipped from the bed without causing more than a small change to the rhythmic log-sawing. *An early morning scratch of the various hairy bits and then into the shower*, summarized his immediate plan.

Despite missing out on what could have been an encounter beyond even his most debauched fantasies, he had to concede that he felt pretty good. His fears of the previous night seemed less of a concern in the light of day. Even without the unbeatable bonus promised, the project itself was definitely interesting. Indeed, sometime during the night, a host of ideas had started to coalesce into a structured plan. *We can't go head-to-head against our opponents, so the key is staying below their radar. This means moving as fast as possible. Getting into the 1F vault is clearly the best option, and Angela's contact could make that possible. The only problem will be getting Angela to Japan to work her magic on her academic admirer. I'm just not sure whether the greatest resistance to this idea will come from the Pharm or from Angela herself. Or, maybe, from Engel when she realizes that we'll have the well-endowed prof on tow for this jaunt.*

Bruce was actually whistling, cheerfully if tonelessly, when he returned to the bedroom and noticed that Engel had disappeared. *Maybe having a workout, polishing her ninja skills.* He pulled on the trousers of a light karate suit then wandered into the living room in search of her. As he walked past the open door of the neighboring bedroom, Engel's voice rang out. "Breakfast's in here."

He entered the room and noted that it was about twice as large as the already sizeable bedroom that he shared with Engel, and that it was dominated by a truly monstrous bed. Compared to its occupants, details of the bed were secondary as far as he was concerned. Engel had managed to squeeze in between the two other women, and all three were helping themselves to a lavish breakfast, which was presented on a table that was supported from the ceiling by a bizarre cantilever system.

"Come and join us," Angela encouraged him, flamboyantly throwing back a black silk sheet, which confirmed that nightwear was not an option here. It also made it clear that Eva was managing to eat breakfast with one hand, which did not seem to be bothering Engel at all.

Well then, I can hardly get into bed with three naked women and keep my trousers on. He stepped out of the gi bottoms and slipped into the indicated place beside Angela, pulling the sheet up to his waist as he did so.

Bruce couldn't decide if he was relieved or disappointed that Angela kept her hands to herself during breakfast. *They must do this a lot.* He noticed that the croissants and bread, although tasting completely natural, seemed to have been engineered to avoid crumbs: something which, normally, put him off the entire idea of breakfast in bed. Of course, the Heath-Robinson table also helped a lot.

His entrance hadn't interrupted the conversation between the woman, which was focused on the pros and cons of physical implants. Engel was strongly of the opinion that, in her line of work, they were absolutely essential. Bruce noted that she was unconsciously rubbing the diamond fiber armoring in the side of her hand while she made her points.

Eva was equally adamant that such surgical invasion was antiquated: any reinforcing needed could be done with a structure-enhancing pharm cream, which gave the same performance but was completely reversible. "Not that I mind your hard bits." A ripple of sheets followed Eva's hand down to Engel's knee. "But soft bits are best!" Bruce traced her hand returning to its previous position between the little warrior's thighs.

Enough of this. We could be stuck in bed all day. Not that that's necessarily a bad idea, but there's some serious work to be done. More importantly, if we don't clear out fast, Angela's Network will have closed in on us before we can get away from one of their concentration points.

"A coffee and a gipfeli is enough for me," he said as he swung his legs out of the bed and bent to pick up his trousers. "We should start to blur. Would the lot of you be ready to get started in about fifteen minutes?" He left the room, carrying his trousers, without waiting for an answer.

He had already dressed when, about ten minutes later, Engel appeared in the bedroom. "I showered with the girls," she explained while she started to dress. Minuscule white tanga knickers, a pelmet of a white mini-skirt and a translucent, almost but not quite, transparent boob-tube, and she was dressed. The entire procedure took less than a minute. Clearly she was sticking to bare feet, Bruce decided, as he followed her into the living room.

To his amazement, Angela and Eva were already there. He conceded to himself, however, that their rapidity in dressing was helped by the limited number of items involved. Angela was again clad in a dark tube under her open white lab coat, which seemed to be the entirety of her apparel, with the exception of black high heels. Apart from flat black pumps, it was not evident whether or not Eva was wearing anything at all under her buttoned white lab-coat.

Angela clutched a brown leather briefcase to her stomach, as if to rest her large breasts on it. "Back to the meeting room then?"

"I don't think that's necessary," Bruce responded. "I've already downloaded the searches from yesterday, which only confirm what I guessed last night. If we want the best option, we need to head for Fukushima. There may be other options, but I don't think any will work out better than an intervention by your tame Nipponese bugs prof."

"Tame Nipponese pharmo-genetics prof," Angela corrected him.

"Whatever! I think your plan could really work. The database on the Ichi-effu vaults is hard to get a hold of, but they've had some strange results from the underground monitoring network over the last few years. Considering the ostrich approach of most top people there, I'm not too surprised that there haven't been any follow-up studies. They're certain to be worried, but nobody wants to discover something that might be bad news. Someone high enough in the Japanese system to take some blame, yet naive enough to want to get involved in the first place, would be welcomed with open arms."

"My prof is anything but naive, I'm afraid," Angela pointed out. "You've got to be pretty astute to move into the higher levels of Japanese academia."

"That's why you're going to have to start wearing knickers, professor. You'll probably need a case full of well-used ones by the time we get to Tokyo."

"Is this absolutely the only way? I can't imagine the Pharm being very keen about me leaving the super-security system that they set up here and swanning off to the Far East."

"It's your choice," Bruce conceded, "but I can't see a better option at present. If we get to Switzerland without picking up a physical tail, then we should be able to lose all electronic traces there. For the Far East, we can follow the black money route from Zurich to the Hong Kong Free Zone. HK to Tokyo should then be a piece of piss."

"Are you sure about that?" Eva asked, skeptically. "We didn't look much into the Far East options but, if we had to go there, the Pharm route from Basel to Shanghai looked like the best option."

"Okay, but how do you get from Shanghai to Japan? They've had one of the bloodiest trading-zone turf wars going on for the last ten years. And, additionally, your Pharm opposition will also think about Pharm transfer routes. No, I'm absolutely convinced that a money route is best, certainly from Switzerland. For this part of the caper, I've really got only two main concerns, how to clear it for you to go to Tokyo and how to get the three of us to Zurich."

"There you can leave everything up to us," Angela stated, confidently. "You've convinced me that the Japanese option is best for us and that's all I need. You were recruited as the expert here, so we should go with your choice. If I decide that I'm going with you, then the Pharm has no say in the matter."

Again Bruce was impressed at the forcefulness of this woman. Even if nothing else, the sheer power of her personality would have convinced him that she was much more senior than she looked on the basis of apparent age. No normal Pharm exec would have a hope in hell of diverting Prof White from her chosen course of action.

"As far as Switzerland is concerned, we've already looked at that in some detail," she continued, "and it should be no problem. This department has a secure transportation system to the docks, which utilizes the old Glasgow *clockwork orange* underground system. We dispatch several containers of active pharms to the docks every week. Not very comfortable, but we have a special container that has been already used to move people out of the country. These containers are always lead-lined and so it's not hard to sneak anything we want past any monitors that might be in place. Unfortunately, we don't import this kind of stuff. The nuclear chemistry department on campus produces all the isotopes that we use. The containers thus return empty and open, so it's very much a one-way system. It's straightforward thereafter. The container goes onto a ship that is just about to sail. Then, somewhere in the Firth of Clyde, we have a pick-up by some kind of veetol jet, with a direct flight to the Pharm airfield in Basel. Oh, and one further thing, there'll be four of us. Eva will come along too. She's a very talented girl."

Bruce raised his eyebrows at Engel. "What do you think, partner?"

"The transportation looks doable, but I haven't the fuckin' foggiest about what we're going to do when we get to Japan."

"We can talk about that when we get to Switzerland. How soon can you get things organized?" Bruce asked Angela.

Eva answered. "This route has actually been set up for ages. I guess it'll take them about twenty minutes or so to get the transit container sorted out, but anytime after that would be possible." She muttered something in the direction of her wrist. "Okay, they've now started getting things prepped."

"Well, if we're going to go, let's get packed up." Angela turned towards her bedroom. "Remember, absolute minimum luggage. There might not be much room for four in one of those little veetols. Any general stuff can be shipped after us."

"Keep your kit down to an absolute minimum in any case," Bruce added. "We're going to be doing a bit of hopping around, so it'll make our lives a lot easier if we can stick to a couple of large pieces of hand luggage, at the absolute maximum. But Angela," he shouted as she disappeared with Eva into their room. "Remember plenty of panties!"

***

All Bruce's tech kit was still packed in his shoulder bag, so he started selecting a minimum of clothing and toiletries to fit into a leather holdall. He threw a companion bag to Engel. "Here, use this. They didn't seem to have thought to provide you with luggage."

Although the bag was not particularly large, Engel's selection hardly half-filled it. "If I need anymore, I can pick it up en route," she explained. "What I really need are some tools, though. I notice my leather top from last night didn't make it over." She noted him shaking his head and mouthing *recycler*. "Fuck, fuck, fuck and fuck! There was a load of useful kit in that top and I feel totally fuckin' naked without it."

Bruce remembered how naked she looked in it, but knew what she meant. "I've got a few top range combat chemicals," he said, passing over his wallet. "Maybe there's something here you could use."

She quickly flicked through the wallet and tossed it back to him. "Thanks for the offer, but it's all crap."

He did notice, however, that she had slipped something out of his wallet, which she surreptitiously palmed into the waistband of her skirt. Bruce resolved to check up later to see what was missing but, for the moment, decided to say nothing. "Well, if you've got everything, let's move."

Angela was sitting at the dining room table, waving her hands about and mumbling at her palmtop holo-interface. "Just got to set up the test program for the next week before we leave. Eva's packing for me."

"I don't suppose you'd happen to have any GBH-chemware handy?" Engel asked. "I'm not really kitted up for operations at the moment."

"Eva's bound to have anything you'd want. Just go and check up with her, dear." Angela sounded quite matronly, in stark contrast to her appearance.

Bruce silently watched the good professor at work until Engel returned about five minutes later with a satisfied smile on her face. "Here, you can have this shit back." She smirked and tossed over two pills and a derm that she had slipped from his wallet earlier.

Bruce reached over and untangled the back of Engel's skirt from her tanga. Unfazed, she merely flashed a grin back at him.

A couple of minutes later, Eva appeared with two synfabric bags that were set up as rucksacks.

"I guess we're ready then." Angela switched off

the palmtop and chucked it into her briefcase. "Let's hit the road."

She set off with the three others in tow. *We must look like Mother Goose and three goslings.* Bruce smiled at the thought and followed her lead towards the elevator.

When they reached sub-basement three, the elevator opened directly to an anteroom. An electronic voice announced with Gallic rolling Rs that they were about to enter a *radiation restricted region.* Angela completely ignored the wall-length list of warnings and precautions and marched straight to the retinal scanner at the side of the entrance. Almost instantaneously, the heavy door into the hot cell opened, and Angela strode in and directly to the second door of the airlock, without even glancing at the racks of yellow isolation suits lining both side walls. "It's okay," she explained over her shoulder. "We don't do active work here anymore, so the place is clean."

Bruce noticed a pallet of two-hundred liter drums, which bore both the radiation warning trefoil and the linked tricycle of chemical hazards. Instinctively, he held his breath as he scurried after Angela into a side laboratory.

She stripped off her lab-coat and threw it on a

bench beside the door then continued up a ramp into a vibrant yellow ISO transport container, which seemed to be covered with every haz-warning known to man. Bruce recognized radiotoxic, chemotoxic, teratogenic, mutagenic, corrosive, explosive and oxidizing. *It's no wonder this container gets through ports unopened. I'd certainly keep well away from anything looking half as dangerous as this.*

Following Angela into the thick-walled container, Bruce spotted that the inner surface was covered with a thin golden mesh. No doubt the thick lead wall was complemented by a bit of more active shielding. Inside, their transportation was brightly lit by a luminous ceiling panel and contained two well-upholstered benches, which faced each other and ran the length of the container. *Not luxurious, but fine for anyone who was not too claustrophobic.*

Angela dropped heavily onto the left-hand bench about halfway in and patted the seat beside her. "Make yourself comfortable, lad. We'll be in here for the next five hours or so. You girls just settle down and behave yourselves," she added when Engel and Eva sat down together opposite her.

She really is in matron-mode today. Maybe it's the thrill of getting out of the Uni for a change. "I suppose we can use the time to sort out what we'll do when we get to sunny Switzerland." He pulled his slim laptop from his shoulder bag. "I presume we've got full EM shielding here and I can use this thing."

"Nul problemo, you can do whatever you like as we've EM, acoustic, vibration...just about every shield known to man," Eva responded. "It's just external comms that're out. But we've got plenty of time anyway. Secure accommodation is already organized in Basel, and we can spend as much time there as we want. That's where the rest of our stuff will be delivered."

"Call me paranoid but, even with your heavyweight sponsor, I don't want to hang around Basel. Remember that your opposition is dominated by major Pharms, which are all likely to be present there. We should get the best out of the start that we have and move on to Zurich or somewhere in the vicinity asap."

"And how do you propose we do that?" Eva leaned forward, elbows on knees and chin in hands.

Bruce became aware that she had also ditched her lab-coat somewhere and was wearing a tight pair of khaki shorts and a loose shirt of the same color. Engel had her hand up the back of this shirt and was rubbing the blonde's back.

"We could drive or take the train, six of one and

half-dozen of the other. Transport is really no problem, so the question is only where to crash until we can get a commercial flight to Hong Kong." Bruce ignored the clang of the door closing and the slight lurch as the container started to move. Although it was all very smooth, the absence of windows made the various changes in direction unsettling.

"What about a private jet directly from Basel to Hong Kong? The Pharm could certainly run to that," Angela said.

"It would certainly be convenient, but I think it's too traceable. What do you think, girls?"

Eva and Engel nodded together. "Bruce has certainly got a good point," acknowledged the former. "We can never be sure how tight the logistical sections of the Pharm are. Anything we can do completely independently has got to make our trail harder to pick up...as long as there're no hackable computer records, of course. Is that doable?"

"Doable? It's a Swiss characteristic. How do you think that a country with no natural resources, no economic zone membership and an extreme climate manages to have the highest standard of living in the world? With my Swiss passport, we can travel internally without any computer record at all, assuming we don't break any laws, of course. Even then, minor offences stay off the record as long as the spot fine is paid cash."

"Okay, okay," Engel broke in. "We all know about Swiss privacy, their draconian regulations and their fascination with cash. But you surely can't get through the country and on to Hong Kong without leaving any records at all."

"Assuming that the Pharm gets us to their airfield in Basel without being spotted, there'll only be a record of the flight itself, without any evidence that we were on it. I'm certain there'll be satellite coverage of the entire Pharm complex, but we'll be okay as long as we don't go wandering around in the open. We leave in any kind of transport that gets us through expected local surveillance and then we're clear. Get over to Kloten for a designated black flight to Hong Kong and buy tickets cash. It's expensive, but very tight. Even your Network can't have the resources to physically place tails on every black transport route out of Switzerland on the off chance that we might use it."

"I'm convinced," Angela said. "But why do we have to go anywhere else? Why not directly from Basel to Zurich airport?"

Bruce projected a transport net-plan onto the blank wall at the end of the container and, with input from Eva, started filling in details.

"ETA in Basel is 5pm, allowing for the one-hour time difference between Switzerland and Scotland. Even with the fastest possible transit to Kloten on the shinkansen, there's no way of making the last black flight of the day at seventeen forty-five."

"It's just as I'd guessed," Bruce explained. "We need to overnight somewhere and get the first flight out tomorrow. This is at eleven forty-five, which gets us to HK just before midnight. It's a hypersonic Airbus, but the black routes are pretty complex to avoid overflying any territories that're formally opposed to such transport, mainly those run by Muslim fundamentalists."

"So what do you suggest, a hotel at the airport?" Angela asked.

"I don't think so. Better to stay away from the airport until the last possible moment. Extra caution never did anybody any harm. I've got a mate with a flat in Baden that he uses only for walking on the wild side. I'm sure that his wife knows about it, but she pretends that she doesn't. I'll check if it's okay with him as soon as we get out of comm blackout and, if it's free, get him to clear access for us. It's small, but I can't imagine anywhere safer."

"What sort of transport should I organize then?"

Eva asked.

"A self-drive car or van to take us to Basel Hauptbahnhof. Anything with dark windows would do. But tell your Basel people that we're taking it to Geneva. We can leave it in long-term parking and the Pharm can pick it up in a couple of days."

"You really take paranoia to new heights," Engel commented in a complementary tone. "I think we're looking pretty good as far as getting to Hong Kong is concerned. The biggest danger seems to be dying of boredom over the next five hours. You don't, by any chance, run to in-crate entertainment?"

"Afraid not," Eva answered, "but you can lie against me if you fancy a snooze." She sat up and Engel meekly lay out on the bench and laid her head back onto the tall blonde's lap.

"I can provide some background muzak," Bruce volunteered, scrolling through screens on his laptop. "It's all a bit old though. I don't usually carry anything pre-null with me. In fact, not only old, but usually fairly obscure," he qualified further as he selected an old piece of late 90s pop-rock.

"Bell, Book and Candle," Angela stated smugly after about thirty seconds of the first track. "They sound Irish, but they're actually German."

Good God, is there anything that this woman doesn't

know about? He wasn't at all surprised when a discussion of bands of the 90s and 00s slowly became an Angela monologue.

Eva was keeping up the minimum response required to keep the professor's lecture going, so Bruce continued with nailing down their travel plans. Basel to Baden and Baden to Kloten train options, HK travel and accommodation and final links to Narita or Haneda, as the two possible airport connections for Tokyo.

By the time he had finished, Angela and Eva had moved onto discussion of the results of some experiments, which were displayed in the form of a palmtop-projected holo. Although he understood only about two words in three of the biochem techno-babble they spoke, he listened with interest, regarding deciphering this arcane tongue as a challenge, like some sort of brain teaser. Engel started to snore, but stopped as soon as Eva started to stroke her head. Bruce made a mental note to remember this useful trick.

After about an hour, Engel woke, stood and stretched on her tiptoes. Walking through the holo between the two scientists, she sat on the other side of Bruce and squeezed his knee in a familiar manner. "How about giving me a bit more background info on this ichy-thing."

Happy for something definite to do, Bruce projected a selection of images from his 1F file. There was a vast amount of material on the accident, regional decontamination, reactor stabilization and subsequent dismantling, and final industrialization of the site. The video footage of the construction of the vast underground reactor pressure vessel storage caverns and the subsequent extraction and transport of the most radioactive innards of the three damaged units was an impressive illustration of Japanese engineering prowess. The caverns were now backfilled with concrete grout, these *storage vaults* including a monitoring system that incorporated a plumber's nightmare of gleaming hardware connected by a jungle of pipes, tubes, wires, optical fibers and waveguides.

Information about the current status was much more limited, which was not surprising in view of the chaos caused by the Tokyo quake of '45. Good 3-D visuals in English were available from the report of the IAEA team who last inspected the site over a decade ago, but these concentrated on the containment measures and the results from the local radiation monitoring network. Further visuals generally had Japanese legends or explanatory audio, but Bruce could usually work his way through the key messages involved with only a little help from his translation demon.

In many ways, it was impressive how little trace the accident had left on the surrounding Fukushima prefecture. The old reactor site was now a regional center for recycling nuclear materials, which served not only Japan but also a large part of Southeast Asia and the Pacific Rim. This huge industrial complex was surrounded by disposal facilities: the original cleanup waste from the 1F accident buried below concrete monoliths that contained the less toxic residues from the currently operational decontamination plants, smelters and plasma furnaces.

Although spent fuel and other highly radioactive wastes went to a deep repository located near the Rokkasho reprocessing complex, more toxic wastes from Fukushima operations were also stored in caverns below the site. Web-cam monitors of these could be readily accessed, but the RPV caverns were a blank area within the labyrinthine maze of tunnels that extended several kilometers out from the coastline, which was now defined by a huge flood defense wall.

"Fuck me!" Engel shook her head in disbelief.

"Are the Japanese really building a wall to hold back climate change? Christ, why don't they just retreat back to high land like anyone else?"

"Good question." Bruce smiled, pleased that he had managed to retain his partner's attention. "Actually, barriers to sea-level rise and storm surges are, like elsewhere, focused on threatened urban areas. Around 1F it's a bit of an exception. The walls are built out of recycled waste, so it's a kind of a win-win situation. An industrial complex that nobody really wants to live beside sits on land that would otherwise be abandoned, defended by a system using material that would otherwise be disposed of. Clever, isn't it?"

Engel did not look convinced but changed the subject by asking what they were actually going to do when they got to the site. Here Bruce became rather vague. Angela had obviously been following this conversation, because she asked to look at 3-D overlays of temperature, radiation dose rate and pH within the RPV caverns. The first two parameters could be derived from reported measurements, but the third had to be guesstimated from cement injection records and its expected interaction with groundwater that would inevitably seep through the vaults.

Extremophile

"I don't know how you sample it, but that's your target zone," Angela concluded, indicating the highest dose rate region between the three-fifty and three-seventy Kelvin boundaries, which had also been exposed to fluids with pH values over twelve for the best part of forty years.

"Now we know exactly what to do, all we need to do now is work out how to do it." Bruce concluded, "But enough of all this work, anything edible in this toxic waste transport container?"

"But of course." Eva gently moved Angela to one side and lifted the bench seat to reveal a refrigerated compartment. "Only beer and sandwiches, though. We've got bottles of McEwan's pale ale or cans of some naff-looking lager." She wrinkled her nose. "Sandwiches seem to be roast beef, salmon or cheese and something." She had already started passing out the bottled beer.

During this picnic lunch, Angela managed to display her comprehensive knowledge of international beers. This developed into a game, with the others trying to identify beers she knew nothing about. A few points were scored with obscure micro-brews, but Angela won the game by a mile.

Bruce was relaxing in post-prandial contentment that was threatening to turn into a doze when he was surprised by a clang and the inrush of humid air as the container door opened. A tech in blue overalls stormed in, carrying a mesh basket loaded with clothing. Trying to mask the way he undressed Angela with his eyes, he grinned a welcome. "Hi, folks. Please kit up as quickly as possible. Your plane is waiting." With obvious great reluctance, he turned and left.

Eva was already passing out white jump-suits, soft boots and full-face helmets. "You don't actually need any of this shit," she noted, "but it messes up any spot observation. We use this kit for all air transfers, so it won't register as anything out of the ordinary."

Angela had kicked off her shoes, pulled up her skirt and was now pulling the jump-suit on over it. Bruce noticed that, despite all his previous comments, she was not wearing any underwear. "Bloody unhygienic things," she muttered, spotting his glance and reading his mind.

"Maybe I should go for a pee first," Engel said, reminding Bruce that a couple of beers were passing their way through his system.

"Don't worry," Eva responded, who was already fully dressed and just about to don her helmet. "The plane isn't as primitive as these suits suggest. You'll have full access to toilet facilities after we take off."

A couple of minutes later, they filed after Angela out of the container and into the hold of some kind of cargo ship. The entire area appeared to be deserted and without any obvious signs. Nevertheless, without hesitation, Angela marched straight ahead and into an open cargo lift. The door closed silently, the entire lift jerked twice and the opposite door opened to reveal a flat stern deck on which a small exec veetol was sitting with door open and stairs extended towards them. As they marched in line towards the plane, drizzle began to spot the visors of their helmets.

The door towards the cockpit was closed and the stairway began to withdraw as soon as Engel, as last, entered the plane. The plane contained eight well-padded leather seats that were set in twos, facing each other, on either side of a narrow aisle. A luggage rack facing the entry hatch allowed them to deposit their baggage as they entered. An aft compartment, separated by an open curtain, seemed to contain a small galley cum bar and a toilet. "Not bad!" Angela commented. "Bigger than the usual bus for this route." Without warning, the engine note changed and they began to lift from the deck.

"Maybe best to sit for a couple of minutes," Eva

suggested. She had already removed her helmet and dropped onto one of the seats in the first row. The others filled the rest of these seats and began to strip off helmets and boots, which were tossed onto the second row of seats. Angela, who was sitting opposite Bruce, also started to peel off her jump-suit, which made for an interesting view when she struggled out of the lower half. By the time she finally pulled the suit loose and chucked it backwards over her head, settling back with her skirt rucked high enough to show her navel, Eva laughingly announced that it was now okay to move about. "The prof just hates to waste time sitting doing nothing," she explained to Bruce.

"The flight is sub-sonic and will take about an hour and a half. Climb out of the suits if you like, we won't need them at the far end as we'll deplane in a hanger." Engel was already out of her suit by this time and headed aft towards the toilet. Bruce divested himself of the suit while Angela pulled her skirt down to a more modest level. *Not actually all that modest, though,* observed Bruce as he caught occasional glances of dark pubic hair when the professor moved about on her seat.

Bruce was last to use the facilities and was amazed at how large the toilet was. *Not only a toilet but also a bidet, by God!* When he returned, Eva was distributing coffee and passed him a double espresso without being asked. *This is the way to travel, or maybe it's just the contrast of the view of the sun shining on the rain clouds below with the claustrophobic transit container.* He decided, however, that discretion was the better part of valor and refused the offer of a *digestif*. Angela was appreciatively sniffing Cognac from a fish-bowl dimensioned glass, while the girls tasted each other's drinks, discussing the relative merits of Williams and Pflumli, selected from a mini-bar that seemed to have been stocked in Switzerland.

The cloud cover broke up somewhere over France and they had an excellent view of the blinding snowfields of the Black Forest, Vosges, Jura and, in the distance, the Alps. The main melt was well underway and, even from ten thousand meters, the swollen Rhine was noticeably brown with sediment. In the Alsace, where barriers had recently failed yet again, the river was several kilometers wide. By then they had already started a steep descent into the private Pharm airfield, adjacent to the Basel-Mulhouse international airport.

They landed gently and taxied directly into an open hanger. Minutes later, the hatch opened and a couple of young men clad in yellow shorts and vests entered, along with a blast of hot air. Without speaking, they collected the various items from the luggage rack and withdrew. When Angela led the group from the plane towards the waiting mirror-window SUV, Bruce noted with amusement that they were all now bare-foot. *Eva's planning isn't perfect after all.*

Angela waved Bruce to the driver's seat while she headed for the opposite side and the baggage handlers slammed the back closed and disappeared in a small electrocart. When he climbed in, he noticed the pair of sandals sitting on the seat and a pair of high heels for the front passenger. Angela turned with a grin after she pulled herself in beside him, as if to prove that her telepathy was still fully functional.

"I'll navigate." Eva leaned forward between the two front seats to point the way. "Straight ahead and down the ramp facing you."

Bruce switched on the hydrogen IC / fuel cell hybrid and drove off into a maze of tunnels. When they emerged into sunlight in the middle of an industrial zone full of warehouses, workshops and the monkey-puzzle labyrinths of chemical works, the air conditioning cut in and they caught first sight of other traffic. Eva projected a heads-up route map onto the windscreen and Bruce followed the specified red path, which was confirmed by a soft audio running commentary.

They were within two blocks of the station when Eva scrambled the route and sent them on a diversion past it. "What the fuck's up?" Bruce asked in an annoyed tone. "We're almost there."

"We're being followed." Eva leaned over his shoulder to tap the screen in the middle of the dashboard. Bruce glanced backwards and saw Engel nod.

Engel overrode the rear-view camera and threw a circle round a small s-car about four places behind them.

"It's all a bit low tech," Bruce commented. "Wouldn't they be better using a tracer or sticking to spot surveillance?"

"I've already checked for tracers," Eva answered, "and any satellite system like spot's pretty shitty in Switzerland. Too many tunnels. So just follow the route shown and it'll be okay." She and Engel pulled a piece of luggage from the back and started rummaging through it.

The diversion had taken them into a rundown area next to the Rhine levee, which was undoubtedly due for demolition within the next river protection upgrade phase. Although holding back a bit farther, the car following them was now the only one in sight.

"Get ready for a bit of action now," Eva warned. "Next left into the levee monitoring tunnel, one hundred meters farther and then into reverse as fast as you can. Straight on the nose of our tail, if you can." The green dashboard light, which normally indicated that the collision avoidance system was engaged, turned red. Another flashing red light warned that the airbags were switched out.

Bruce felt his palms begin to get damp when he realized what Eva was up to. Nevertheless, there was no time for argument. He turned into the tunnel, driving straight through the flashing *Eintritt Verbotten!* hologram, and counted to six before jumping on the brakes, slamming into reverse, and flooring the accelerator. Tires screamed as everyone was thrown forward against their seat belts.

Bruce was now steering by the rear camera and trying to center on the white line displayed as they shot backwards. Eva's estimate was right on: the following car turned into the tunnel just in time to present itself as an unmissable target for the SUV, now reversing at a good fifty kays. Bruce noted two pairs of saucer-like eyes before a deafening crash forced him back into his seat and caused the rear display to vanish.

Extremophile

He was hardly aware of the two rear doors opening but, by the time he turned, he saw that the girls were at opposite sides of the car. Two cracks came almost simultaneously as the side windows were punched in. Although his view was limited by the height of the jeep and the airbags which filled the front of the wreck behind them, Eva seemed to be reaching into the car on her side, while Engel was pumping in a series of punches from hers, accompanied by rather wet-sounding impacts.

Not more than ten seconds later, the girls were back in their seats, slamming the doors. "Move it," Eva shouted. "The route's loaded."

Bruce switched on with a feeling of trepidation. To his surprise, the emergency cutout light went off and the car moved off smoothly. The girls seemed in high spirits as each pulled off one member of a pair of black gloves. Reinforced with something, Bruce guessed, given the way they had punched through the toughened windows. Apparently Engel's glove was soaked in blood, leading to a mock scolding from Eva. Two kilometers farther along the levee tunnel and then right into a storm sump, ignoring even stronger warnings of danger and the consequences of unauthorized entry.

"Aren't we likely to be setting off a lot of alarms

down here?" Bruce asked.

Angela, who had been unusually silent since their tail was spotted, answered in a somewhat shaky voice. "We've got Pharm transponders and, because the Pharms have to continually monitor for leakages from the vast number of plants above, there's nothing especially unusual about us being down here. As soon as they find that wreck, though, it'll be another kettle of fish."

"Not far now, anyway," Eva reported. "We can exit here," highlighting a ramp about five hundred meters farther on, "then it's across one open road and into a car-park complex that connects directly with the station."

At the exit ramp, they sat at the end of the tunnel while Eva stripped off a rather conspicuous roof rack. They then waited until the road was clear and shot across and into the entrance opposite in a matter of seconds. A spot pick-up was possible but, given the usual image-refreshing interval of about 30 seconds and the change in appearance of the car from above, not very likely. In any case, they drove to the end of the park nearest the station and immediately bailed out.

The rear door of the car was jammed closed but, otherwise, the damage to the rear end was surprisingly light considering the mess of the other vehicle. "Four-pi fiber steel reinforcing," Angela answered Bruce's unspoken question, while the girls dragged luggage over the back seats.

Bruce left the door open with the lock-card lying conspicuously on top of the dashboard. "I know it's Switzerland, but there's still a chance some foreigner will steal it," he explained as he picked up his bags.

Following signs for *Hauptbahnhof: Schweiz*, they arrived in the concourse of the Swiss national part of the station. Seeing the queues for international arrivals, Bruce was extremely glad they had slipped into the country through the cross-border Pharm without going through the rigors of entering Switzerland as a normal tourist.

Bruce purchased tickets at an automat for a first-class compartment on the limited-stop shinkansen to Zurich, turning down Angela's ecs and paying cash with Swiss Francs. Although it would sit at the platform for another quarter of an hour, the train was ready for boarding and Bruce led them directly to their compartment.

As they settled down, Bruce used some small denomination notes to purchase beers from the mini-bar. The post-mortem of the previous half hour started immediately. Eva was convinced that the tail was a fluke, a stroke of luck—bad as it turned out for them—by some gate-watcher. Engel was equally convinced that a leak within the Pharm was to blame. By the time the train moved out, the argument was beginning to get heated, as evidenced by Engel's increasingly colorful use of the vernacular.

"Ladies, ladies!" Bruce broke in. "It really doesn't matter who's right. We've got to assume both that the Pharm is leaky and that there are hoards of lucky observers sitting about in unexpected places. Look on the bright side though. Basel was always the trickiest part of the trip and now we know for certain that we can't take Pharm protection for granted. Assuming, of course, that you didn't take out a Pharm protection team," he added.

Eva and Engel looked at each other in surprise. This option clearly hadn't occurred to them.

"At least mine was only tranked, the worst he'll have is a brutal hangover," Eva responded defensively.

"Well, a broken neck isn't necessarily that fuckin' serious these days," Engel added. "Especially as he's tranked to the fuckin' eyeballs as well. Fuckin' expensive, but completely curable," she concluded, with a clap of her hands for emphasis.

"There'd also be the plastic surgery expenses to

put his face back together," Eva added, and the two girls broke into giggles.

At least they're not fighting with each other. "Anyway, we have to assume the opposition knows we're in Switzerland and, probably, that four of us are travelling together. I hope it takes a while before our compartment for six to Zurich is picked up, but in any case, we jump out at Baden, according to plan." He flicked his wrist. "In thirty-seven minutes, second stop after Aarau."

The girls happily started to discuss how to handle the rest of the trip. Bruce glanced at Angela and noted that she was rather pale, and the hand holding her beer quivered slightly. He moved closer to her and put his arm round her shoulder. He could feel the tension on her body relax slightly when she leaned her head onto his shoulder with an almost silent sigh. For the first time, Bruce realized that the omnipotent professor was a stranger in this strange land of physical aggression. *She probably knows the history of every major armed conflict in the last two millennia and might have black belts in a half-dozen martial arts, but looks like she's never been in a fight where blood was spilt. No wonder she was so freaked-out when her lab was broken into.*

He squeezed her shoulders, reassuringly. He was

almost ready to conclude that the woman finally seemed switched off sex for the first time since he met her, when he noticed that her nipples were sticking out like a couple of thimbles.

Well, violence does seem to affect some women that way. Let's just try and make sure that this is the last time that it happens during this trip. Deep down, however, he felt that the chances of this were negligible.

***

As agreed, they disembarked at Baden from two separate doors of the train, Eva with Bruce and Engel with Angela. *Engel the angel and Angela, what a contrast. Next to the statuesque professor, Engel looked just like a child in adult's clothes, even more so due to the fact that Angela had taken her by the hand in a motherly manner, which was probably completely inadvertent.*

Bruce headed off directly for the flat known to his Zurich drinking mates as the *Bear Pit*—this transmogrifying into the *Bären Hüetli* when claiming to wives or girlfriends that the time was actually being spent in a mountain hut, the men enjoying the pleasures of the great outdoors. Thinking about his motley group of Swiss pals, he could not help half-hoping that, against all likelihood, he would be spotted by one of them. *Heading for the BP with three such lovelies, my street cred would reach an undreamed-of pinnacle. On the other hand, I'd need a bloody big stick to keep the bastards away from this kind of temptation.*

Two minutes' walk brought them under the Stadtturm into the Löwenbrunnen Platz. Bruce glanced up at the very sorry-looking lion topping the fountain that gave the square its name, before turning to the scanner on a modern glass entranceway next to an extremely dilapidated English-style pub. As Bruce muttered his name, the door slid aside to reveal a small, shabby lift. He squeezed in with Eva, making space for the others to join them.

The doors closed and the lift began to squeak its way upwards. In a flashback, Bruce suddenly remembered, one time about five years previously, sharing this same lift with three rugby-players and four crates of beer. Now, here he was with one hand crushed between Eva's bottom and the wall, his other arm jammed against Angela's breasts and Engel pushed against his chest, her head tilted upwards to look innocently into his eyes while her fingers slid up the leg of his shorts. *I'm not quite sure what I'm doing, but I'm bloody certain that I must be going in the right direction.*

All too soon for him, the lift groaned to a halt and ejected them into a small hallway facing a single door. Another retinal scan was needed to gain entrance to a large, high-ceilinged attic room that was dominated by a massive four-poster bed. Bruce rapidly cancelled the wall displays, which presented live action enactments of some highlights of the Kama Sutra, replacing them with pseudo-window views of the roofs of Baden's old town. "Kind of a chap-flat, you know." he mumbled, wondering if this was actually such a good idea after all.

Engel was examining a shelf containing a selection of silk cords and handcuffs, while Eva lifted a pile of magazines off the sofa to make space for their luggage. "Have a look at this," the tall blonde called, lifting a gaudy magazine entitled *Anal Lesbians* from the top of the pile. All three women broke into peals of laughter as they discussed the possibilities of the various positions on display. "Keep that handy," Angela commanded. "We could get some hints for tonight."

Bruce rolled his eyes and wondered if it was too late to find somewhere less esoteric to crash out.

By the time they had sorted through their luggage and freshened up, it was almost seven thirty. "We should eat early," Bruce recommended, "so that we can get moving tomorrow morning by about six thirty."

Extremophile

"Why so early?" Angela asked. "Our flight isn't until about eleven, as I remember it."

"Two reasons, actually. The first is that the Swiss are early risers and their rush hour is from about six until seven. That's when we'll be hardest to spot. Secondly, we don't have flight tickets yet. Economy will be mobbed, but we shouldn't have a problem with business class. All the same, we should get to the airport early to be on the safe side."

"Remember we're not on a restricted budget here, the Pharm will cover us first class."

"No chance. First class is small, select and far too obvious. Additionally, it'll probably have been booked out for weeks. So it's business class or nothing."

"Okay, you're the boss," Angela conceded. "Where are we going to eat?"

"I had been thinking of fish." His brow wrinkled. "But, as we're heading for Japan, we'll probably get enough of that in the near future. It's too hot for anything Swiss like fondue or raclette, so how about French or Italian?"

"Italian," Angela decided without consulting the others. She picked up a small black shoulder bag and waved towards the door to forestall any further discussion. "Let's go!"

Although it was still bright, Baden old town looked seedy in the evening light. The entire area seemed to consist of bars, nightclubs and brothels. These were now beginning to open for business as office workers drifted in from all directions. Bruce explained that this was one of the main red-light areas of the Zurich suburbs. Being Swiss, activities started early, tended to finish early, and were very expensive and relatively safe. It also contained a few excellent restaurants. He led the others, again walking as two couples, to an old Italian restaurant, which was almost hidden by the gaudy facade of a Macdonald's joint offering junk food and soft drugs.

Probably due to the buffering effect of the Mediterranean, the climate of central and southern Italy had changed less than most, and the country was still a major wine producer. Their meal provided an opportunity for Angela to compare a couple of recent white wines from Gavi and Orvietto that accompanied their mozzarella and tomato salad. This was followed by a vertical profile of three bottles of Chianti, covering almost thirty years. Only Eva could face Suppa Inglese for dessert; the others stuck to espresso, although Angela complemented hers with a Grappa de Barolo.

It was after nine when Bruce paid the hefty bill

for the meal: Swiss Francs, cash. Although by no means sober, due to the hour time difference they were all wide awake and, especially the girls, reluctant to return to the small flat. Abandoning the pretense of two couples, the girls were hamming up as spoiled children to the mummy and daddy figures presented by Angela and Bruce.

They had clearly convinced Angela that going to a bar was a good idea, so Bruce was now mainly concerned with damage limitation. "Okay, okay, we'll go for a drink, but I'll choose the place."

"What's wrong with the bar under the flat, you know, the dingy, English one?" Engel asked.

"Not a good idea, with the three of you dressed the way you are. That type of bar will be packed with Kosovans, Iranians, Sudanese and loads of other types here on temporary refugee visas. They pay a fortune for short-term residence and spend the entire time trying to find a wife who can get them some kind of European citizenship. They would pounce on you three like flies round shite. We would be pestered to death. No," Bruce huffed, "the best place would be either a strip joint, where we could get a table to ourselves, or a gay bar. Which would you prefer?"

Bruce was rather relieved when, after some debate, the final consensus was for a gay bar. He wasn't sure his blood pressure could take the strain of a strip show in this company.

Bruce led the women back past the flat and along a dubious side alley to Cordulaplatz. The ground-level bar of the Paradies club was relatively empty, although the cabaret upstairs seemed to be packed. The three women caused a few appraising glances when they entered, but their clothing actually fitted in well with the ambience of the place. There were quite a few members of both sexes wearing much more outrageous rigouts.

Bruce managed to find a table for them against a back wall and called over an extremely camp waiter, who was wearing only a massively padded jock-strap and some very graphic tattoos. *At least, I hope it's well padded, otherwise I'm going to get a serious inferiority complex.*

While he took their orders, the waiter tapped his fingers on the table in front of Bruce. The fingernails were painted with a sequence of stills of a growing erection. Whether this was completely accidental or some kind of come-on, Bruce wasn't sure, but he placed his hand on Engel's back anyway, hoping to make his position clear. Engel nudged against him and slipped her fingers down the waistband of his shorts, without breaking her animated discussion with the other two women about the possible sex of two androgynous creatures who were groping each other in an alcove opposite them.

Sipping the peaty Caol Isla, Bruce could feel the accumulated alcohol dissolving the tensions from his body. He was fairly sure that a similar process was resulting in the rather exuberant behavior of the others. Angela, in any case. Engel was certainly tough enough and no stranger to physical action. Eva was more of an enigma: she was obviously much more than a simple research assistant. More, indeed, than the *prof's little bed-warmer*, as Engel had put it. The woman had serious security training, which was clear from the way she had handled the fracas in Basel. *She also looks as happy as Larry, sitting squeezed between the other two women. Certainly not at all out of place in a gay bar.* Bruce had to force himself from going further with that line of thought. It helped that the clientele of the bar was every bit as good as a club floorshow, providing endless topics for the ladies' conversation.

Bruce said very little over the next hour, beyond ordering a second whisky from a buxom waitress who was wearing spiked heels and a very uncomfortable looking leather corset-like contraption. The waitress seemed to be especially interested in Eva, but didn't complain when Angela stroked her thigh while she served their drinks. Angela paid for this round with a wad of ecs pulled from her shoulder bag, tipping the girl outrageously, despite the usurious exchange rate for ec transactions charged in the bar. She was rewarded for her generosity by a drawn-out, noisy kiss. Bruce noticed, however, that the girl's eyes were glued to Eva during the entire proceedings.

By the time they left, at about ten thirty, the bar was fairly packed and the air-conditioning was beginning to lose its battle against the ambient heat outside and that generated by the hormone-charged bodies within. It took only five minutes to return to the flat, Bruce hand-in-hand with Engel and Angela arm-in-arm with Eva. While Bruce was opening the door, the latter couple attracted a lot of ribald commentary from a group of swarthy men who were smoking as they lounged around outside the English pub. Engel suggested to Eva that they have a competition to see who could collect the most foreskins, a small stiletto materializing in her hand. Worried that they might be serious, Bruce dragged the two girls into the lift, assuring them that their potential victims were very unlikely to possess foreskins in any case.

Back in the attic, Angela took Eva by the hand.

"We'll use the facilities first, so you two can sort out the sleeping arrangements."

Bruce looked at Engel. "The bed is big enough for four, I know from experience." *Although I'd never admit that the experience actually involved three other totally pissed blokes.* He remembered the two girls with them on that occasion had spent the night together on the sofa, after throwing the lads in a pile on the bed.

"Nope," she decided, "the clients get the bed. I suppose the sofa converts?"

Reluctantly, Bruce moved their luggage into a corner and converted the sofa to a small double bed. He pulled some bedding from below the four-poster, along with a commercial-size box of condoms and a pile of porn holos. Before he could kick them back into place, Engel had picked up a couple of the chips. "Mega-boob, fist-fucker?" she asked with a smile. "You guys certainly go for the top-end of the market. Should we see if this gets the old girl's juices going?"

"I don't think so." He grabbed the videos from her and tossed them back under the bed. "Just help me make up this bloody bed."

After they finished with the bed, Engel commented on the relative tidiness of the flat. "It's as seedy as I expected, given its purpose, but I didn't think it would be so clean."

Bruce explained that Ollie, the owner of the flat, had a housekeeper. She was one of the whores from the bar downstairs and she even gave discounts to occupants of the flat for extra services rendered. "She's very Swiss. She'll start cleaning the room, stop to give somebody a blowjob, and then start cleaning again. She does special group discounts." He raised his eyebrows suggestively.

"You can't even handle the three of us without thinking about anybody else." She grabbed his groin and squeezed. "How about a shower as soon as beauty and the beast are finished in the bog?"

Bruce had just taken off his shirt when the aforementioned duo emerged, both naked, carrying their clothes. Eva simply dropped her clothes on the floor and bounced directly onto the bed. Angela, however, folded her clothing onto a chair and then looked around the room. "I don't suppose there are any books in this place, are there? I get fed up looking at screens and holos. I need some real paper." She lifted a magazine. "Although viewing little girls being rodgered by big, hairy beasts has only limited attraction." She smiled as she looked over at Bruce's hairy shoulders and belly. "Present company excepted, of course."

Eva laughed in delight until Engel jumped on

top of her. "What're you laughing at, ye skinny bism? I'll show you a bit of rodgering by a wee hairless beast." She started to tickle her captive.

Angela dragged Bruce away from this cabaret. "Books," she reminded him.

Trying to avoid staring at her naked body, Bruce padded over to a shelf in the corner of the attic. He lifted down a large format postcard to reveal a line of books behind it. Angela was looking at the card, which portrayed a line of about a dozen naked women of wildly different ethnic types, ranging from Eskimo to Masai. "Very nice," she commented. "Quite out of place next to *anal rampage* or whatever that card on the next shelf displays."

Bruce pretended not to hear that comment. "These are old Uni books of Ollie's, so I don't know if there's anything suitable. There's something called *A brief history of time*…"

"Absolute rubbish," Angela broke in. "Probably the worst-written best-seller in the history of the printed word. It makes the bible seem transparent and logical. What else do you have?"

"*Sophie's World* by…"

"God! What was your lad studying: lowpoints of twentieth century literature? That's probably the second-worst book ever written."

A well-read woman with very strong opinions. Bruce skipped over a suspiciously virginal *Quantum Chromodynamics* and a *Thermodynamics of Aqueous Solutions* by a couple of Swiss-sounding authors. "How about *Swing Hammer Swing*?"

"I stand corrected." She fumed. "*Sophie's World* was third worst, and you've just reminded me of number two. I'd go back to the porn mags, if it wasn't for the increasing evidence that such literature not only makes you go blind, but rots your brain in the bargain."

"I'm afraid that's all there is, apart from some old manga things."

"Why didn't you say so? Let's see." She pushed past him. "*Akira*, that'll do." She lifted down the thickest of the shabby tomes. "I've read it a couple of times," she explained, "but I always see something new in it. Anyway, I can't think of anything more appropriate before visiting post-quake Tokyo. Would your friend mind if I took it with us?"

"He'd never miss it." Bruce brushed dust off his hands. Clearly even the super-Swiss cleaning lady hadn't been near these books for years.

In the interim, Engel had managed to shed all her clothes and was kneeling on Eva's shoulders. She was haggling over a price to sit on Eva's face, while the latter was describing in gory detail the damage she would do with her teeth if Engel even tried. As much as he would have loved to follow the next move in this game, he reached over to grab Engel round the waist, carrying her off towards the bathroom.

"Oh, you big hairy beast, be gentle with me for I am but a little girl." She screamed in mock terror, setting Eva's laughter off again. "Please don't put your willy up my bum, for it's very small and wrinkly and tickles me fit to burst."

Bruce slapped the aforementioned bum loudly as they entered the bathroom. It sounded like Eva was going to choke and even Angela was guffawing in the background.

Bruce stripped off his shorts and they took turns using the toilet and the cleansers at the sink. They then showered together. After shaving, Engel's hands again performed their magic to reduce the ache from his testicles. Afterwards, however, she looked directly up into his eyes, took hold of his ears and flicked a heel round to push the back of his legs. With a surprised gasp, he fell painfully onto his knees and felt his face pulled against a wet and salty quim. "Go for it," she commanded. "Now you can see what Eva's missing out on."

Whether it was due to the foreplay with Eva or

their previous activities in the shower, Engel was already fairly far on and required little in the way of ministrations from his tongue and fingers before she had an extremely noisy orgasm, during which she literally pulled out a handful of his short-cropped hair. He wasn't sure if his scream of pain contributed to her orgasm, but it certainly didn't detract from it in any way. *I'm definitely going to have to get a complete skinhead cut before I try anything like this again.* Bruce rubbed a bleeding patch of scalp.

They re-entered the bedroom to chuckles from the two women. Angela was sitting up with the manga comic in one hand and her other arm round Eva, her thumbnail unconsciously stroking the girl's left nipple.

"That sounded like fun," Eva commented. "Could I have a shot?"

"Behave yourself, girl," Angela said, slapping her protégé's nipple with her index finger. "You'll embarrass Bruce. Are you sleeping with us tonight?" She patted the space next to her with *Akira*.

"It's okay," Engel answered. "The beast and I will sleep on the couch." She then proceeded to go through a goodnight kissing routine, which reminded Bruce of excerpts from the holos lying under the bed.

Bruce was attempting to slide into bed before his

erection got too obvious when Angela spotted him. "Bruce, after all we have been through today, a goodnight kiss is the minimum required. Get your lips over here."

Resistance was clearly out of the question, so Bruce attempted to slide towards her in a way that minimized her view of his engorged parts. As he neared the bed, she dropped the comic and pulled his head towards her face. To his surprise, however, she nuzzled softly against his ear. "Thanks for everything," she murmured and kissed him gently on the lips. The tension in his shoulders dispersed as he lifted his hands to the side of her face and relaxed into the kiss. After about twenty seconds he drew back and looked straight into her brown eyes. Suddenly she pulled his head forward and crushed his lips against hers while her tongue forced its way into his mouth. Shocked, he pulled back, managing to pull his mouth free after a few moments of struggling. "No-one expects the Spanish inquisition," she said with a smile and picked up her book.

"Me too!" Eva insisted, evidently much amused at his discomfiture.

Giving up all attempts at subtlety, Bruce walked round the bed with a prick like a bowsprit. Pushing Engel to one side, he put his arms round Eva and kissed her deeply, their tongues sliding together and deep into each other's throats. His aggressive move very quickly softened as Eva's blue eyes looked directly into his. Time started to slow when he was shocked back to reality by the feel of a set of teeth closing on his glans. When he drew back, Engel released her hold on his family treasure.

"Not bad, for a man," Eva commented, reaching down to pull Engel back to her. "But, on balance, I'll stick to girls." Their sloppy kiss was, however, quickly broken. "Yuck! You taste of willies!" She made theatrical spitting noises. The giggling girls fell back into each other's arms.

I don't believe it, they all become comediennes when it gets round to time for sex. Is this my best wet dream or worst nightmare?

He slouched into bed and lay, with eyes closed, listening to the noises coming from the bed. He was still wondering if they would notice if he engaged in a bit of self-relief when he drifted off to sleep.

This time it wasn't simple restlessness, it was a fully-fledged nightmare. The events of the day replayed while he looked on like some kind of external observer. Despite all their precautions and a seemingly undetectable escape from Glasgow, they had been made within minutes of hitting the streets in

Extremophile

Basel. That shouldn't be possible. So, what more impossible things could their hunters do? He woke in a cold sweat and lay in the darkness, listening for sounds on the roof, outside the door... Maybe this really was too much for him, but it wasn't just the threat to himself he was worried about. He now also had to worry about risks to his increasingly close companions.

Day 4 ...it's a wonderful life

Bruce woke with a vicious cramp in his left shoulder, which Engel had been using as a pillow throughout the night. He gently eased his arm free, causing her to roll over with a muttered curse. It was five-to, just right for him to cancel the alarm set for six. The flat was lit by the projection windows recreating the glow of a pre-sunrise sky that silhouetted the Läggern and filled the room with soft light. The sheet on the four-poster had been thrown back, displaying Eva spread-eagled on her stomach, which showed off her fine buttocks to great advantage.

Angela emerged from the bathroom just as he reached it. "Bad timing! Five minutes earlier and you could have shared a shower with me."

"Morning," Bruce mumbled, trying to avoid thinking about what such a shower could have led to.

He closed and locked the bathroom door and sighed at the luxury of being able to relax during his morning ablutions.

He had just finished his shower when the banging on the door started. "Open up, Beast! We're busting for a pee. We won't laugh at your naked body, honest."

Bruce unlocked the door and was unceremoniously pushed aside by the two girls, who started fighting for possession of the toilet. He closed the door rapidly behind him and turned to face Angela, who was standing by the luggage, wearing only a miniature white tanga. "I hope you notice these." She sighed, dramatically. "The things I do for this damned project. Anyway, what else should I wear?"

"Anything that minimizes the attention you call to yourself," he answered, hopefully, while pulling on shorts and a loose cotton shirt.

"I'm not sure that I've got anything quite like that here," she responded. "I have only the compact stuff that fits into hand luggage, although I certainly have clothes that would fit the bill in Basel." She pulled on a tube that was, by Angela standards, modest—like about three coats of paint. "I could wear one of Eva's shirts over this."

"Maybe not. Here, try this." Bruce took off his shirt and tossed it to her. The shirt strained to button over her chest, but the overall effect was certainly less provocative than the tube on its own. Bruce noted his approval and pulled on the shirt he had worn the previous day.

Bruce and Angela had completed packing when the girls exploded from the bathroom. "What's for breakfast?" Engel demanded. "Those fuckin' detoxicants make me starving."

Bruce had prudently dropped a tab of an alcohol destructor before leaving the bar the night before. Engel obviously preferred to wait until the hangover began to kick-in before taking counter-measures.

"We'll get something on the train. Get into some respectable clothes now and we can be on our way."

After a rapid debate, both selected shorts and shirts. With a concerted effort to pick up scattered clothing, all the luggage was packed by six forty. Bruce assured the women that the Pützfrau would look after tidying up, so they were able then to head directly for the station.

They were in perfect time for the regional express to Zurich. Although slow compared to the shinkansen, they could buy tickets to Kloten from an automat on board and had time for a very quick coffee and gipfeli in the buffet car before they arrived in the Hauptbahnhof. A connection to the airport sat on the opposite platform; only fifteen minutes later, they were disembarking in the sub-basement of the international terminal. Bruce went directly to an automat, which happily paid out a wad of large denomination notes as direct debit from one of his numbered Swiss accounts.

They took a transit capsule directly to the satellite terminal handling all black flights. The business class entrance hall warned, in at least twenty languages, that entry to the terminal was strictly one-way and subject to a support tax of one thousand Swiss Francs per person. Bruce purchased four tickets on the eleven forty-five to Hong Kong at an interactive terminal that exchanged a considerable number of large banknotes for a single small note and two check-in vouchers.

"I can't get four together, so we have two pairs. 18ab and 20ab, both upper deck." Bruce led them past baggage check-in, directly through the airlock-like double door into the subdued lighting of the executive lounge. "If you're still hungry, you can have a proper breakfast here."

They selected a privacy alcove, set the *engaged* sign, then piled their hand luggage into the corner.

Eva and Engel wandered off to pick up coffee and some other breakfast things from the self-service buffet while Angela dragged out *Akira*. Bruce set up a link from his laptop to the business lounge travel center and set about organizing accommodation in HK and a continuation grey flight to Haneda. As a member of the Pacific Rim econo-bloc, Japan was formally opposed to black transport. Nevertheless, given the continuing chaos of the Japanese economy, a blind eye was turned to flights to Tokyo that paid a special facilitation fee. In a complex series of maneuvers, Bruce bought four single tickets for un-assigned business class seats by different purchasing routes. The only link was that each specified a halal menu. With the bookings coming very close together, there was a good chance that neighboring seats would be assigned.

Breakfast was a drawn-out affair, the women having decided to add sparkle to the boredom of travelling with a jug of Buck's Fizz. Bruce utilized the secure booking system to reserve a suite in a hotel in Shinjuku for a week, not knowing how long it would take to set up the work in Tokai.

By the time priority boarding for business class was announced, Angela and Eva were beginning to show the effects of the champagne. Engel had drunk as much, but was clearly on an inhibitor, acting boisterous, but actually completely sober.

As expected from the outrageous ticket prices, the supersonic flight from Zurich to Hong Kong combined comfort with anonymity. Bruce sat with Angela at the window, while the girls were two rows behind. In addition to a continuous food and bar service, a full interactive entertainment system was on offer. Bruce accompanied Angela in a meal that slipped almost unnoticed from lunch to dinner. Fifteen wines were on offer, all of which were sampled and subjected to Angela's critical review. Bruce was, despite a post-lunch alcohol blocker, feeling pretty fazed by the end of this marathon and declined a cross-comparison of the three brandies available.

During breaks between courses, Angela was working her way through the manga tome. It was only after the first time that she enquired about the English translation of a German word that it dawned on Bruce that it was a German language version of the comic that she was reading. *Having picked it up in Switzerland, not so surprising really.*

Having never read this comic, he was severely challenged by the twentieth-century high-German translations of Japanese slang. It did, however, provide an insight to Angela's past, following his surprise that she spoke German. Apparently she had post-doced for three years in Heidelberg and actually came very close to accepting a permanent post at the university there. Only a better offer from Oxford had dragged her back to England. All other things being equal, she would certainly have rather lived in the academic elitism of Heidelberg than the class-snobbery of Oxford. The Oxford research groups, as opposed to the spoiled undergraduates, were the deciding factor. Both the Medicine and Molecular Biology departments at Oxford were then considered to be at the forefront of life-science research. So, there was no real choice for an extremely talented, ambitious and, as she freely admitted, arrogant researcher. With the exceptions of sabbaticals to LBL and UCLA in the US, Chalmers in Gothenburg, Sweden and Napier in Edinburgh, she had spent her entire academic career climbing up the academic ladder at Oxford.

As if worn out by this revelation of her past, Angela gradually slumped against him and started to snore, just as they commenced their descent into HK. Bruce waited until they touched down before gently shaking her awake and giving her a CLEARUP pill and a large glass of water, which he had already prepared for this purpose. By the time disembarkation had started, Angela was again bright-eyed and bushy-tailed.

With hand luggage only, they passed directly to the free zone exit, Eva and Engel following closely on their heels. They walked fifty meters or so along a bare steel corridor before emerging into a rather plush reception area. An oriental man in his late fifties wearing a dark green uniform immediately stepped forward. "Doctor Quigley, welcome to Hong Kong," he boomed with a surprisingly deep voice and attempted to relieve the entire party of their luggage. After he had managed to take possession of a couple of token pieces, Bruce managed to convince him that they could handle the rest. The chauffeur then led the party out to the executive pick-up zone where a green Rolls Royce was waiting.

The blast of tropical heat between leaving the airport and entering the air-conditioned luxury car was enough to bring sweat to Bruce's brow. Settling into the deep green leather upholstery, he began to feel the weariness of air travel and changing time zones bear down on top of him.

"The Peninsula, what a good idea," Angela commented, as she plumped down beside him. Engel squeezed into the other side of the back seat, while

Eva elected to sit in front with the driver. As soon as they were all settled, the car slid off soundlessly. Conversion to hydrogen obviously had no effect on the performance of a car that dated back to the end of the previous century.

"It's not cheap, but it is one of the tightest hotels in the world. Very popular with the clientele on the black flights, as you can see." Bruce pointed out three other identical green Rolls Royces, which were emerging into the stream of traffic behind them.

The road between the islands leading to Kowloon offered panoramas of the lights from clusters of skyscrapers and myriad boats every time they crossed one of the long suspension bridges. The traffic was relatively light as it was almost midnight, local time, so the trip to their hotel took only about forty-five minutes. As the car drew up, a squad of porters opened the door, each of whom welcomed Doctor Quigley and party to the Peninsula and ensured that there was no possibility of anyone else carrying luggage.

An extremely polite, extremely English under-manager welcomed them profusely. The rather eccentric, heavy-framed glasses that he wore almost certainly contained retinal scanners, to match Bruce to the registration, but this was done once only.

Thereafter, the hotel expert system recognized guests, allowing human staff to greet them by name without fail.

This welcome was sufficient to conclude all registration formalities, and a young oriental man with a marked Oxbridge accent walked them to a lift, which, without any obvious command, took them silently to the top floor of the old building where their suite was located.

Angela was delighted by the pot of fresh tea that awaited them in the living room, and she settled down to pour cups for the entire party. Meanwhile, their guide provided instructions on the various facilities available in the bedrooms, into which their luggage had already been deposited.

With a cheerful, "Goodnight," the man disappeared before a tip could even be considered. Eva observed that Bruce and Angela's luggage had been put together into one of the rooms and mischievously suggested that they give this a try.

"Some chance," Engel responded, immediately setting off to re-organize the bedrooms. "The beast almost pegged out in his attempts to satisfy the needs of a wee skelf of a thing like me. A big wummin would be the very death of him."

Both Angela and Bruce were rather bemused by

the entire proceedings and sat together drinking tea while the girls rearranged luggage. The high ceiling and heavy furniture conveyed a feeling of a vanished era, which seemed eminently conducive to silent relaxation. Having lost another six hours, they were not yet physically tired, but more mentally exhausted.

By the time the girls joined them for tea, it was clear that Bruce's original idea of getting to bed early and then maybe rising early to have a look around before their mid-day flight to Tokyo was going to meet resistance. As a compromise between Engel's suggestion to visit some of the exclusive clubs at the top of Hong Kong Island's super-skyscrapers and Angela's outrageous alternative of ordering in some plastic sheeting and a couple of liters of extra-virginale olive oil, it was decided to have a quick visit to Bottoms-up. This was probably the most famous bar in the city and was, conveniently, within five minutes walking distance.

Bottoms-up was quaint, with a faded tackiness that all four found very amusing. The decor had been frozen in the 1960s when the bar was featured in a cult movie, a policy which paid off when, in the 2050s, *The Man with the Golden Gun* was remade in holo and Bottoms-up returned to its original Kowloon location and was featured more prominently in the film. At one-thirty in the morning, the club was rather quiet. Angela led them to one of the circular bars at which two young men were sitting in animated conversation with a topless barmaid.

The bottle-blonde barmaid had a truly enormous chest, which was clearly the main focus for both the lads...and for Angela. As they sat, the girl turned to them. "Hi, I'm Fi. What can I do you for?" She spoke in some kind of North English accent. Bruce noticed she was actually rather big all over: *definitely built for comfort rather than speed, but very pleasing to the eye regardless.*

By the time the extremophile-hunters were half way through their first drinks, the hostess had introduced them to the two accountants who were also en route to Japan. After another drink, however, the barmaid managed to move the conversation from introductory chit-chat to the topic of breast size — very obviously leading on to tacit offers of services available after the bar closed. Not one to be outdone, Angela removed her shirt and rolled down the top of the tube. Although not quite as big as the barmaid's boobs, Angela's tits were certainly a spectacular sight, especially as she appeared to be very aroused.

The accountants were certainly impressed.

"Yours are certainly bigger," Angela said, "but

are they as firm?" She took the waitress's hands and placed them on her own chest, and then started to squeeze the blonde's breasts while her thumbnails rubbed the dark nipples. At this point, the younger-looking of the men choked on his beer, which started off Eva's giggles. Obviously very embarrassed, the lad turned away and managed to make things worse by knocking his beer into his lap. Engel, who was sitting nearest to him, offered to dry him off with a handful of paper napkins, serving only to increase his discomfort and Eva's amusement.

With evident reluctance, Angela released Fi and ordered a full round for all at the table as an apology for causing the young accountant to spill his drink. The barmaid had just finished serving the drinks, accepting a glass of champagne herself, when Bruce caught a mischievous glance passing between the girls. Just as their victim started to take a first mouthful of his beer, Engel leaned over and took two large handfuls of the goods under discussion by the two well-endowed women. "Pretty good, but I think mine are firmer: do you want to feel them?" As the choking fit recommenced, even his colleague joined in the general hilarity.

Poor guy, he'll probably be scared to touch his drink for the rest of the night.

Extremophile

The game had, however, developed further, with all three males considered fair targets any time they attempted to sip their drinks. Both accountants were caught several times by outrageous exhibitionism or salacious suggestions. Even Bruce spluttered when Angela asked him, mid-drink, if he was going to have anal sex with all three of them again tonight, although she cheated somewhat by grabbing his groin at the same time. The two lads may have been financial wizards but, as they tried to get into the spirit of things and attempted to shock the women, it was clear they were totally outclassed.

While Angela was, apparently seriously, debating whose room they should head for now, Bruce slipped a fast detox pill into her drink. Engel caught his eye and drew Eva into a boisterous hug, dropping a matching pill into the colorful cocktail that they had been sharing. Within five minutes, Angela began to calm down as the alcohol disappeared from her system, by which time Eva had slumped against Engel. Bruce dragged his party to their feet, paying the bill in Swiss Francs and leaving the hostess an excessive tip. *It looks like Fi's lucky night.* He noted that, although obviously reluctant to lose the other three women, the accountants seemed to have decided to take up the blonde's offer of going back to her place for *fun and games*.

Even though it was almost three in the morning, the air was still warm and sticky as they left the club and walked the short distance back to the hotel. The doorman welcomed the party by name and guided them to a lift that, again without any obvious instruction, took them to their penthouse suite.

Although now completely sober, the girls were in high spirits, recapping the various ways in which they had shocked their poor victims. Undressing as they went, Angela and Eva wandered towards their bedroom while Engel took him by the hand and led him towards the other. "Have a shower and we'll meet in your bedroom for a nightcap," Angela shouted through the open door of her room.

The en-suite bathroom contained not only a sizeable shower but also a circular glass hot tub on a raised platform by a window that looked directly out onto the lights of Hong Kong Island. Bruce set the program to fill the tub, start the massage jets, and provide some background Chinese-classical music. He then entered the shower for a quick shave, which he drew out as long as possible in the hope that Engel would join him.

After about ten minutes, feeling both disappointed and more than a little frustrated, Bruce reluctantly turned off the shower, which allowed him to hear the chatter from outside and note that the main bathroom lights had been dimmed. Emerging, he was met by the sight of the disparate bodies of the blonde, brunette and red-haired women, lit by the underwater lights of the Jacuzzi and silhouetted against the skyscraper panorama. Bruce gasped. *I've seen many spectacular sights in my life, but this is certainly the time that I most wished I had a holo-recording system handy.*

Without a word, he slowly slipped into the scorching water between Engel and Angela, positioning one of the jets between his shoulder blades. Without breaking their conversation, Engel slipped onto his knees and Eva took her place against his side. Bruce closed his eyes and concentrated on the sensation of hot water and smooth skin against his body. Almost in a trance, he realized that it was only three days since this entire adventure had started. *Not only has my whole life been turned upside down, but I'm starting to build up incredibly strong feelings for each of these women. It's not just that they're all gorgeous and fun to be with, but there's some kind of empathy and closeness that's more intense than in any relationship I've ever experienced.*

He opened his eyes and saw that Engel had

twisted in his lap and was now kissing Eva. Turning to Angela, he was just in time to meet her lips as they opened and her tongue slipped into his mouth. Time slowed down and Bruce lost himself in a miasma of the sensations of touch and taste. He had no idea how long it was before the girls started to get restless and clambered out, heading for the shower.

From the noises, it was evident that a lot more than washing was going on. Angela straddled his lap and laid her brow on his shoulder. Bruce looped one arm round her waist and rubbed the back of her neck with his other hand. He was rewarded by a deep, almost sub-base growl of contentment that sent a shiver up his spine. Slowly, Angela straightened up and presented him with a face-level view of her impressive frontal system. She teased the side of his nose with a nipple the size and hardness of an acorn before shoving it between his lips. As he squeezed the succulent nipple with lips and teeth and caressed it with his tongue, he felt a contentment, which was certainly sexual, but not the fire of his previous encounters with Engel. *Undoubtedly, shrinks would attribute this to some kind of throwback to a childhood suckling experience, but who cares? It's bloody good fun anyway.*

Angela changed nipples and Bruce closed his

eyes, the better to drown in the flood of tactile sensations. Almost without him noticing, Angela had raised herself up so that her lower lips were poised over the tip of his penis. With infinite slowness, she lowered herself onto him. Releasing her nipple, he looked straight into Angela's deep brown eyes, which were certainly not those of a shy young virgin. *This is a fully mature woman who had seen and done a lot...and had had seventy-five years to do so*, he reminded himself.

Her features were even more striking in the shimmering underwater lighting, giving him the impression of some kind of primitive earth Goddess hovering over him. She was a big woman in every way. Even though he felt himself to be fully erect, he had slipped into her without any resistance at all. *Like throwing a sausage up a close.* He smiled at the irreverence of the thought.

She slowly leaned back and he took hold of a nipple between each thumb and forefinger, a wrinkling of her eyes indicating that he had done as she intended. Without losing eye contact, they started to move together with the rhythm matching that of the increasingly hard squeezing of her nipples.

As her breaths began to come in gasps, she tore her eyes away from his and sank her teeth into his shoulder. The pain hit him as her muscles clamped round his dick, squeezing him like a vice. He groaned loudly as the orgasm caused his back to arch, the sound lost in a scream from Angela as, with head thrown back, she started to bounce on his lap, splashing water from the pool in fountains. It probably lasted only twenty seconds, but the violence of her orgasm was beginning to frighten him when she finally slumped on top of him with a satisfied, if inelegant, grunt.

As awareness of his surroundings began to slowly drift back, the giggles from the two shapes silhouetted in the bathroom doorway became noticeable. Despite the happenings of the last seventy-two hours, Bruce felt somehow embarrassed. *Something to do with being caught making love to someone old enough to be my mother, I suppose.*

Angela's telepathy was clearly still functioning. "Don't worry about that pair, they're just jealous," she whispered into his ear.

Could be, he mused as he started rubbing Angela's neck again, *but jealous of whom?*

About five minutes later, Angela hugged him tightly then clambered over him and out of the pool, standing painfully on his thigh in the process. Bruce hardly reacted at all, entranced by the view as she bent to pick up a towel. *Callipygous, that's the word for it. Indeed, the very epitome of callipygousness, if that's a word. If not, it certainly should be.*

"Stop ogling, dear, and come to bed," this personification of Aphrodite commanded in a schoolmarm-like tone that was in shocking incongruity to her appearance. With this she strutted off towards the bedroom, rubbing her hair vigorously.

Bruce pulled himself out of the pool and set off the cleaning-draining cycle. As he splashed though the surrounding puddles, he noticed just how much water the good professor had displaced in the height of her passion. He slipped into the shower for a mini splash and blow-dry, emerging within seconds: dry and smelling slightly of some kind of designer-pheromone. *Pheromones that drive the girls wild, what a laugh. I've been dowsing myself in that shit for years, with marked lack of success. Now I'm living in a wet dream come true, and this little dab of musk-from-a-vat hasn't a hope in hell of cutting through the stink of excited women that permeates the entire suite.* He inhaled deeply. *Can't beat that with a big stick.*

He was not surprised to see the three women piled together in the center of the king-size bed, but hoped his disappointment wasn't too obvious as it became clear that Angela and Eva were kissing their goodnights to Engel. Eva pulled herself loose, crawled towards Bruce and pulled him into a kiss that was surprisingly gentle. Sweet, he would have called it, had the tall blonde been wearing any clothes. She pulled loose, stood and bent over to give Engel a last peck and walked towards the door. Angela then crawled over a squirming Engel to take Eva's place.

Bruce looked directly into Angela's eyes. In the brighter light of the bedroom they looked, paradoxically, even darker than in the pool. In a way that was extremely intimate without being sexual, she ran the tip of her tongue along his lips before rubbing them with her own. Before he could work out how to respond, she had given him a quick hug and bounced to her feet to follow Eva.

He stood mesmerized watching her departing back...or departing buttocks, to be more accurate. The spell was broken by a whisper. "Put your fuckin' eyes back in their sockets and get your sad pallid arse into this bed."

Bruce obeyed without a word and lay back while the small body squirmed against him and organized his limbs to suit her desired sleeping position. He gently stroked her head as she mumbled into his chest. "That was a mistake, Beast. You're getting far too personally involved. In any case, she's too big for you. And too old. You like young girls. Remember your fuckin' psych profile."

Bruce filtered out this background until it had transformed itself into rhythmic snoring. Somehow the noise was reassuring, a solid benchmark in an environment that was rapidly becoming as bizarre from an emotional point of view as it was technically. He commanded the lights to dim, rather than off, so that he could still make out the profile of the head on his chest.

Well, it looks as if we've done it, finally slipped away from our pursuers. The longer we're invisible, the harder it'll be to catch up with us, as the search problem increases exponentially with time. He should have been re-assured, but his thoughts kept returning to the attack in Glasgow and pursuit in Basel. It niggled and he kept coming back to it, like a tongue probing an aching tooth. *Am I missing something here and, if so, am I leading these three women into a lethal trap?*

Ian Mckinley

Day 5 ...big in Japan

Bruce was violently ejected from a dream in which he was having a long, drawn-out bath with someone who seemed to alternate between Angela, then his long-deceased mother, and then an aunt whom he hadn't seen for at least twenty years. The small, naked body bouncing on his chest only contributed further to his confusion, as the sequence that seemed so normal in the dream showed its weird absurdity on waking.

"Come on, Beast. Time to move. It's ten o'clock already."

"Fuck!" Bruce exploded from the bed, effortlessly pushing the small figure to the side. "We've got only about an hour to get to—"

He stopped when Engel's face broke into a grin. "What's so funny?"

"It's not quite ten yet, but it will be in a couple of

hours. I just wanted to see if I could get your blood pressure as high as the fat pensioner did last night."

"You little shite." He threw himself at her.

She tried to roll out of the way, but was hindered by both a tangle of sheets and an attack of giggles.

Bruce used his weight to hold down the wriggling girl, while ensuring that her knee-jabs to his groin stayed wide of their mark. He managed to get a hold of both wrists at the cost of a slim thigh that was pushing up increasingly painfully into his groin, when the noise brought in the others.

"God, they're frisky this morning," Eva said to Angela. "Tomorrow night we shouldn't go so easy on them, Prof."

Eva's voice was enough of a distraction for Engel to pull Bruce forward and bite his chest hard, using his reaction to slide loose and jump to her feet. Adding insult to injury, she retained a grip on his left wrist and hammered on a wristlock, which forced his face deep into the thick pile of the bedside rug.

"Okay, Blondie, if you're in the mood, we can continue where we left off last night," Engel offered. "You probably couldn't even excite me enough to give the flabby-arsed old Beast here a chance to escape."

Eva hurled herself at the smaller woman. The

pressure on Bruce's wrist vanished, and by the time he had crawled to his knees, a tickling competition was well under way on the bed, with Eva having the distinct advantage of being fully clothed.

"Come on, lad, time for a bit of breakfast." Angela pulled him towards the lounge and handed him a yukata that had been sitting folded on a stool at the bottom of the bed. She was already dressed in a cheongsam that was, by far, the most modest item of clothing that he had yet seen her wearing. It was, nevertheless, slit to waist level and cut to make her breasts look even more spectacular. When she sat down opposite him at the low coffee table, which was set for a sumptuous breakfast, Bruce could not help noticing that she seemed to be wearing self-supporting stockings and nothing else beneath it. "The Chinese are a bit shy," she explained without prompting, "but there's no need to get unhygienic."

"You know," he started as he poured himself a coffee, "I've been thinking about this jaunt and there's something bothering me. Longevity and rejuvenation are worth an absolute mint. Any crumbly would pay a fortune for this treatment, and there are a hell of a lot of mega-rich geriatrics about. I'd have thought that your Pharm would stake you for a hundred labs, if that's what you need. And that also goes for your opposition *network*. With something this valuable up for grabs, it's amazing that they haven't mobilized equivalent resources."

"It's not so easy," she responded. "Think about the consequences of having a treatment like this available. Population pressure was already our number one problem before global climate change made things even worse. Greater longevity is just the thing that most governments don't need. Of course, individually, all old politicos will want to get a hold of it for themselves and their buddies."

Angela was now in full lecturing mode. "Rejuvenation is, by no means, a boon for mankind. In fact it could be the greatest curse ever. Because of this, the project is classified ultra-top-secret. Even in my Pharm, there's probably less than a half dozen people who know about the longevity side and not many more who have even heard of a rejuvenation project. Even our opposition, whoever they are, must be aware that we're playing with fire here. I'd guess, in fact, that they're probably even more worried about any word of such a drug getting out than we are. It really is a tricky balance, having a project big enough to get results but small enough not to attract unwelcome attention. We still haven't a clear policy for what we do if I ever manage to develop a marketable product. Something to think about, though."

Bruce continued his breakfast in silence, his mind spinning as he tried to grasp the wider aspects of a longevity drug. *The more I think about the potential problems, the more I understand the desire of all those involved to maintain secrecy. Even the knowledge of the existence of such a treatment could cause worldwide chaos.*

Bruce was finishing his second cup of coffee when a couple of disheveled but grinning girls emerged from the bedroom. They were both wearing khaki shorts and white blouses, which tied between their breasts. Eva was wearing light boots while Engel was, as usual, barefoot. This further emphasized their difference in height: the slight redhead well below shoulder height of the tall blonde.

Bruce left to dress while the girls descended on the breakfast spread like a pair of starved wolverines. *How do they stay so slim? If I ate half as much as they do, I'd be plumper than I am already.* He threw the yukata onto the bed and pinched the roll of fat around his waist. *As soon as I get back from this jaunt, I'm seriously going to get myself into shape,* he promised himself, although not for the first time.

After enjoying undisturbed ablutions, it took only a few moments for him to slip into shorts, sandals and a loose, raw silk shirt. Then only a couple of minutes more to repack the few items that had been removed from his luggage. He returned to the lounge just as the girls were finishing their breakfast.

Angela, feet propped up on her packed bag, was screening through various news servers. Sitting beside her on the sofa, Bruce accessed the hotel mainframe on his laptop and checked the travel bookings. The Cathay eleven-ten to Haneda was confirmed, with seats 11a, b, f and 12f. Not perfect, but not bad. He booked the Rolls for the trip to the airport, giving the departing flight as the JAL eleven-thirty to Narita. *It'll make the check-in a bit tight, but as we have hand luggage only, this shouldn't be a problem. Despite the security of the Peninsula, you can't be paranoid enough in this game.* He couldn't shake his foreboding of the previous night but was determined to prevent Angela from worrying about concerns that might be figments of his over-active imagination.

All were packed and ready well before the assistant manager, accompanied by two bellboys, arrived to guide them to the car. Checkout was restricted to the question, "Was everything to your satisfaction, Dr. Quigley?" His confirmation was sufficient to debit his account and close all records of their stay.

The drive to the airport through a bright tropical drizzle was uneventful. They managed to discourage the driver from carrying their bags to check-in, waving him away cheerfully. Immediately after the car had left, they headed to the Cathey lounge rather than the JAL desks that they were now facing. The grey-flight exec lounge was less secluded than the black lounge in Zurich, but they could complete ticketing there in the anonymity of a shielded terminal.

This formality was just completed when a first boarding call for their flight was announced. Their seats were at the front of the upper deck of the 797-megatop. Because the flight was half empty, Bruce was easily able to exchange seat 11f for 12g, so that he and Angela could sit together. The airhostess confirmed their halal meals and, with only a slightly raised eyebrow, took their orders for champagne as a pre-takeoff drink.

The flight was mainly sub-sonic and took a full three hours. Angela managed to draw out lunch to cover most of this period, while the girls restricted themselves to a snack, allowing more time for some kind of combat game they had accessed from the entertainment system. The sonic neutralizer eliminated all noise coming from their seats, but their vigorous hand movements indicated that some very serious mayhem was going on.

At Haneda, the group passed quickly through passport control, using a set of Swiss Pharm VIP-passports that took them through a diplomatic channel with hardly a glance from the bored-looking inspector. With no luggage to collect, they continued directly to the unoccupied diplomat/VIP customs area and then straight through to the exec pick-up point. Most of the chauffeurs in the area were holding cards with the names of firms or individuals, predominantly in English but a few in kanji.

To the far left was a row of stretched Mercedes under a banner proclaiming *Executive ground transportation*. Bruce led them to the first in line, the door of which opened by itself as the group approached. "Shinjuku Hilton, dozo," he ordered into a grill set in the smoked glass divider, while the ladies settled themselves into the deep leather upholstery. The car moved off silently down a long ramp, which emerged moments later into bright afternoon sunshine.

As they cruised along the freeway towards Tokyo Bay Bridge, all four peered out of the one-way windows to view the latest miracles of reconstruction in what, even after twenty years, was still one of the biggest construction sites on earth. Bruce filled-in the others on some of the details.

Although the epicenter of the H-57 quake had been under the Bay, the 8.1 magnitude temblor had completely flattened many of the main commercial areas of the megalopolis, including Shinagawa, Ebisu, Shibuya, Rippongi and Ginza. The pattern of maximum destruction curved through the city, but still left some districts relatively unscathed, although many of these were subsequently devastated by fires that burned for days in areas such as Akasaka.

The sky-towers of Shinjuku could be seen through the haze, looming in the distance. The earthquake engineering of the Shinjuku skyscrapers had proved its worth. Paradoxically, however, several of the buildings that appeared unaffected by the quake had to be torn down and rebuilt afterwards when the new post-disaster building codes were introduced, at a total cost higher than that of replacing the structures that had collapsed.

The Great Kanto Quake unfortunately coincided with the increasing frequency of Pacific super-typhoons, during a season that now extended from early May until late November. During 2045 alone, the devastated city was hit by no less than eight storms with peak winds over 150 km/h, wreaking further havoc and making rebuilding almost impossible. Nevertheless, with typical Japanese ingenuity, the form of Tokyo was redefined, creating an almost continuous plain of connected three to five-story buildings, separated by roofed-over streets. The only things emerging above this layer of concrete were a forest of aerials, occasional domes that covered parks, monuments and sports centers, the glass-walled freeways, and the sky-towers.

Tokyo had never been an attractive city, but now it was positively ugly. As before, however, some of the more audacious skyscrapers were eye-catching and impressive examples of engineering hubris. One definite improvement, though, was that freeway traffic moved much smoother than ever before.

Shinjuku was still dominated by the Tokyo metropolitan buildings, which looked much as they had at the end of the 20th century, their iconic appearance like something from Fritz Lang's *Metropolis*. The retrofitted exoskeleton and DLC skin was completely invisible, but allowed these monsters to withstand the worst that the turbo-charged climate could throw at them. Many of the other towers in the area retained the names of past blocks or hotels—Sumitomo, NKK, Keio Plaza, I-land Plaza, Washington—but had been totally rebuilt or transmogrified by supports and armoring. The Hilton was a featureless light-brown curved wall about forty floors high, but further details were lost as an off-ramp from the freeway took them into a warren of tunnels. The driver was clearly familiar with the area and confidently snaked his way through a bewildering series of junctions to pull smoothly into the underground Hilton reception area.

Bruce authorized a credit transfer from one of his Swiss accounts then the taxi door slid open. "Domo, arigato gozaimasu," he muttered in the direction of the unseen driver. Assuming, of course, that there had been a driver; automation was very extensive in Japan, but superfluous use of manpower in make-work jobs was also common. This latter point was emphasized as a swarm of bellboys and bellgirls descended on them, insisting on carrying all items of luggage. Trying to assure them that the hand luggage was light and that assistance was not needed didn't help. Giving up the fight, Bruce asked for the Executive floor. The party was then led to a special elevator that took them directly to a lounge on the thirty-seventh floor. As they ascended, Bruce noticed that the hotel catered to both Eastern and Western superstitions, having neither a fourth nor a thirteenth floor.

Extremophile

Well, if you've had as much bad luck as the Japanese, you can't be too careful.

The registration formalities needed little more than a retinal scan for Bruce to authorize transfer of a deposit, which would more than cover the cost of their planned stay. He and Angela had already discussed various payment options while in Japan and had agreed that working off a range of his private Swiss accounts was the least risky. Cash would have been more secure but, unlike Switzerland, paying large bills in any way other than electronic transfer would call attention to them here. Real money still existed in Japan, but was rarely used. Charge chips were ubiquitous, even for the smallest purchases.

By the time they had been led to their suite, conveniently located only a few doors along the corridor from the lounge, their luggage had already been laid out on a rack in the entrance hall. From the dimensions of this rack, it was clear that guests were generally accompanied by a lot more than hand luggage. When his offer to unpack was gently declined, the porter set the voice recognition to respond to 'Doctor Bruce and party' and withdrew. It wasn't exactly the most sophisticated deception, but for one of his numbered accounts with a small private bank, he had simply reversed his Christian and surnames. The bank would have happily accepted any name for the account; there were probably quite a few M. Mouses, D. Ducks and C. Kents among the list of patrons of that venerable institution.

The hall led into a sitting room that featured a full wall depiction of the drab city stretching out to the distant mountains dominated by the perfect cone of Mount Fuji. On command, this idealized picture was replaced by reality, showing exactly the same view, except that now Fuji and the other mountains were lost in a sickly-looking orange haze. At the extreme edge of their view was a suggestion of darkness, which seemed out of place in this early summer evening. Bruce pointed this out as an indication that the weather might be about to change, an opinion which was confirmed when he called up a spot weather map showing the giant black spiral of a typhoon heading directly for them. "Looks like we're due for a bit of weather," Bruce commented before he called pristine Fuji back onto the screen.

Angela and Eva grabbed their bags and took the door to the left, while Bruce followed Engel into the small but neat bedroom to the right. The en-suite bathroom was positively claustrophobic when compared to the facilities in the Peninsula, but it contained all the very latest gadgets in a miracle of ergonomic planning. Engel was examining the bed, which, although just big enough to qualify as *double*, seemed to have all kinds of built-in goodies. She drew out some silk cord from a compartment in the headboard. "Look, we can play at bondage again. See if it has the same effect on you as it did in Glasgow."

"Don't tempt me," he responded, uncomfortably aware that even the memory was beginning to affect his composure. "I'll definitely take you up on your offer if you can find a bull-whip in there."

Engel chucked her blouse into the recycler and walked round the bed towards him, grabbing him by the shirt front and standing on tiptoes for emphasis as she stared into his eyes. "Maybe that wouldn't be a bad idea. At least it might take your mind off the old, fat one. You're getting emotionally involved and that's a fuckin', fuckin' bad idea. You, mate, are just a big soft dod of shite." With that, she kneed him in the groin, twisted under his grab at her, and threw him onto the bed with his elbow held in an excruciating lock. "See what I mean, I'm cute as shit and give you a boner if I even look at you sideways, but you've still got to be careful."

A hard nipple rubbed his earlobe and he attempted to bite it, only to be rewarded with a shock of pain that took his breath away and slammed his face into the hard mattress. The pain then vanished as Engel bounced back out of range of any possible retribution.

"Thus endeth the lesson," she stated smugly and started to peel off her shorts. "Do you think we can squeeze into that micro-Japanese shower together? If we can, and if you can get it into your fuckin' thick Jock skull that a quick BJ in the shower isn't a fuckin' commitment to marriage, well, you never know your luck."

***

Emerging to the sitting room about twenty minutes later, Bruce was greeted by a grin from Angela that increased his confusion even more. "What?"

"My good news is that I've contacted Hideki and arranged to meet him tomorrow." She raised an eyebrow. "Eva tried to book the gym, but the only free block is at nine tomorrow morning. We could go for an open session before then, but I guess we might attract too much attention."

What an understatement, this trio attracts attention in the West, fully clothed, standing still. Cavorting about in a Tokyo gym, they'd be the talk of the town in nul-comma-nul. "I think you're right there. I'll wait until we've talked to your bugs prof before I go further with Tokai. What about dinner? The best option would be room-service," he suggested, hopefully.

The chorus of objections to this proposal came as no surprise. "Well, at least, somewhere in the hotel," he suggested as a compromise. "What about tepanyaki or tempura, those are two options in the penthouse restaurant here?"

"What's the tepan-thing...?" Engel started to ask before she was over-ridden by Angela.

"Tempura, my favorite, that'll do nicely."

Engel limited herself to rolling her eyes behind the tall brunette's back.

Angela left to dress and quickly reappeared wearing her usual ephemeral tube, this one a smoky grey-pink, which made it difficult to assess if it really was as outrageously transparent as it appeared to be. Bruce thought of sending her off to change back into the cheongsam but, realizing that any chance of changing the prof's mind was negligible, restricted himself to an audible sigh.

The girls flowed out of Angela's bedroom, wearing mini-dresses that, by their standards, were almost modest. As if sensing his satisfaction, they lifted their hems to reveal one pair of completely transparent knickers and a blonde bush. The expression on his face was enough to send them into a fit of giggles.

Following the glares that greeted his suggestion of a drink from the minibar, Bruce reserved a window niche in the restaurant, making sure that it was Western-style seating, then herded the women to the executive lounge for a pre-prandial drink. "Look at the bright side," he announced to nobody in particular, "the chance of any men noting what your faces look like is pretty remote given your rig-outs."

The lounge was relatively quiet and most window alcoves were still free. Despite the low lighting, Bruce's companions attracted several long stares from the solitary businessmen and even managed to bring the intense wheeler-dealing of some of the smaller groups to a grinding halt. Eva's smile managed to cause a grey-haired Japanese salaryman to choke on his martini, but Bruce managed to intercept her before she could do further damage by bending to pick up the napkin that he had dropped on the floor. "Cut it out," he whispered hoarsely into her ear, "we don't need the fuss of some exec pegging out just at the present moment."

They were still seating themselves when a petite Japanese girl in a navy-blue uniform appeared to take their drinks order. Within a minute, she was back with three glasses of champagne, a bottle of Sapporo beer and a dish with an assortment of Western and Eastern nibbles. Bruce glared at Angela when she started in with an obvious chat-up line, raising his eyebrows in surprise when she backed off immediately, allowing the rather flustered-looking waitress to escape.

The lounge looked onto a number of other sky-towers, which, as the light faded, became increasingly interesting as their bland walls became translucent, building up a kaleidoscope pattern of offices, bars, shops and the wide diversity of other premises therein.

Angela launched into a monologue on Japanese cuisine. Even Bruce, who was much more familiar with Japan than the others, learned a lot over the next half hour. Their little waitress approached shyly about halfway through and also seemed engrossed in Angela's presentation. She seemed flustered when she noticed Bruce's empty bottle and, without a word, hurried off to bring a second round.

Although the women seemed settled, Bruce dragged them off before they could be talked into a third round. It was becoming increasingly obvious that their table was having the effect of a black hole, causing all men entering the lounge, and a couple of women, to gravitate towards it.

Their departure was evidently a disappointment to many and caused a number of stares at Bruce, which ranged from jealous to downright hostile. *Well, many times I've cussed these old rich bastards with their entourages of foxy ladies. I may not be rich, but companions don't come much foxier than this bunch.*

The lift disgorged them into the forty-first floor foyer, which led towards the specialist tepanyaki, tempura and French/Alsatian restaurants. A waiter met them at the entrance and led them to an alcove with a candle-lit table set next to a full-wall window, which presented a view that was not for the vertiginous. The non-reflective glass was obviously a source of amusement for the staff, as the waiter enquired politely, but with a gleam in his eye, if they would like the view blanked or amended.

"Not at all," Angela responded, while she shoved Eva into the window-side seat.

"No, no problem at all," Engel confirmed, standing back to allow Bruce to take the equivalent position on the other side of the table. Bruce and Eva grinned at each other, for once clearly in a dominant position.

"Tempura Set A for four," Angela ordered after a perfunctory glance at the menu, and as usual without consulting the others.

"And," Bruce added before the waiter turned to leave, "four large Ebisu and a bottle of whatever sake you'd recommend, cold."

Angela started to launch into a critique of sakes, but Bruce broke in to point out almost continuous lightning in the distant wall of clouds, which defined themselves by blackness against the grey of the horizon. Engel stood to get a better look but sat again rapidly as she caught sight of the precipitous view.

Bruce could not resist teasing his partner with a couple of anecdotes based on accidents during construction of the sky-towers, to which Eva added gruesome descriptions of people being thrown out of skyscraper windows during earthquakes or sucked out when windows blew during typhoons. Bruce had just noticed that Angela's knuckles were white from her grip on the table when, exactly on cue, the entire building gave a noticeable jolt to the side.

"Fuuuck!" Engel gasped, grabbing hold of Bruce's arm with a grip that threatened to stop the flow of blood. "Christ! Shit, what the fuck was that?"

Angela had dropped forward onto the table with eyes closed, knocking over two water glasses. Even Eva was sitting bolt upright with eyes like saucers.

"It's okay, it's okay." Bruce crushed Engel to him

with one arm and reached forward to stroke Angela's cheek with his other hand. "It's just a wee tremor. They happen regularly, a couple of times a day maybe. Most of the time you can't even feel them. However, if the frequency is right, you sometimes get a shake that's noticeable in the towers. Safe as houses, though."

"As long as the glass doesn't crack and you don't get sucked out," Eva added with a grin. She seemed to have completely recovered and started to debate about whether it was more likely that your heart stopped during the drop of forty stories or whether you hit the ground fully conscious.

Bruce glared at her.

"Enough...please," Angela requested with a quavering voice, and Eva stopped mid-sentence, with a smooth segue into a question about the various components of the first course.

Angela described what to expect by the time the food arrived, along with the drinks. The waiter also dabbed-up spilled water and refilled the glasses. "Only micro-quake," he clarified in an apologetic tone. "Less than four point five, maybe."

"I wouldn't fancy a bloody mini-quake then," Engel commented after he left. "Much less a midi-quake...and I don't even want to think about maxi-quakes."

Bruce almost commented on the likelihood of these various events but, glancing at Angela's strained face, directed the conversation back onto the topic of sake.

Thereafter the meal progressed smoothly, tension relaxing as a sequence of picture-book-quality presentations of different types of vegetable and fish tempura appeared, to be matched with Angela's choice of sake to accompany them.

By the time the final course of fresh melon accompanied by green tea was reached, the women were getting quite merry. Reluctantly, Bruce slipped down a tab of alc-detox and felt the warm buzz of alcohol slowly fade from his body. As he tried to surreptitiously drop a tab into Angela's tea, Engel nuzzled his ear. "Leave it, Jim, auld fat-arse could do wi' a drink in her the noo," she whispered in an exaggerated version of his own Glasgow accent.

"Well then, I guess it's time to go back to the room for a quick bit of ménage-a-quatre." He raised his eyebrows hopefully.

"Dream on, Beast," Eva responded. "Don't you know that *girls just wanna have fun*?"

Engel spontaneously joined her singing the ancient Cyndi Lauper refrain.

"Early to bed seemed like a fun idea to me," Bruce mumbled under his breath while the women discussed options.

"Just a drink or two," Angela insisted, "somewhere outside this bloody hotel. We're in Japan but, in here, we could be anywhere in the world."

"Apart from the view out of the window," Eva added mischievously, ignoring Angela's glare.

"Yea, exactly," Engel chipped in. "A nice claustrophobic wee basement would be the very dab."

Bruce's token objections were completely ignored, as he knew they would be, so he focused on damage-limitation. "Okay, okay, but we stick to somewhere within walking distance."

He led them from the table to the lift, which took them directly to the basement level one. A labyrinth of tunnels with moving walkways spread out in all directions, but Bruce set off confidently in the direction of the Sumitomo building. Ignoring access to the sky tower with its characteristic triangular cross-section, he veered off towards the Keio Plaza hotel and the main artery to Shinjuku station. At this time of night and with the imminent storm, there were very few people in the underground walkways: a few extremely tired looking salarymen, the odd gaijin and one large group of young office workers, all of whom were extremely drunk. The girls certainly caused a few turned heads but, as miniskirts seemed to be common wear for most of the Japanese women they encountered, they didn't look out of place. Even their blonde and red hair attracted little attention, as Japanese hair dyes seemed to cover most of the visible spectrum.

Bruce led the party up to ground level at a shopping complex that filled the old Shinjuku post office. Although the roads here were also roofed-over, the surrounding shops and bars dropped them into a barrage of lights, colors and sounds that gave the impression of being *outside*. In contrast to the tunnels, the streets here were packed with a jostling throng, mainly Japanese, but with occasional tall foreigners standing out.

Bruce squirmed through the crush of bodies, allowing the others to follow in his wake while he set off up one of the small side streets. After about a hundred meters, he pushed right into a dingy stairway that dropped down into what was clearly a pre-quake building. The stairs opened up into *The Shamrock*, an Irish bar that certainly fit Eva's requirement of a claustrophobic basement.

By a stroke of luck, a group of raucous Japanese

girls were getting up to leave a cubby to the left of the bar. Bruce guided the women towards the vacated table, thus not having to fight farther through the crowded bar.

As he ordered drinks, three Bushmills and a pint of Guinness, Bruce noticed that his companions had attracted the attention of a group of five very large Westerners who were blocking the far end of the bar. *Rugby or American football, I'd guess, probably the latter.* This seemed to be confirmed as he caught a marked Yankee accent from the tallest of the group. The heavily-built man must have been over two meters ten; his head almost touched the ceiling.

Bruce squeezed back with the drinks and noted that Angela appeared to have completely recovered and was well ahead in the game of naming an Irish pub in each of the major world cities. Eva had just lodged an objection based on checks via the pub datalink, but she had to concede defeat when a further search confirmed that the pub involved, *Delaney's* in Hong Kong, had indeed been there thirty-five years ago when Angela had last visited the city. The pub database also informed them that they were actually in the third incarnation of *The Shamrock* at this particular location; it seemed to close and reopen on a ten-year cycle.

Extremophile

They were just discussing options for a second round when the huge American pushed his way to their table, his companions in tow. "You guys wanna havva drink with us?" he drawled, trying without much success to keep his eyes off Angela's chest.

"We're not guys, we're gals," Engel pointed out. "Anyway, thank you very much for your kind offer, but no thanks."

"A'm not talking to you, boy-girl. You wanna join us, Honey?" He addressed his question directly to a smiling Angela.

Bruce reached a restraining hand towards his partner, but was far too slow. Engel jumped onto the bench, which still left her a head shorter than her tormentor, and waved a finger under his nose. "Right, fuckwit, no more Little Miss Polite. Which part of take a flying fuck to yourself don't you understand?"

The big guy's attempt to slap her hand away from his face was not even close. Before he knew what was happening, she had grabbed his pinkie. "It's not gentlemanly for a big man to hit a small woman," she pointed out in a polite Anglicized voice, just before his finger snapped with an audible crack.

Bruce shrugged and sat back. *If I mess in now, it would probably just encourage the others. As it is, this fuckwit's friends can hardly move in to help him against a girl a fraction of his size.*

Chivalry clearly took second place to pain, as a seriously pissed-off Yank attempted to grab Engel by the throat. Bruce winced at the noise of the poor mug's teeth snapping together following the kick to his jaw. The intake of breath from a couple of the watching football-players was probably more due to their view of Engel's crotch rather than admiration of the beauty of the move.

Being shown up in front of his buddies had obviously robbed the big idiot of whatever sense he may once have possessed. He swung a haymaker at Engel, which even Bruce saw coming ages in advance. The slight girl froze, as if terrified, long enough for a grin of satisfaction to begin to light up his face. Her hands blurred and the loud cracks were almost simultaneous when she broke his arm in two places. His face went white and his arm slumped to his side. Engel's leg came up to waist height, showing off a bare foot with toes pulled back. Two blurred motions caused wet breaking noises when she kicked in some ribs on the left and right sides of his chest.

Now Bruce stood and put his hand gently on her waist. "That's enough now, don't kill him."

"Fine, fine, fine but never-again-raise-your-hand-to-a-woman." Engel made her points with a series of fast kicks to his face. "Cunt!" With this last expletive she whirled into a back-roundhouse kick—to Bruce an apparent impossibility in the restricted space available—which landed with a sickening thud against the side of poor Goliath's head. His eyes glazed as he dropped towards his friends, who managed to catch him before he hit the floor.

The bar was so crowded and the action so fast that most of the clientele had missed everything. Nevertheless, attention was turning in their direction while Bruce easily lifted down the triumphant nymph and pointed her towards the door.

He immediately steered Engel up the stairs, checking that Angela was behind him with Eva bringing up the rear. He turned again at the top of the stairs, just in time to see a couple of the other Americans rushing up the stairway behind them. The one in the front was probably rewarded with a beautiful view of Eva's golden pubes in the instant before her kick landed on his nose, sending him backwards in a spectacular fountain of blood. The second jumped to the side and managed to avoid being bowled over. He could not help reflexively glancing down when his buddy crashed into a heap at the bottom of the stairs, so he didn't even see the kick that caught him just below the ear and catapulted him on top of his groaning pal.

With an arm round Angela, Bruce propelled his party towards the nearest entrance to the underground walkways, muttering a litany of curses below his breath. At the last moment, however, he changed his mind and shepherded the group past the entrance, and pointed them in the general direction of the Keio Plaza. *On balance, the crowds should provide more cover than anything available in the quiet lower levels.*

Sticking to the upper levels, they got as far as I-land before Angela asked if they could stop for a quick drink. Bruce tried to argue that they were only a few hundred meters from the Hilton, but the deciding factor was Eva, who pointed out that it might be advisable for her to wash blood off her leg before entering the hotel. They settled for a small Yebisu beer hall in I-land. After the girls headed off in search of the toilet, Bruce ordered a large creamy-top stout and three cognacs. He held Angela's hand silently while she breathed deeply and slowly in some sort of calming exercise.

The drinks had arrived before the girls bounced back, obviously in very high spirits. "Now what the fuck was that all about?" Bruce challenged Engel before she even managed to sit down. "We're supposed to remain inconspicuous and you decide to kick the fuckin' brains out of a brick shithouse in a packed bar. Three quarters of fuckin' Shinjuku will hear stories about the redhead ninja before the night is out."

"Sorry, sorry, sorry...all right. The guy was just such a total wanker. Look at it as a free workout. And, in any case, it's our job to protect our clients from such tossbags," she finished, obviously clutching at straws.

"On the bright side," Eva added, "there's no way they're going to go to the police. Could you imagine some hundred-fifty kilo running forward admitting that a fifty kilo girl pulped him?"

"On the bright side, they may still be capable of going to the police," he responded. "I wouldn't be the least bit surprised if one or more aren't in intensive care by now."

"Or in the morgue," Engel added gleefully, before realizing that she wasn't doing her case any good.

"The fight itself isn't the problem," Angela broke in with a shaky voice. "I don't suppose anybody noticed who was standing at the bar just at the other side of that bunch of overgrown idiots? Unless I'm going blind in my old age, it was the two guys from

Bottoms-up."

"No Chance!"

"No Way!" Engel and Bruce responded almost simultaneously.

"It couldn't possibly have been deliberate," he continued. "How could anyone know that we would end up in that pub...out of all the places in Tokyo?" Even as he asked the question, he felt a shiver down his spine, reminding him of his hidden worries.

Engel raised her eyebrows and, catching his eye, mimed checking her watch against something imaginary hanging from her nipple.

"Whatever. If it was the same guys, then I think we can forget about coincidence as an explanation. I can't think of how it's possible, but it looks like somebody is successfully tailing us despite all our precautions. Anyway, we're much too obvious as a group, especially now." He glared at Engel. "Whenever possible, we need to split up. You women will also have to change your appearances. At the very least, dyed hair, all hair, if you can't wear something that covers it." The glower this time he directed at Eva. "We'll move out of the Hilton tomorrow. Anything needed to change your appearance can be sorted out en route to our next accommodation."

"Right, let's get back to the room," Angela announced, knocking back the remnants of her drink.

It was a rather muted party that entered their suite. *Somehow, after Basel, this trip had become a bit of a game. More like tourism than the buildup to some high risk breaking and entering. Now we've been reminded that we're playing against serious opposition with frightening resources. All we needed is one slip-up and the consequences could be fatal for us all.*

Nobody suggested a nightcap so, although it was still relatively early, they headed off to their bedrooms after agreeing to have breakfast after the booked dojo session. There was no objection to Bruce's suggestion of sticking to room service for that.

As the door of their room closed, Engel pulled Bruce round to face her. "Yea, right, I admit that I fucked up. I've been so busy busting your balls about getting emotional that I've not been watching myself. I've actually had more fun in the last few days than I can remember. Fuck, fuck, fuck! The wrong fuckin' time, in the wrong fuckin' place with the wrong fuckin' people! So what do we do now, partner?"

Bruce was taken aback by the intensity of her outburst, which was emphasized by her weird oscillation between polite enunciation and the vernacular in mid flow.

Ian Mckinley

"For a start, you could try to help me keep the other pair under control instead of encouraging them to be even more outrageous. Secondly, you could get your bare ass onto that bed and prepare to be shagged till you die of ecstasy."

Bruce jumped back in time to avoid the grab at his groin.

"I may be sorry," Engel responded, "but not that fuckin' sorry. I'd have to be guilty of at least genocide and fifty cases of child abuse before I'd let you near me with that shriveled-up wee thing."

Bruce peeled off his shirt and threw it at her before heading off for a shower. He had just got the temperature exactly to his satisfaction when he felt the small frame squeeze into the tiny cubicle behind him. "Just a back rub, don't get your fuckin' hopes up, or anything else for that matter," she warned him before starting to rub a hard bar of soap up and down his spine.

His involuntary groans of pleasure got deeper as she pressed her body against him and reached round to soap his chest. As she worked lower, she encountered his erection, which she slapped playfully. "I told you, none of that," she scolded. Nevertheless, thirty seconds later she was massaging his penis with one hand and squeezing his balls with the other. A timeless period of pleasure suddenly peaked in an orgasm that shook his entire body.

Turning to the diminutive woman, he wrapped his arms about her and held her tightly.

"What did I tell you about gettin' too fuckin' soppy," she grunted into his chest, but he noted with satisfaction that she made no attempt to pull away.

After a couple of minutes she gently stood back. "Look at this, you pig, you've smeared spunk all over my belly!"

As was obviously expected, Bruce took over the job of washing the indicated piece of anatomy. This required him to drop to his knees, a very intimate position in a Japanese-dimensioned shower. After the cleanup was completed, Engel grinned down at him. "Well, seeing as you are down there anyway, you may as well make yourself useful." She pushed her groin into his face.

No doubt about it, he thought, as his tongue entered the hot, wet proffered void. Violence certainly does seem to turn this woman on.

***

So much for paranoia and an over-active imagination. Could this profiling shit really be so good? Glasgow was one thing, but Hong Kong and Tokyo seemed impossible.

Then again, taking out the Basel opposition was probably a red flag. If the opposition focused all available effort on Switzerland, they could have picked us up in Kloten. Then they'd set up an intercept in Bottoms-up, which would probably fit my profile. Fuck! On top of that, we'd blabbed to the guys in the bar that we were also heading for Tokyo.

Rather than protecting the women in my care, I've been leading them straight into the lion's jaws.

Extremophile

Day 6 ...violence grows

Bruce drifted gently awake, aware that his left arm was dead under the weight of the small body that was wrapped tightly round him. He grinned as he felt her light pink nipple rub against his much darker one, in rhythm to her gentle snoring. He slid his arm loose with only a low grunt in response and winced as returned circulation caused a sharp attack of pins-and-needles.

He padded into the small bathroom and halted in indecision on spotting a large sponge lying in the minute bath. Twenty seconds later, a cry of shock greeted the splash of cold water squeezed onto his partner's chest. Avoiding her flailing arms, Bruce jumped to one side of the bed while the struggling dervish fell out the other side in a tangle of bedding.

"You bastard, cunt, shite, arsehole," she screamed, hauling herself free of the sheets. "You are so going to fuckin' die for that. Painfully."

"Hold on, hold on." He backed carefully towards the refuge of the bathroom. "I'm just putting you in the mood for our workout."

"That was the biggest fuckin' mistake of your entire bastardin' life. Get your sorry arse down to that gym. Time to die!"

Bruce threw the irate nymph a towel and pulled on a pair of briefs. Watching Engel storm out of the room, he surreptitiously reached into the side pocket of his bag and selected a tab of SLOWDOWN from his pharm pouch. *I've never before used enhancement in a training session.* He picked up a bathrobe. *But it's certainly better to have the option in case I need it.*

All three women were in the sitting room as he entered: Eva and Angela wearing light yukatas and Engel lost in a huge bathrobe. Angela put her hand on his shoulder and pecked his cheek. "Good morning, dear. I hope you know what you're doing." She was looking at the glaring redhead.

A smiling Eva led them to the lift, which dropped to the thirty-first floor. The exec gym was at the end of the north corridor. The changing room contained a range of shorts, T-shirts, training suits and gis. Bruce selected heavy judo trousers, noting without surprise that he was the only member of the group wearing underwear. Bruce had already decided that stripped to the waist maximized his chances of surviving the session, but this choice was made for him by Angela, who gently nudged him aside and took the matching judo jacket.

"Well then, if we're being eco-friendly and minimizing the washing up..." Eva smiled, throwing a light karate jacket at Engel as she pulled on the associated trousers. Bruce tried to avoid staring at Eva's fine breasts.

Additional distractions are just what I don't need.

Eva and Angela preceded them into the dojo, which was a simple rectangle of tatami matting with three mirrored walls and the fourth, containing the door, plain pine with racks of weights, a range of martial arts training weapons and an assortment of other work-out equipment. The two taller women went to the far end of the mat and started a series of warm-up exercises while Engel stomped directly to the weapons rack and selected a mid-length bo. "This is going to fuckin' hurt," she muttered.

Discretion is certainly the better part of valor. Bruce slipped the tab of SLOWDOWN from the waistband of his briefs and surreptitiously palmed it into his mouth. He could feel it begin to kick in when, without warning, Engel swung round with the bo at full extension whistling towards his head.

Bruce had plenty of time to throw himself into a side roll, which took him well out of range, but was grateful for the speeded reflexes that allowed him to catch the stick that was thrown straight at his face. He brought the bo to guard position while Engel wrenched a matching stick from the rack.

Engel repeated the cut to his head but, this time, Bruce blocked the blow, the crash of the sticks sending a shock though his upper arm. Flicking Engel's bo upwards, he dropped to a crouch and scythed his stick forward at waist height. With a loud crack, her raised foot blocked the bo. *Fucking body armor*, Bruce cursed silently, *as if she doesn't have enough advantages already.*

Still standing on one leg, Engel changed her grip and directed a blow at his throat, using the stick like a snooker cue. Such a showy move indicated that Engel was still unaware of Bruce's chemical acceleration, which gave him an opening. Dropping his stick as he slid forward around her blow, his hands closed over hers while his shoulder slammed into her stomach.

A loud grunt turned into a squeak as he twisted forward, sending her flying over his shoulder. This throw should have slammed her onto her back but, somehow, she managed to land on her feet, push against his thigh, and throw him over her hip. The reversal was so smooth that Bruce was still clutching the stick tightly when he crashed onto the mat. With a twist, he used the end of the bo to put a lock on her wrist, which she immediately countered by dropping heavily onto his stomach.

His grip loosened as the breath was driven out of his lungs, but he managed to push the bo above his head, which threw Engel forward on top of him. Abandoning the stick, he grabbed the small form with both arms and crushed her against his chest.

"Not a very clever move, Beast," came a muffled voice from his chest. The bo rapped him several times on the head, a set of sharp teeth clamped onto his left nipple, while armored heels kicked hard into his thighs to emphasize the point. "That was fun, though. How about best of three?"

Bruce relaxed his grip and patted a bare buttock. Engel bounced to her feet, her smile miraculously replacing the previous glare.

Beating up guys clearly does wonders for her mood. I now need to work out how to cheer her up further without getting seriously damaged in the process.

As he walked over to recover his bo, Angela put her arm round his waist. "Let the girls play with each other for a bit. You can train with me."

A series of loud cracks indicated that play had already started, Eva aiming a barrage of blows at Engel's head and shoulders with a bokken, causing a blur of blocks and counters by the bo.

"Shawari-waza," Angela said, pulling him to his knees. "I want to minimize the advantage of your drug." She bent forward and peered into his eyes. "SLOWDOWN, I'd guess, or one of its clones."

"SLOWDOWN, indeed," he confirmed. "You don't miss much, do you?"

"Not very difficult. It's a bit of a giveaway that your body isn't lying in a bloody heap in the middle of the floor. Normal humans don't last for a second against warriors like Miss Maiden. Remember last night! Anyway," obviously wanting to change the subject, "don't use your normal detox. I have something upstairs which has much milder side-effects."

They sat on their heels facing each other in *sieza* position and formally bowed.

"Okay, big boy, do your worst," she taunted.

Aware of his advantage of speed, Bruce lunged forward and cut towards her neck with the side of his right hand. As he was holding back slightly, Angela had time to enter inside the blow, take control of his arm and apply the wristlock *ikkyo*, which forced him face-first to the mat. Bruce resisted the lock with all his strength, but was forced to slap the tatami with his left hand as the pain became excruciating.

The lock was instantly released and Angela had moved back to a safe distance by the time that he had rolled onto his knees.

Bruce worked through a series of cuts and punches from both right and left sides, in all cases being smoothly restrained by a wrist, elbow or shoulder lock.

"Very nice," he commented. "Now you should have a go at attacking."

As they kneeled, facing each other and sitting on their heels with knees wide apart, Angela slowly reached down and pulled the lower part of her jacket apart. Bruce gaped at the sight of her open lips, gleaming wetly, surrounded by the bush of black hair. He could feel the color rising to his cheeks when she suddenly lunged forward and her open palm touched his nose.

His full blush was now brought on by the shout of glee from Engel and Eva's burst of giggles. "Combat drugs are very useful, but you should be careful not to get overconfident," Angela commented, increasing the girls' amusement even more.

"Good one, Prof," Engel conceded. "I'll have to

remember that move, anytime I'm fighting with no knickers on, that is."

"Like now," Eva pointed out, lifting the front of Engel's jacket to reveal her bald parts.

"You'd be able to distract the poor old Beast with your tits if they weren't so small and droopy," Engel responded, flicking a nipple on a breast that was anything but small and droopy.

"You wee Irish toerag!" The bokken would have taken off Engel's head if she hadn't ducked.

The cracks of wood against wood became a continuous rattle as the girls whirled around each other in a blur of blows, blocks and counter-blows.

"Wipe the saliva off your chin and let's go for a shower," Angela suggested, tugging his elbow. With a sigh, he tore his eyes from the flesh on show and followed the professor towards the changing room, turning only for a last glance as he formally bowed out of the dojo.

"We'll shower upstairs," she announced as she hurled her jacket into the recycler, to be replaced by the yukata.

As they entered their suite, Angela took his hand and pulled him towards her room. "You can wash my back."

The restricted size of the shower was even more

obvious when Bruce squeezed in after the statuesque brunette. Washing her back was difficult when he stood behind her and, although made easier after she turned to face him and pulled his arms round her, it was much more distracting as her breasts pressed into his shoulders.

Trying to ignore the erection that was rubbing against her thick pubes, Bruce kneaded the base of her spine and squeezed her solid buttocks. Her brow gently pushed against his neck and she whispered "Bruce, lad, you're really a very nice guy." Her arms went round his neck. "Much though I'd like to go on with this jape, I'm really not sure I'm up to it. It's one thing sitting in Glasgow planning all this stuff, but totally something else when it is real life. One mistake could be fatal, for yourself or someone you love." She nuzzled his ear with her nose.

Bruce slid his hand up her spine till he had a handful of dark brown hair. He gently pulled her head around until he could look directly into her eyes. "You're the boss. If you want to pull the plug, then we're out of here on the next flight to Scotland. Alternatively, set us up with your tame prof and Engel and I can finish things off. You zip off back directly with Eva and we'll be with you in Glasgow within a week or so. What do you think?"

"You're right, of course." She straightened up, seeming to physically pull herself together. "You and I can meet up with Hideki today and set up the sampling while the girls move us to another hotel. We can decide this evening whether we split up or go on to Tokai together." She grabbed him in a bear-hug and crushed him till his spine cracked. "Thanks, Bruce, as a special reward you can wash my hair."

Bruce palmed a handful of shampoo and started rubbing it into her scalp. After two rinses she took a hold of his wrists and directed his hands between her legs. "If a job's worth doing..." she murmured.

Bruce's fingers brought Angela to her toes, her entire body shaking and breaths coming in ragged gasps, before he took her left nipple between his teeth and began to bite. Just as her head leaned back, the cubicle door opened to show a very startled Eva. "Oh, fuck, sorry!"

Angela's heels slammed down as her head whipped round towards the closing door. "Christ almighty!" She banged the back of her head against the wall of the shower. "God, this is stupid! It's like being caught at it by your parents. We're adults, in fact I'm bloody ancient, so I shouldn't be bothered by this."

Bruce pulled her to him and patted her bottom.

"Don't worry. The mood comes and goes quickly, but when it's gone, that's it. Just give me a shout when it comes back."

Bruce glared at Eva as he strode, dripping, through her bedroom.

"Sorry," she whispered again with an apologetic shrug.

Bruce ignored Engel while he crossed their bedroom to the bathroom to pick up a towel.

"Well then, Beast, been shaggin' the old fat one have—" Her question was cut off when a damp towel hit her in the face. "I guess not," she finished under her breath.

***

Japanese business culture was not something to be driven by either climate change or economic collapse. Although summertime *CoolBiz* style was already established at the beginning of the 21st century, this never developed as far as the shorts and sandals common in most of the Western world and, indeed, with plentiful nuclear power to allow cheap air conditioning, the current trend was back towards increased formality.

With marked reluctance, Bruce donned a white short-sleeved shirt, an ultra-lightweight, light-blue business suit and forced himself into socks and shoes. Finally, he pulled out a tie from his bag, a gaudy Spiderman classic, and put it in his jacket pocket. "I hope I can remember how to put this fucking thing on," he muttered.

"Very smart, Beast. I guess I won't kill you this time. I wouldn't try that fuckin' trick with the cold water again, though," Engel warned. She was already dressed in light shorts and blouse, which emphasized how over-dressed he was.

The others were already in the sitting room, with the wall set to real life. The mountains were completely obscured by a wall of black cloud, while the light seemed unusually intense, giving the scene the unreal clarity of poor quality computer graphics. Angela turned to them, clad in a dark grey tube that was tight enough to clearly show the profile of the tanga she was wearing under it. "Okay," she pre-empted his objections, "it's not exactly normal business wear, but our main aim is getting a Tokyo Uni prof to do something that he doesn't want to. Trust me, this is the uniform for the job. Anyway, I've arranged to meet him at his house in Akasaka, so we can get there by taxi."

"Fine, it's your show," he conceded. "You girls know what you're doing?"

"Nul problemo," Eva answered, looking extremely elegant in a white mini-dress and high heels. "We'll just do a bit of shopping and then move hotels."

"Good, use this for your shopping." He tossed over a coin-shaped credit chip. "There're a lot of small shops in the towers and several big department stores like Odakyu and Takashimaya over by Shinjuku station. All within easy walking distance."

"Although it offends my Scottish soul greatly," he continued, "don't bother checking out of here. Leave bags and any non-essential stuff here. If you pick up a couple of backpacks, you should be able to move all the rest. You could then walk over to the Park Hyatt and change en route. What've you got for docs and dosh for check in?"

"We'll have to go for the Pharm stuff," she answered. "We can use the VIP docs we used for passport control. I've got a personal Pharm account drawn on Basel, which should be okay. We can book a twin bedroom. I guess we'll just have to rough it for a couple of days."

"I guess it's the best we can do," he said. "Book in for a couple of days, but if all goes well, we should be off tomorrow."

A buzzer announced the arrival of breakfast,

which was wheeled into their room by two uniformed girls. They fussed around setting things up neatly on the coffee table. When everything was arranged to their satisfaction, the waitresses wheeled the trolley to the door before turning to bow together. "Have a nice day," they chanted in singsong voices before they disappeared.

"Very cute." Engel winked at him before pouring coffee for everyone. "These Japanese women just look so young. You must feel like you've died and gone to heaven, eh Beast?"

Bruce ignored the jibe and settled back with his coffee and a croissant, only half listening to the discussion of the relative sexual attraction of women of different races.

After breakfast was finished, the girls set off shopping while Bruce and Angela took the lift to the basement reception area. Angela passed an address card to a bellboy, who sang something to the driver of the little electric taxi, which set off as soon as they sat down, the door sliding closed while they were already moving. After weaving through a maze of tunnels, the taxi took a ramp up to the freeway.

With a sigh, Bruce pulled the tie from his pocket and put it on. "Lurid." Angela grimaced, causing him to smile.

Extremophile

After about ten minutes on the freeway, they dropped down to ground level and wound their way through streets that became increasingly narrow. *Just as well we didn't take a limo. We'd never have gotten it through some of these tight twists and turns.* The area was clearly very affluent, though. Traditional style houses with blue-tiled roofs sat in minute but perfectly manicured gardens. It could almost have been pre-quake Tokyo, if not for the occasional white ceramic pillar which supported the translucent roof covering the entire district.

The car pulled up in front of a large house. Bruce transferred credit, the door slid open, and he clambered out with a muttered, "Arigato gozaimasu."

"Have a nice day," the driver responded. The door slid closed and the taxi glided silently away.

The heavy wooden front door opened at their approach, allowing them into a small entrance hall. Bruce untied his shoes and stepped backwards up to the raised floor of the inner hall in his stocking feet. Angela, less elegantly, flipped her sandals carelessly into a corner and stepped up in bare feet to join him.

Angela led the way, parting a small curtain that hung at the end of the hall and striding into the center of the large wooden-floored lounge. She looked around at the sparse furniture: a number of heavy, over-stuffed, leather chairs, a small lacquer chest and a glass-topped coffee table. Two windows that were closed by white paper screens and three large traditional-style pictures, which seemed to have been painted directly on them, dominated the walls.

A small grey-suit clad figure suddenly exploded from the opposite doorway. He rushed directly towards the tall woman and stood directly in front of her, his neck craning upwards and his chin almost touching her beasts. "Angela? My God, Angela, is this you or your daughter?" His shaking voice could not hide his perfectly enunciated Oxbridge English.

Taking his hands in hers, she smiled warmly. "Hideki, great to see you. You always were a flatterer. You're looking pretty good yourself. You may have a touch of grey at the temples but you still look about twenty-five."

"But, Angela, you look miraculous. You told me that you were working on rejuvenative cosmetics, but this is outrageous. Tell me what Pharm you are sponsored by, so that I can invest my entire savings in their shares."

He disengaged his hands and walked round her, looking her up and down like some prized possession. "You are completely and utterly stunning. Of course, you always were," he added, "but now even more completely and utterly stunning."

"Anyway, us oldies both seem to be in good shape. Let me introduce my young colleague, Doctor Bruce Roberts. Bruce, Professor Hideki Yamakawa."

The small Japanese professor looked startled. He clearly had not even noticed Bruce's presence. When Bruce stepped forward, proffering his business card, reflex took over and he accepted the card carefully, shook hands, drew a small silver case from his pocket, and offered his own card. Bruce in turn carefully read the card, noting the small hologram in the corner that probably contained a full CV with links to all his ongoing research work.

Before Bruce and Prof Yamakawa had an opportunity to do more than exchange names, Angela collared the small Japanese scientist and drew him towards one of the chairs, sitting down herself in one at right angles to him. Bruce noted that her dress rode up as she sat, revealing the tiny knickers that were failing to contain completely her bush of black pubic hair. A slight intake of breath indicated Hideki had not missed the view.

Bruce withdrew to the far side of the room and sat as quietly as possible, to avoid perturbing Angela's fishing work. *From the look of it, though, I could open up with a shotgun and the poor Japanese prof still wouldn't be able to tear his eyes off Angela's body.*

Angela launched into their agreed spiel, which contained two main items of disinformation: that the product of interest was a complex hormonal-based rejuvenating cosmetic and that the extremophile organisms were essential to the catalysis of its production. He broke into her lecture several times with questions, which in one occasion diverged off into a discussion of the pros and cons of doing full DNA sequencing of all organisms involved. Several times, Angela declined to go into details, simply noting that these were *commercial*, which seemed to be readily accepted by Yamakawa-sensei.

After she had described the assistance that they needed for the Tokai sampling, she added the bribe of first access to any rejuvenant produced, noting that production would probably be very limited and cost outrageously high. His horrified reaction amused both Westerners. "Oh no, Angela, I already have lots of problems because I am so young. I actually dye my hair grey," he confessed, to Angela's great amusement. "I'm afraid your cosmetic will not sell well to Japanese salarymen but, as it is their wives who spend all their money anyway, this is not going to be a problem for your Pharm."

Angela leaned forward and took hold of his right

hand, stroking his palm with the nail of her thumb. "This would be a very great favor, Hideki. I'd be very happy to do something for you in return. Is there anything at all that I could do for you?" She looked straight into his eyes and raised her eyebrows.

"Yes, well there could be something." A slight tremor of excitement in his voice was emphasized by the way his slight frame squirmed on the large chair. "First of all, I need to see what I can do for you." He bounced to his feet. "I need to contact some colleagues, so what about a bite of lunch? It's probably going to take me a little while."

"Something small and light would be nice, but don't go to any trouble."

"No trouble at all." He disappeared through the doorway he had originally entered by, and then a rather heavily built Japanese girl appeared. She wore a light blue kimono and carried a large round lacquer tray.

She bowed into the room with a shy, "Konnichi-wa," knelt to set the tray on the coffee table, and then proceeded to pour soy sauce into a couple of small bowls, open beer bottles, and generally fuss about.

Bruce walked over and took the vacated seat beside Angela. The girl was in the process of pouring beer into very small glasses when she evidently caught a glimpse of the view up Angela's dress. With a ring of crystal, the neck of the bottle touched the glass and beer spilled onto the table. While the flustered girl mopped up the spill, Angela leaned forward. "It's all right, dear, we can manage now. Thank you very much."

The girl rose smoothly to her feet and bowed. "You are welcome." She shuffled to the doorway, turned and bowed again. "Have a nice day."

Angela knelt beside the table, and using chopsticks, she deftly transferred pieces of vegetable and seafood sushi to a triangular plate. She mixed wasabi into the soy sauce contained in a small triangular bowl, which then fitted neatly into the apex of the larger plate. As she sat back in her chair, she accepted a glass of beer from Bruce, which she drained in a single gulp.

"How long have I been talking?" she asked, rhetorically. "God, but I'm dry."

Bruce refilled her glass from the bottle of Kirin, took a mouthful of beer, and then topped up his own glass. "Nice beer, but the glasses are far too small." He helped himself to a few pieces of tuna sashimi, rather disappointed that Angela hadn't taken up the chance to lecture on Japanese porcelain, beer or food. Painfully aware that the room was probably wired for sound and vision, conversation was stilted and focused on small talk about the food and furnishings.

While he leaned forward to open a second bottle of beer, Bruce noticed the delicate carving of the legs of the glass-topped table. "What do you think of this?"

Angela crouched beside him to peer at the centimeter-sized figures, which seemed to be acting out positions from the Kama Sutra or some other manual of sexual debauchery. She turned to pull a palmtop from the shoulder bag that was lying by her chair and scanned one leg with the video pickup. She then produced a holographic projection of the scanned image and started to step up the magnification. The detail was stunning, up to the limits of the mini-scanner's resolution. Not only were the bodies reproduced in full anatomical detail, but the expressions of lust—or perhaps pain—on the carved faces was breathtaking.

"You like my table?" Professor Yamakawa's question caused both of them to jump. "I did the carving myself," he announced, proudly. "Nano-sculpture is my one hobby, although I cannot seem to find much time for it. The table took me almost ten years to complete."

"It's absolutely amazing, Hideki. I had no idea

that you were also an artist. Maybe I could sit for you sometime." Angela threw herself back into her chair with a flash of white underwear. "So, how is it going?"

"Everything is arranged. There now is a formal collaborative project between Tokyo University and the University of Saint Andrews on bioremediation of radionuclide and heavy metal contamination. A friend at Sendai University has responsibility for water chemistry monitoring at Ichi-effu and has cleared sampling with the NRA, the regulator. Ask for Doctor Ito. He will organize things for you. In case of any difficulties, contact Professor Umeki at Sendai directly. Here are all the details." He handed over a coin-shaped memory chip.

"I can't thank you enough," Angela gushed. "I really don't know what I would have done without you."

The little Japanese man was clearly very pleased with himself and looked at the large woman expectantly. "Well, you know, there is a little something you could do for me." He offered his hand, hesitantly.

"No problem." She bounced from the seat and took the offered hand. "Anything at all you want."

Almost like a boy leading his mother into a

toyshop, Yamakawa drew Angela out of the room. "Excuse us, we may be a little time," he threw over his shoulder.

Bruce returned to Angela's palmtop, scanning in the rest of the table leg carvings and set up a copy for transfer to his own laptop. The magnified holos were impressive, not only in terms of their realism but also the imagination of the artist. As far as he could determine, the coupling possibilities with up to four participants of all sex combinations had been comprehensively documented, with no repetition.

Bruce started as the girl drifted in silently to take away the lunch things. Although Bruce felt as if he had been caught looking at pornography, the Japanese woman seemed completely unperturbed by a holo that depicted a well-built woman simultaneously satisfying three men. Bruce did a double take when he noticed that the exquisitely carved face of the woman bore a marked resemblance to the serving girl. *Probably coincidence*, he shrugged mentally. *Japanese women probably look pretty similar while attempting to swallow a dong that wouldn't disgrace an elephant.*

It was almost an hour later before a tight-lipped Angela returned alone. "Yamakawa-sensei apologizes and asked me to say goodbye on his behalf," she stated rather formally. "There should be a taxi waiting for us." When she bent to pick up her bag, Bruce couldn't help but notice that the line of her knickers had disappeared.

The journey back to the Hilton passed in complete silence. They didn't even need to inform the driver of their destination, as he had confirmed, "Hirutono," as soon as they climbed in.

At the Hilton reception area, Bruce guided Angela through the throng of porters and was directing her in the direction of the walkway to Shinjuku station when she stopped abruptly and turned towards him. "Let's go to the room here first, I need a shower."

Bruce started to object but, noting the look in her eye, gave in and turned back towards the executive lift.

As soon as they entered the suite, Angela headed straight for her bedroom, abruptly declining his cheerful offer to scrub her back. Somewhat miffed, Bruce ordered the window to reality. Although not yet four o'clock, it was almost black outside, brightening only occasionally when illuminated by distant lightning. Surrounding towers were discernible only by the faint glow of lighted windows. Large individual drops of rain splashed against the window. *Not long now before the ladies get a chance to experience a Tokyo typhoon.*

Ten minutes later, Angela emerged in her chuong sam, which had originally been abandoned in the move. "Okay, what now?"

Bruce checked his e-messages; as agreed, the note with no sender or topic contained the single number 4006. "Ten minutes' walk and then we can find out what the others have been up to. I'll have to pop into a toilet en route to change, but that'll take only a couple of ticks."

"Why bother, why not change here or in the other hotel?"

"Search agents," he explained. "Just like you can use pattern recognition to follow cars, or even people, on spot satellite images, it's not hard to hack into the Tokyo metropolitan CCTV network to look for four gaijin matching our descriptions. Of course the database is gigantic. There are actually more CCTVs in Tokyo than in the entire US of A. But, if you knew, or suspected, that we were here and had a fast enough search engine, you might just strike lucky. Changing appearances and our groupings just makes it harder to pick us up, especially if we change away from a fixed location, which they might already have nailed down and targeted for a more detailed search."

"Sounds reasonable," she conceded. "Okay, let's go"

From the Hilton lobby, they walked over separately to the facing Sumitomo building, where Bruce headed straight to a public toilet and re-appeared a couple of minutes later in shorts and an electric blue shirt. He met up with Angela, who was staring into the window of a travel agent, put his arm round her waist, and headed off into the maze of subterranean walkways. Five minutes later they were in the lower lobby of the Park Hyatt, where they were allowed into the elevator after it had been confirmed that Doctor Lomperski was, indeed, expecting them.

The door to room 4006 opened as they approached and a small black-haired figure looked out. "Well then, how did it go?"

Angela bustled into the room with Bruce in her wake. "Fine, fine, we should be able to go on to Tokai tomorrow."

Engel gave Bruce a confused look as he passed her, but he only shrugged silently. "Well then, what do you think about the hair?" she asked, rather loudly.

"It's great, reminds me of someone I kicked the shit out of in Glasgow." By jumping forward, her kick hardly touched his buttocks.

Extremophile

"Come into the room before you start squabbling," Eva scolded gently. She was now also transformed: raven hair, black eyebrows and brown contacts changed her appearance completely, but she was still a beauty.

Angela had already disappeared into the bathroom. The bedroom was very spacious by Japanese standards, with twin queen beds and a monolithic wall unit with all kinds of drawers, cupboards, minibar and other such fitments. At the far end of the room, two small sofas separated by a rectangular coffee table sat beside a window that, under normal circumstances, would look onto the dome covering Shinjuku-Chuo Park. Currently it showed only sheets of rain that, as walls of water impacted the window, he could relate to vibrations of the entire building.

Bruce pulled out his laptop and threw his shoulder bag onto the bed nearest the window. He then ordered the window to a less distracting view of Shinjuku by night and settled down on one of the sofas to look at the info that Yamakawa-san had given Angela. While Bruce was at it, he confirmed that the copy of the scan of the coffee-table carving had transferred over.

As he glanced at the holo of the magnified

image, a small body squeezed in beside him. "Mmm, porn, you dirty old beast. No wonder the Japanese have slanty eyes, if they do that all the time. It makes my own eyes water just to think about it."

She leaned closer to him and whispered in a more serious tone. "What's up with the prof? She looks really upset about something. Was there some kind of screw up?"

Bruce then noticed that Eva had also disappeared into the bathroom. "As far as I can see, everything's hunky-dory. Look at this." He replaced the holo with a cross-match between his original plan and the info from Yamakawa. "We're bang on plan. It's almost too good."

"Well, if it's all *hunky-dory*," she mocked his archaic expression, "what's with the big yin?"

"I really haven't a clue, but it's something to do with the favor that she had to do for her little Hideki. She was off with him for quite a while and came back minus knickers. Other than that, I've no idea what went on."

"If that little fucker screwed about with her I'll..."

Engel's colorful description of the violence she would inflict on Yamakawa faded away when the others returned to the bedroom. Angela had clearly showered yet again and was wrapped in a large bath towel. With atypical modesty, she turned away when she dropped the towel and pulled on the black tube that Eva handed her.

"We've booked a hot bath and masseur," Eva announced. "Anybody else interested?" Noting the nods she continued. "Okay, let's move."

Somewhat taken aback by the speed of developments, Bruce quickly initiated the pre-programmed sequence of messages that would provide background info to Ito-san of Sendai Uni and a few of his own personal contacts in more junior positions. The women had already left the room, but he caught up with them halfway along the corridor.

The onsen was also on the fortieth floor. A standard hotel door led into a delicate little garden through which a path of polished natural stone led to a steaming tub that appeared to have been carved out of a single block of granite. The window, which curved round the far side of the bath, was partially blocked by paper screens but appeared to show the view from a hilltop down towards a little traditional Japanese fishing village. Further paper screens defined a changing area that contained a washing pool and a massage area dominated by a low table, which again appeared to have been carved out of granite.

They stripped off clothes and sat together on very low stools while Bruce demonstrated the formal washing protocol, using wooden buckets to scoop hot water from the pool for rinsing while they soaped themselves all over. The full-body washing procedure was repeated twice.

After washing, they proceeded to the main pool and lowered themselves gingerly into the scalding water. Bruce settled his buttocks on a small ledge, which brought the water to mid chest height. Angela sat against his right side, half turned away to wrap her arms around Eva. Engel squeezed against his left arm, water coming to her chin. She elbowed him sharply until he raised his arm, allowing her to settle her head against his shoulder. He closed his eyes with a sigh and felt tension soaking away, leaving his body along with the sweat that had already begun to drip from the end of his nose.

After an indefinite time, Bruce's reverie was broken by a high-pitched voice. "Okay, guys, who wants a massage?" He looked up at a blond Adonis standing by the side of the pool. He was about two meters tall, with the physique of a serious body-builder—the male model type rather than a weight-lifting hulk. Engel whistled her appreciation, which was probably enhanced by the fact that he was wearing only a very small loincloth that, from their present position, left nothing to the imagination.

"You go first," Eva suggested to Angela. Bruce felt her shrug against his side before she clambered from the pool and sighed into a large white towel, which the masseur wrapped round her.

Eva moved closer to Bruce, lifting his arm and draping it round her shoulder. He was then pushed slightly backwards, so that she could talk more easily to Engel. Both girls were clearly concerned about Angela and the fact that she would not even talk to Eva about what had upset her.

"Maybe a good rodgering by that big hunk would sort her out," Engel suggested.

"I'm sure it would," Eva agreed, "but I think that he would rather be rodgering wee Brucie here."

"It is indeed a cruel world." Engel sighed melodramatically. "All the best looking guys are gay."

"On the other hand," Eva put in, "so are all the best looking girls." Reaching over, she pulled Engel forward into a passionate kiss, her tongue sliding into the smaller girl's mouth.

"No, no!" Engel pulled back, shaking her head. "The very best looking girls are AC/DC." She kissed Bruce playfully on the chin.

He closed his eyes and let the exchange of increasingly outrageous insults wash over him. At least it had diverted them from discussing Angela, his main concern at present.

About twenty minutes later, Angela returned, looking much more relaxed.

"Right, Beast, get your spotty arse onto that massage table," Engel commanded while she stood to help Angela into the pool. "See if he can give you some training hints. If you build up a body like that, I'll let you father my children."

"Just as well you're so weedy," Eva added, "otherwise you might get more than a massage." She grinned at him as Angela took his place between the two girls.

"Physique isn't everything," he retorted as he picked up Angela's towel. "I bet your Big Blondie knows bugger-all about quantum chromodynamics."

"Quantum chromodynamics!" Engel laughed as he padded towards the massage area. "Aye, right, bet that helped ye get shagged loads o' times."

Bruce approached the massage table with trepidation but could not help being relaxed by the big man's easy smile. The masseur took his towel and placed it over the thick mat which covered the stone table. As Bruce lay face down, the masseur rubbed pine-scented oil into his back and started a monologue that lasted for the next quarter of an hour. To his amazement he could hear laughter from the pool, which cheered him up immensely.

Just as well I'm not a betting man, Bruce thought while he listened to the life story of Walt, the big Canadian, who turned out to be a post-grad in the Information Engineering department of Shinagawa University. *He probably knows a lot more about quantum everything than I do.*

To be able to afford to live in Tokyo, Walt moonlighted as an artist's model as well as a barman in a Shibuya nightclub. After he playfully slapped Bruce's buttocks to indicate that he was finished, he gave him directions to the Shibuya club, "... just in case you want to see what alternative Tokyo is all about."

Bruce thanked Walt for the massage, making it clear that their chances of having a free evening to visit the club were negligible, but promising to return for another massage if time permitted.

Walking towards the changing area to rinse off the massage oil, he noticed that the women were already dressed and waiting for him. Angela looked straight into his eyes and smiled, obviously back to her usual self. He started to question her on her improved mood, but stopped abruptly as she caught a hold of his scrotum. "Later, maybe." She grinned.

A very quick rinse and then the girls helped to dry him down. *This'd be quicker and a lot less painful doing it myself, but I guess I'll just let them have their way. Anything at all to avoid dampening their current good spirits.*

Back in their room, the topic of conversation immediately turned to dinner. Bruce didn't even dare suggest room service. Skimming through the hotel services directory, Angela quickly decided on everybody's behalf. "Tepanyaki, that's what we need. I could just handle a chunk of beer-fed, pampered Kobe cow."

Bruce made the reservation while the women selected clothes for dinner. Sitting at the window, he quickly checked progress in setting up details for the next day, but made no pretense that he was not also enjoying being a voyeur in the ladies' dressing room.

They went directly to the tepanyaki restaurant on the forty-second floor and were immediately seated around a stainless steel hotplate. A very well dressed young Japanese couple sat at the other side of the counter and greeted them with a cheery, "Konban-wa."

"Konban-wa," Bruce responded automatically.

"Sumimasen." He waved at a waiter. "Dai bin bieru, mitsu, arigato gozaimasu."

"Why did you ask for three beers?" Angela inquired as the waiter bustled off.

"Simple. We can split bottled beer and I don't know the Japanese word for four."

This sent the Japanese couple into giggles. "Yottsu," the young Japanese man informed him in a distinct Southern-American accent. "We don't get so many foreign visitors in Tokyo these days. I guess they're scared off by the quakes and typhoons. Any that do come don't often attempt to speak Japanese. Our economy is not strong anymore, and gaijin don't want to work in Japan. We must all speak English."

"Don't be so rude, Hiro," his partner interjected in perfect Oxford English. "Japanese is a horrible language and we would never bother with it if we weren't forced to in school. The sooner we adopt English as our first language the better."

A conversation on the pros and cons of preserving local languages developed naturally, Angela siding with Hiro while the girls supported his partner, Junko.

Bruce stayed out of the main discussion, quietly watching the show provided by the chef, a complete extrovert who prepared their meals with flashing knifes and spatulas, spinning spice shakers and repeated flares of flaming spirits.

The Kobe beef was ridiculously expensive but tasted exquisite, melting in the mouth yet with a rich meat flavor. In addition to the beer, Angela ordered a range of sakes that she considered particularly suitable for beef. The Japanese couple agreed to join them in the sake-tasting and complemented Angela on her choices.

Hiro and Junko excused themselves just before the team reached a final course of green-tea ice cream. The women were keen to go somewhere for a nightcap, but Bruce decided that it was finally time to put his foot down, insisting that they should return to their room and, if anything, restrict themselves to a quick drink from room-service.

He played his trump card. "I've booked tickets for a shinkansen to Mito at eight thirty tomorrow morning, which means that we need to get a taxi to Ueno at seven forty-five, at the latest. We should be up at about six thirty if we want to have breakfast."

"Stuff breakfast!" Engel responded. "We can get a coffee on the train." The other women nodded. "So we've plenty of time to go to the panorama bar for a drink," she concluded triumphantly.

Bruce shrugged and dropped behind Angela

while she led the way towards the elevator to the 'Starlight' bar. It certainly was a spectacular sight, he had to admit, when they entered the large bar with its high pyramidal glass roof. The typhoon was really hitting hard now and lightning was almost continuous, revealing walls of water which crashed into the building in time to gusts of wind that could be felt as gentle taps on the soles of their feet. Angela looked as if she was having second thoughts, but evidently decided that it was now too late to back down. She compromised, however, by selecting a table near the center of the room, rather than one beside the sloping glass walls.

All ordered coffees from the kimono-clad hostess, who appeared as soon as they sat down and knelt elegantly by their table. Bruce restricted himself to a Calvados, while the others had double cognacs, enormous measures that were served in glasses like goldfish bowls.

The girls were keen to know more details of the Tokai trip. Bruce mentioned the option of Angela and Eva dropping out after the contacts had been established at Tokai, but Angela had now changed her mind. "No, Bruce, we've started now, so we'll finish. If all goes well we should be done in a couple of days, and then we can head back to Scotland together. Also, we don't want to miss Maria's birthday, the day after tomorrow, isn't it?"

Engel looked startled, unable to decide whether to be annoyed that Angela knew her personal details so well or flattered that she would remember the date of her birthday.

Bruce outlined the basic plan for the following day; Angela and Eva were being picked up from Mito station by Doctor Ito, who would take them directly to the 1F R&D coordination group at Tokai. There they would get the administrative side of things sorted out. Engel and Bruce would continue on to Katsuta, where Bruce's friend, Ryu, would meet them. They would then drive to Fukushima Daiichi with the required sampling kit.

Theoretically, the sampling could be done in a couple of hours. However, knowing how things worked in Japan, Bruce guessed that it would probably take at least two days, especially allowing for travel to and from Ichi-effu. He had looked at options for the sampling team to overnight in Fukushima, but decided that the risk of leading opponents to the target of their search was too great. Finally, he had booked four single rooms in the Mito Plaza hotel for two nights.

Angela took Bruce's arm as they strolled back

towards their room. "By the way, it's your lucky night. You're sleeping with me tonight."

Bruce's eyebrows shot up, taken aback by the calm statement. "Well, that's certainly fine by me, but I'm not sure that the girls will be very happy about it."

"Don't be silly, dear." She grinned. "It was their idea."

***

Bruce lay in a tangle of sweaty sheets, the post-coital relaxation of his body contrasting with his worried thoughts. *We've now had a full day without any sign of the enemy. This could mean that we've managed to lose them or, following the fracas last night, they're calling in reinforcements and allowing us to walk into a trap when we leave the relative safety of central Tokyo and move out into the boonies. But we're so close now that we can't turn back. Angela was clear enough on that. So it's off to Ichi-effu tomorrow, regardless of the risk. And, one way or another, it'll all be over within a couple of days.*

Somehow this thought was not as reassuring as it should have been.

Ian Mckinley

Day 7 ... you can't always get what you want

Bruce woke lying on his side, facing towards a window that showed only continuous hosing rain, lit more by lightning than by the first greyness of dawn. He was aware of the well-padded body pressed against his back, one arm draped over him with a hand lying against his chest. Breath sighed gently against the back of his neck. As he attempted to slowly lift the arm, the hand slid sensually down his front to start fondling his rapidly growing erection.

"Time for a quickie before the girls wake?" Angela inquired.

As he turned towards the big woman, she threw a leg over his thigh and ground her pelvis against his penis. He looked into her deep brown eyes as she raised her eyebrows suggestively. A movement caught his attention as Eva sat up in the next bed. "Too late. I'll have to take a rain check on that." He groaned as Eva yawned and stretched, showing off her beautiful breasts to great advantage.

Angela smiled while she took hold of his erection and rubbed it against her lower lips. Feeling the warm wetness, Bruce thrust reflexively, sliding smoothly into her well-lubricated vagina.

Angela gave a satisfied sigh.

Looking over her shoulder, Bruce caught Eva's eye. "Morning, Bruce. Do you want to shower first?" she chattered cheerfully.

Only gradually did she seem to become aware of the profile of the thin sheet covering Angela and Bruce, the deep breathing of the former and the embarrassed look on the face of the latter. "Maybe not," she concluded quickly and turned to grab hold of the small form at the other side of her bed. "Come on, Maria. Time for a shower." She smiled at him while dragging the half-sleeping girl towards the bathroom.

As the bathroom door closed, much more noisily than necessary, Angela rolled over on top of him, throwing off the sheet and drawing herself up until only the tip of his glans was still inside her. With a series of moans, she started bouncing up and down on him, her pendulous breasts swinging heavily from side to side. Bruce noticed that her eyes were half-closed and her face had a look that might be best described as intense concentration. She was blatantly riding him, using him for her physical satisfaction.

Bruce relaxed back against his pillow with eyes closed, trying to focus on extending the experience for as long as possible. She was very wet and wide open, which resulted in audible slurping noises at the extremes of her thrusts. An old Stranglers song ran irreverently through his head, *...making love to the Mersey Tunnel, with a sausage, have you ever been to Liverpool?*

Her thrusting became more urgent and he could feel her fingers touching his penis as they rubbed hard between her legs. Opening his eyes, he located nipples as large as thimbles and squeezed hard.

She started to scream, which was enough to finish off Bruce's control, and his back arched as the orgasm hit him. Squeezing even harder, he tried to bring the big woman to her peak, but her screaming went on long after his flaccid dick had slipped out of her vagina.

Finally, with head thrown back, she hit her highpoint in a strangely silent scream, which contrasted markedly with the previous noise. As Bruce felt the shudders shake her massive frame, he noticed for the first time that some rather loud afro-jap pop music was playing. Obviously Angela's shouts had carried well into the bathroom.

He released his hold on her breasts then she flopped forward on top of him, squirming to rub her well-padded, sweat-soaked body against his. "Mmm, much better than a poke in the eye with a sharp stick," she mumbled cryptically into his ear as he slowly rubbed her back.

They were still lying in that position when the girls emerged, both grinning broadly. "Best orgasm I ever heard," Engel commented in a stage whisper, and then grunted as Eva elbowed her in the ribs.

"We better get moving." Eva ordered the background music off and called up news on the window to replace the storm.

Angela rolled off Bruce and stretched unselfconsciously. As he turned over onto his stomach, he couldn't help noticing that her labia were still swollen and wetly open. He tore his eyes away from the sight, trying to control his reaction as she turned and padded off towards the bathroom.

"Look!" Engel's voice caught his attention. "How about this for attention to detail?" She pointed at Eva's black pubic hair. Bruce groaned and pushed his face into the pillow, starting to silently count backwards from one hundred in German, in the hope that he would be presentable before he had to walk to the bathroom.

After a bit of a last-minute rush, partially caused by Engel's initial resistance to Bruce's insistence that she wear not only a modest mini-dress but also neat black slippers, they managed to reach the basement taxi rank at seven forty. A doorman in a formal uniform helped them into the waiting car. "Ohio gozaimasu. Ueno eki, dozo," Bruce said.

"Good morning, sir," he responded.

"Ueno station," he instructed the taxi driver. "Have a nice day!" He waved as the taxi door closed automatically.

When the taxi emerged from the tunnels onto the freeway, the full fury of the typhoon became apparent. The transparent walls were clearly designed to offer protection from the wind, but offered only limited diversion of the rain. Despite conditions like driving through a car wash, the driver held a constant hundred-twenty, switching onto full automatic and calling up a vidcast on the front windscreen.

They dropped into the tunnel that led to a basement level of the station with plenty of time to spare. Emerging from the car, they were swept up in a flood of humanity that seemed to flow through the station in distinct rivers, disintegrating into turbulence only at points where they crossed.

Although the main flow seemed to be leaving the station, Bruce managed to edge his group into a stream heading towards the sign that read: *Shinkansen Tracks*. At the entrance to track eleven, a uniformed man nodded passengers through a gateway after confirming their reservations on a handheld reader. Bruce didn't need to take his palmtop from his shoulder bag. "Carriage two, green car, 12 A, B, 13 A, B," the attendant confirmed in a sing-song voice. "Have a nice day."

Although they were almost a quarter of an hour early, the train was already sitting at the platform. They settled themselves in their seats in an empty carriage, which started to fill up five minutes before departure, yet appeared completely full when the train pulled out, exactly on time.

The monorail accelerated smoothly into a tunnel, which made speed difficult to judge. It was twenty minutes before it broke into the open, clear of the outskirts of Tokyo. By this time they were finishing coffee and croissants, which had been served almost immediately after the shinkansen drew out of the station. The rail was unprotected and the entire train shook as it was buffeted by the wind. Nevertheless, due probably to its aerodynamic shape, the shaking seemed to lessen as the bullet-train accelerated up to its four-fifty cruising speed.

They had time for a second cup of coffee before they began to decelerate into Mito. Angela stood and leaned to peck Bruce gently on the cheek. "See you later. Just keep out of mischief." She pulled Eva to her feet and they set off along the corridor while the train pulled into the station, exactly on time.

The train sat at Mito for only two minutes before it pulled out for the short run to Katsuta. Bruce and Engel were the only ones in their compartment disembarking at Katsuta, and they almost walked into the tall, thin Japanese man waiting for them on the platform. With a wide grin, he punched Bruce playfully on the shoulder, causing him to step backwards and bump into Engel. "My God, you old bastard, you really look like shite!" boomed out a surprisingly deep voice, with an even more surprising Glasgow accent.

"Great to see ye, ye wee slanty-eyed bugger!" Bruce shook his hand enthusiastically. "Yur clearly going blind from too much self abuse. A told ye wankin' wid be yur downfall. Me, a'm the picture o' health, thrivin' in ma prime!"

A small foot pushed against the back of one

knee, causing Bruce's leg to buckle. "Oops! Sorry, let me introduce my colleague, Doctor Maria Maiden." His broad Glaswegian disappeared, returning to a less noticeable Scottish accent. "Maria, Doctor Ryu Toyota."

The accent of the tall Japanese had also almost disappeared when he turned to shake her hand. "Very nice to meet you, Doctor Maiden. Please call me Ryu." He turned back to Bruce. "What's a beautiful, respectable woman doing with a despicable old reprobate like you?"

"Nice to meet you too, Ryu. I'm Maria. Bruce sometimes calls me Angel, but that's only because he's besotted with me."

Bruce rolled his eyes.

Ryu guffawed and punched him again on the shoulder then pulled him and Engel forward as the door hissed closed behind them and the monorail accelerated out of the station. He shepherded them along the platform towards an escalator that took them down into an underground garage, chatting away constantly, alternating between insulting Bruce and blatantly flirting with Engel. They past normal-looking city cars and moved toward a massive, squat and rounded foonvan: a vehicle specially designed for driving outside during storms. The doors slid open as they approached.

"Chuck your stuff in the back," Ryu called out as he clambered behind the steering console. "There's plenty of room for three in the front, with Maria in the middle of course."

He drove through a long tunnel and then a maze of covered streets at ground level. Crossing an area of hydroponic gardens at the outskirts of the town, the van passed through a long tunnel that released them to an open, unshielded road. Ryu flicked on the autopilot as they drove into a wall of water and the first gust hit the van. He then turned to Bruce and asked in a more serious tone, "Okay, bwana, what's all this about? I get an e in Rokkasho, which orders my sorry ass down here to meet you and help liaise with the Ichi-effu people. Sampling highly active material, no less! If you're just looking for radwaste, we've got tons of it at Rokkasho. You can have as much as you want for free."

"Sorry, Ryu. I can't go into details. Commercial, very hush-hush. But I'm just the techie here, in any case. Go, fetch, package, deliver. That's it. But I can say that it's bugs we're after, which must have been pretty obvious if our sampling kit has already shown up."

Ryu nodded and pointed a thumb into the back

of the van. "All there, I guess, but why it came to me personally at JNFL and not directly here, I've no idea."

"I asked for you specifically because this is very sensitive. We shouldn't be here, and I expect records of the sampling will be buried somewhere after we leave. Officially, you're simply doing a guided tour for a couple of Uni buddies. A block of active zone monitoring probes will go offline for routine maintenance, we haul them out, get the samples, and then leg-it. Simple."

"Simple, the man says." Ryu waved his hands theatrically. "Even with my clearance, it would take me days to get into the inner hot areas. It's the RPVs of bloody melted-down reactors, remember, with fuel debris still therein. NRA and IAEA inspectors go in about once a year, but Tokyo Disneyland it ain't. I can't just wander in with a couple of gaijin pals for a quick look-see."

"Don't get your knickers in a twist, mate. Let's just see what happens when we get there."

"The other thing I don't get is that, if you want to piss about in Ichi-effu, why didn't we meet up somewhere closer, like the Futaba research center or even Fukushima city? Why bloody Tokai?"

"Yes, it's not at all obvious is it?" Bruce grinned.

"Which is actually the point of the exercise."

"Well, I'm quite happy to skive off on a road-trip along the sunny Tohoku coastline." Ryu glanced at the navigation computer and grinned back. "And, as there's little other traffic out enjoying this weather, I reckon we should be there in just under two hours."

Toyota-san was evidently unbothered by the tropical downpour and almost zero visibility. He concentrated on interrogating Engel during the rest of the trip. Although he did manage to find out that she was Irish, wasn't a microbiologist, and had known Bruce for a relatively short time, Engel managed to twist his questions round, so that he ended up talking more about himself and, in particular, his first encounters with Bruce while he was a post grad at Strathclyde and later ski trips together when he spent time as a postdoc in Grenoble.

Signs as they approached the 1F complex noted in Japanese and English that this was a restricted access area, which should not be approached without prior authorization. The warning was repeated as they approached the dome covering the nuclear complex. A heavy gate slid open on their approach and closed behind them before interlocks allowed the inner door of the airlock to open. Within the main dome, a number of smaller domes or blocky buildings enclosed individual facilities, each with their own security system. The access to the ramp leading to the underground storage vaults was at the far side of the site where, under better weather conditions, the sea would have been discernible through the semi-transparent wall of the main dome.

An automatic gate allowed them into another airlock, which opened into a car park beside the low curving roof of the waste reception and transfer building. They piled out of the van, taking their bags from the back along with three red coolbox-type containers with rugged handles. Bruce passed his shoulder bag to Engel and hefted one container in each hand. Ryu lifted the third with a grunt. "What the fuck you got in here, man?" he muttered. "Depleted uranium?"

"Right in one," Bruce responded, causing the eyes of the tall Japanese to widen in surprise.

Ryu led the way to the entrance, where two armed guards checked the authorizations downloaded from Bruce's palmtop. Extensive discussion in Japanese between Ryu and the guards was caused by the redheaded holo of Engel, which caused Bruce to curse under his breath. "Fuckin' multi-D planning software's supposed to spot these fuckin' things," he muttered to Engel.

Ian Mckinley

"Never trust anything that has evolved from generations of work by geeks and anoraks," she responded, smugly.

Engel eventually solved the problem by pulling out a small pair of scissors and cutting a few strands of her short black hair. With Ryu's assistance, the guards accessed an analysis of the black dye and a clear image of the un-dyed red hair on their screen. With evident relief, the guards were then able to wave them into a short corridor, undoubtedly packed with every remote sensing device known to man, which led to the open door of an elevator. The cool boxes were placed in a separate goods hatch and transported off to a buffer store.

The door closed as soon as they entered and the lift dropped silently to the minus-ten level. The door slid open to reveal two Japanese men and a young woman in white labcoats. They bowed together and the older man stepped forward to shake Bruce's hand. "Welcome to Ichi-effu waste storage complex. I am Naito," he turned slightly, "and these are Saito and Miss Aoki." He drew a holder from his pocket and offered his card with a bow.

After all members of both parties had been introduced and had exchanged cards, Naito-san led them along a bare corridor with lime-green painted walls and into a small meeting room with an oval wooden table and large black leather chairs. Miss Aoki disappeared into a side room, returning with a tray holding six cups of green tea as the others were settling down. After exchanging general pleasantries while drinking their tea, Naito launched into an obviously often-presented overview of the reactor accident and the subsequent clean-up and decommissioning activities. Voice activated holo sequences appeared over the center of the table to illustrate key events based on documentary footage, mainly from the original TEPCO records and IAEA investigation, together with animated 3D simulations.

The presentation dragged out for about an hour, at which point Ryu was rolling his eyes at a bored-looking Engel. The offer to answer questions was obviously added only out of politeness, but Bruce used the opportunity to quiz Naito on the layout of all present monitoring equipment and the latest readings of conditions in the hottest areas of the RPV storage vaults. In general, all data matched the info Bruce had compiled, with the exception of a prototype multi-parameter measurement tool that had been emplaced in the grouted zone around the corium-filled bottom penetrations of the RPV from unit 1.

As Bruce inquired about further details, it was

clear that Naito was getting out of his depth so he requested Aoki-san to take over. It transpired that Miss Aoki was actually a member of the team that had developed the new monitoring equipment and was able to call up both full technical specs and real-time measurements from the probe. Located at one of the few points where significant amounts of liquid water were found, the sensor was able to continuously measure profiles of alpha, beta, gamma and neutron dose rates, redox couples, pH, temperature and concentrations of a range of dissolved species.

Bruce broke off an increasingly technical discussion with Aoki-san on the possible mechanisms causing inversely coupled variations in Eh and pH when he caught a hard stare from Engel. "Well then, I guess we ought to get on with our visit." He looked at Ryu expectantly.

Naito-san squirmed uncomfortably. "We are still awaiting your final visit clearance, sorry," he apologized. "The project leader, Ito-san, is having a meeting with some very important, above-the-clouds people. They are the ones who make the decisions about these things. But, anyway, it is time for lunch," he finished on a more cheerful note.

Lunch had been booked in a TEPCO guesthouse

outside the site, an arrangement that Bruce was convinced had been intended to waste time but would be very impolite to refuse. A large chauffeur-driven van was waiting for them as they emerged into the car park. All six members of their party had plenty of room in the back, and Naito kept up a tourist-guide description of the various facilities as they drove through the site.

The guesthouse was less than a kilometer from the main site airlock, built completely into a small hill, its presence indicated only by large picture windows and a tunnel into an underground garage. Two uniformed girls guided them into the guesthouse and led them to a small dining room set out for a traditional Japanese meal. As they entered the room, the blanked window forming one wall flicked to full transparency, revealing a small roofed-over Zen garden. With guests seated facing the window, Naito welcomed them again to Tokai and raised a small glass of beer to toast them with an enthusiastic, "Kampai!"

After the glasses were topped up, Bruce formally thanked his host, which led on to a second toast to the success of international collaboration.

The meal preceded slowly, course after beautifully presented course, with regular toasts. By the time a final dish of melon was produced, Naito was markedly flushed, his red face clearly indicating that he was one of the many Japanese with low alcohol tolerance. Bruce again thanked his host, while Naito-san slurred a formal response.

The van was waiting for them when they were led from the dining room, but Bruce took up the offer for a restroom visit, which gave him an opportunity to slip down an alcohol detox tab. Back in the original meeting room, Naito-san announced with evident surprise that their active zone visit clearance had come through and that they could go directly to the changing rooms.

The group set off through a maze of green tunnels that led to a small individual airlock, which refused passage to Naito until he took the offered superfast detox drink. His eyes were bulging as the detox brutally blasted through his system, its progress registering by the ruddy color draining from his cheeks. They all took white overshoes from the rack and slid them on.

The short corridor was now pink colored and had large glass windows revealing well equipped, but completely unoccupied, laboratories and waste transfer facilities. At the end of the corridor, Aoki-san led Engel into the ladies' changing room. Ryu then managed to convince the other Japanese that, as specified in their authorization, he could guide the visitors through the hot zone and hence they did not need to be accompanied further.

Bruce and Ryu stripped completely, setting off a slagging match focusing on what a bad shape the other was in. They then fought their way into tight one-piece suits that had integral slippers, gloves and hoods, like some kind of baby sleeping garment. Thermally-activated digital readout dosimeters lit up, displaying dose rate in red and cumulative dose in blue on patches at wrists, chest and waist. They then passed through another airlock into a red-painted corridor where they waited for Engel, who emerged a couple of minutes later accompanied by Aoki-san. Ryu immediately launched into outrageous flattery of both women, causing Aoki-san to blush. As Bruce looked over the two small women in their tight suits, however, he had to concede that Ryu had a point.

Miss Aoki led them to a vehicle that looked like a heavily-shielded golf buggy, and then drove through a maze of downward-sloping ramps walled with rough red shotcrete. While she chatted cheerfully to Engel, Bruce noted that Michiko was now on first-name terms with Maria. As they descended, Ryu pointed out that the dose rate had now jumped above background and, although still in a range which would not be harmful, was slowly ramping up as they neared the various storage areas.

One further twisting corridor and they emerged into a large cavern, which was about twenty meters square and about three meters high.

"This is it," Aoki-san announced, "monitoring station G three." This was confirmed by the large *G-3* painted in white in the middle of each red wall.

The cavern was divided in two by a wall of thick lead-glass. On their side of the wall was a long shelf extending its full length and a row of eight high-back stools. The other side was packed with equipment connected by a rat's nest of cables and tubing to a number of holes extending into the floor and the facing wall. In addition to the analytical equipment, Bruce recognized a tele-operated drilling rig and a laser auger-reamer.

Michiko Aoki went directly to one of the central stools and picked up a VR headset with easy familiarity. Bruce and Ryu took places beside the small Japanese scientist, with Engel then sitting beside Bruce. "Is this really necessary?" she inquired. "Couldn't you do all this from upstairs...or Tokyo for that matter?"

"Of course it is technically possible, Maria-san,"

Michiko responded. "But there are two reasons why all handling is done by local operators. You know that we have many earthquakes in Japan, and there is always a risk that a remote link could be broken in the middle of some delicate operation. Even though it is much less likely, there is even a possibility that a typhoon could disrupt communication. In this room, which is over three hundred meters below the surface, we have full power and support system backup, so it's okay even in a mega-quake. We have very good equipment, but we work in a harsh environment in Japan."

"The other reason is not technical," she continued with a little embarrassed smile. "We have had several nuclear accidents in Japan which were not handled very well."

"Actually," Ryu broke in, "they were totally screwed up by inept attempts at cover-ups. Japanese culture is not very good at allocating responsibility for accidents. It's always better to pretend that nothing at all happened. This tendency is made worse by distant VR operations, which make the impact of a balls-up less visceral. Get the operators as close to the action as possible, and they're not only more careful, they're also much more responsible about handling incidents."

After this explanation, the sampling team activated their headsets and settled back in their stools while Michiko slaved VR navigation to her set and took them off on a virtual tour of the other side of the wall, calling up holos to explain particular technical points. The key technical problem was clearly hydrogen, produced by radiolysis and chemical reaction of both steel and corium with slowly penetrating groundwater. Initial attempts to maintain inert conditions in the hotter areas were complicated by air leakages from the network of ventilated access and monitoring tunnels. Although tunnel sealing had been attempted, the main focus involved extensive use of catalytic recombiners. This system had worked well for twenty years. However, over the last few months, large pulse releases of hydrogen gas had been causing difficulties in ensuring that concentrations stayed below explosion limits at all times.

"Would it be possible to haul out these four probes for our sampling work?" Bruce used data-gloves to mark them on the holo. "We'd like to get both water samples and swabs from the probes themselves."

"I'm afraid that would not be possible, Doctor Roberts-san," Doctor Aoki replied apologetically.

"We can only take out probes at planned maintenance times." She called up the project plan for all operational work on the monitoring system. "Oh, you are very lucky," she corrected herself with surprise. "The check times for all probes in this sector have been moved forward to this month...actually today." She stared at the corrected date on the plan and looked at Bruce with suspicion.

Bruce cast his eyes heavenwards. "I guess we have assistance from above the clouds."

Ryu and Michiko both looked very impressed.

Although clearly still a bit uncomfortable with the situation, Aoki-san helped Bruce and Ryu set up the operational plan for the remote manipulators. The sampling boxes were called up from the buffer store and cycled through an airlock directly into the hot cell. The Japanese woman checked times and concluded that it would not be possible to complete the sampling program before 5pm, after which another special clearance would be needed. Bruce decided not to push his luck and agreed to postpone the fourth probe until the following morning.

The work program was formally logged and received immediate authorization, causing Aoki-san to relax a little. As the work started, Bruce was pleased to see how well they worked together as a team: Michiko handling removal, calibration checking, and eventual replacement of the probes, Ryu sampling water and himself swabbing the probes and monitoring borehole walls. Engel coordinated the recording of all their activities and also monitored gas levels, which shot into the red when each probe was removed, requiring work to be stopped until the catalytic oxidizers had done their scrubbing.

Sampling of the first three locations was finished by sixteen thirty, almost exactly on schedule. Bruce complemented Aoki-san on her work plan—particularly the way she had set up the explosion risk buffers—and was rewarded with a glowing smile. She led the party back to the changing rooms where, after they had discarded their active suits and showered, they passed into the clean zone and could dress again in their street clothes.

The party finally made their way back to the meeting room. Naito-san was already waiting for them. "Have you seen everything that you want?"

"It has been very interesting for us watching Doctor Aoki servicing the monitors," Bruce responded. "Tomorrow she will carry out the maintenance of the new prototype, and we would like to see that also. I think we have clearance for that, if it is okay with you."

Extremophile

Doctor Naito seemed less than enthusiastic but clearly could not refuse this request. A nine o'clock start for the following day was agreed.

***

While Aoki-san led them back to their van, Ryu managed to talk her into agreeing to have dinner with them, arranging to pick her up from Mito station at seven thirty. As they drove off, Engel checked in with Eva via Bruce's palmtop and found that she and Angela were already at the hotel and were meeting Ito-san and a couple of other senior managers for dinner at seven.

Emerging from the outer airlock, Bruce and Engel were amazed by blue skies, already darkening with the approaching evening. The air was completely still and crystal clear. "It's the eye," Ryu explained, cheerfully. "We're just about the middle of it just now." He called up a spot image of the typhoon on the screen. "We could get another few hours in a slow moving bugger of this size, before the other half of it crashes into us. Anyway, it should make for a fast drive back to Mito."

Conversation drifted slowly from a technical post-mortem of the work carried out to an exchange of insults about Japanese and Scottish food. Ryu dropped them in the underground reception area of the Mito Plaza just before seven. With a wide grin, he announced, "I've got just the very place for you, Bruce ma boy, one of Japan's ultimate dining experiences. I'll quickly change at my digs, pick up Michiko at the station, and be with you in about an hour." He managed a reasonable simulation of a theatrical cackle as the door slid closed and he drove off.

"I don't much like the sound of that," Engel commented as she followed Bruce to check-in.

"Don't worry," Bruce reassured her. "The lad's sound as a pound, even though he talks a heap of shite sometimes. Don't know where he picked that up."

Engel rolled her eyes, but refused to respond to this bait.

The hotel was very quiet, so they had no problem getting neighboring rooms on the fifth floor. Taking the lift to floor five, they walked past their rooms to the fire-stair and climbed to the seventh floor. On their knock, Angela opened the door to her room, already dressed for dinner in one of her outrageous tubes.

"Just in case I need any more favors from these guys," she answered his unspoken question.

Extremophile

When they entered, they could catch glimpses of Eva through the open connecting door to the next room. Bruce attempted to concentrate on summarizing progress to Angela while, out of the corner of his eye, watching Engel help a naked Eva squirm into a tube. He lost the thread completely when Engel started tickling the taller woman while she was caught halfway into the dress.

"Girls!" Angela caught everyone's attention with her sharp tone. "We have to be downstairs in ten minutes. Now, Bruce, you were saying?"

Bruce forced himself to turn his back to the open door and continued with his report on their work. They squeezed together round a small table to discuss the sampling details projected from Bruce's palmtop. Eva's discrete cough brought them back to reality, reminding Angela that it was time to go.

Agreeing to meet later in Angela's room, Bruce and Engel set off back to their own bedrooms. They opened the connecting door and sat together on the end of Bruce's narrow bed to plan their evening. Bruce was happy with progress but was uncertain how to handle Michiko Aoki. *In an ideal world we'd have done all sampling ourselves, but external involvement limited only to Ryu and Michiko was a lot better than it could have been. Ryu can handle himself, but there's a difficult line to walk with Michiko, being as upfront as possible but trying to ensure that nothing backfires on her if the shit eventually hits the fan.*

Leaving this problem to be played by ear, Bruce worked over the options for getting themselves and their swag back to Scotland. The water samples in their shielded containers would have to be freighted back. Ryu would drive them back to Rokkasho, where they would be shipped or flown to Sellafield and there picked up by Pharm staff for transportation to Glasgow. As a backup, Bruce intended to take the swabs and filter samples back with them in their luggage. *From a practical point of view, this'll be tricky. I'll be carrying unknown radioactive microbes in a depleted uranium container set with a UV burster wired to detonate in the event of any unauthorized attempts to open it. Not exactly the kind of thing that anybody would want to load into the hold of a passenger plane.*

The optimum option from the MAA analysis was clearly to take a tourist shuttle to Hawaii, followed by private Pharm jet to Bend, Oregon, where first tests could be carried out. Then, if necessary, samples could be repackaged for transportation via normal Pharm channels. Bruce set up an order that would book a first class ticket for himself and three business tickets for the others on the eighteen thirty *Waikiki*

Express. Poorly named, Bruce recalled. *Waikiki disappeared below the waves years ago, although the upper slopes of the Hawaiian chain of volcanoes still hosted a range of expensive resorts.* "These JAL megatops fly out of Narita every half hour," he explained to Engel, "full of Japanese tourists having a break away from the awful climate. Economy is always packed but, since the economic crisis hit, first and business are usually available."

"All very well," Engel responded before they broke to change for dinner, "but why do you get first class while we have to slum it?"

"Because I'm carrying the radioactive shit," he answered. "The chances of having checked-in luggage searched is even less in first. We can swap, though, if you want. Do you know what the penalty is for smuggling this kind of crap onto a passenger flight? On this side of the Pacific, you'd need Angela's longevity to have any chance of breathing fresh air again. And that's the good news. On the other side it's straight onto death row."

"You've convinced me. I didn't really want to fly first with all those rich bastards anyway," she mumbled as an afterthought before she disappeared into her room.

Engel bounced back into his room ten minutes

later, wearing a tight white top and a loose miniskirt. She whirled into a back-roundhouse kick that brought the armored side of her foot against his Adam's apple. "Bare feet okay, I guess?"

"Nul problemo, but knickers would be a good idea if we're going to be kneeling on the floor," he pointed out. "Don't want old Ryu choking to death on his natto, as we're going to need him tomorrow." He flicked a kick at her exposed groin.

Not only did she back flip out of range before his foot had reached knee level, but she flicked his nose painfully with her big toe as she did so. *Maybe just as well.* He blinked tears of pain out of his eyes. *Saves me needing to go for a cold shower after the view that I've just been presented with.*

Engel re-emerged seconds later, lifting up the hem of her skirt to reveal a miniature, semitransparent tanga. "Okay, now?" Accepting his sigh and eyes raised towards the ceiling as agreement, she took him by the arm and led the way towards the lift.

***

Ryu and Michiko were waiting for them in the lobby, evidently in the middle of an animated discussion. Engel nudged Bruce in the ribs as she caught sight of Aoki-san's white blouse, short navy skirt, white knee socks and black slippers. "Schoolgirl-look, just the thing for a randy old pedophile beast," she whispered.

"Best to leave the van here," Ryu explained while he slapped Bruce on the shoulder and blatantly leered at Engel. "We can take a cab."

The taxi took them from the hotel reception through a long tunnel, eventually disgorging them into a maze of very narrow streets under the Mito dome. Bruce could now understand Ryu's decision to leave the van as it would have been far too wide to enter half of the streets in the old town. In addition, there seemed to be absolutely no parking available anywhere.

They pulled up in front of an ancient-looking building, which had the appearance of something disreputable, like a brothel or an opium den. Ryu led them confidently through the sliding paper doors into a stone-floored area containing a number of large granite troughs that were stocked with a diverse range of fish. Two chefs with tied headbands and happi-coats stood behind a massive stone counter and bowed when they entered.

A diminutive woman in a kimono bowed to Ryu, followed by an explosion of rapid Japanese.

Following his response, she bowed to the others. "Welcome, welcome, good evening," she sang at them and led them to one of the small side-rooms. Before they stepped up to enter, the two men removed their sandals and slipped on socks from the rack by the door. Following a glare from Bruce, Engel also selected a pair of the short socks, with their characteristic separate big toe, pulling them on with marked reluctance.

Michiko knelt elegantly at the low table while Engel dropped into sieza, with knees apart. Bruce and Ryu both decided to save their knees and adopted a cross-legged sitting position. Ryu ordered beers and then scanned through a hand-written menu. After the waitress poured their first glass of beer, Ryu offered a toast to friendship and McEwan's Pale Ale, all joining in the ceremonial cry of "kampai!"

Engel and Michiko refilled the glasses and Bruce proposed a toast to the Scottish sense of humor. Just when Ryu started to drink, Engel opened her legs a bit farther, giving him a full view up her skirt. Bruce slapped the back of the choking Ryu enthusiastically. "One point to Doctor Maiden." He recorded this with his index finger on an imaginary chalkboard.

"Totally below the belt, in every sense of the word," Ryu spluttered, increasing Michiko's evident confusion and the gaijins' amusement.

After some picturesque starters, the first main plate arrived, sashimi of some kind of flounder served on the body of the fish, which was impaled by a wooden stake to bend it into an artistic curve on its bed of ice. Engel looked rather dubious and sipped her beer, trying to avoid eye contact with the fish, which seemed to be looking directly at her.

Suddenly the fish's mouth moved in a silent gasp, causing Engel to splutter and Bruce to spill beer from the glass that was halfway to his lips. "It's still fuckin' alive," she gasped, to the amusement of both Japanese.

"Two points to me," Ryu claimed cheerfully, marking them on the invisible scoreboard. "I told you it'd be a special meal. Now tell me one time when you've had fish fresher than this." He lifted a piece of the thinly cut, translucent flesh with his chopsticks, dipped it in soy sauce and chewed it with relish. "Fantastic."

Michiko followed his lead, enthusiastically sampling the fish. "I have heard of this restaurant, but I have never been here before," she chattered between mouthfuls. "It is very famous. It requires much skill to prepare the fish while it is still alive."

With a feeling that he was backed into a corner,

Bruce gingerly tried a small piece of sashimi. "It's really good," he had to concede. "You ought to try some Engel...um, Maria."

Ryu spotted the slip, but Engel was spared further teasing while he recalled the nicknames of some of the girls they knew in their university days. "Engel, no' bad, German for Angel if I'm no' mistaken. Remember that *Thunder-thighs*, God that was a big wummin. Mind that time when we wur pished in the Frog 'n Firkin..."

Bruce rolled his eyes as Ryu rambled on with a series of anecdotes about amorous encounters in Glasgow, focusing his attention on Engel. He was grateful that Michiko could obviously understand only about one word in ten of the exaggerated dialect. Trying to divert her from Ryu's hyperbole and character defamation, Bruce asked her about raw fish preparation.

Engel had carefully lifted a piece of fish to her lips, looking as if she expected it to start wriggling at any moment, when she picked up Michiko's explanation of the fish being kept in tanks of clean water for at least a week to reduce concentrations of hormones and other organic pollutants. She glared at Bruce as if being commanded to make some major sacrifice, gulped down the sashimi without chewing, and turned to devote full concentration to Ryu's continuous stream of waffle.

With little help from Engel, the first course of sashimi was finished. Ryu poked the head of the fish with a chopstick, just as the waitress came to remove it. Another slow yawn from the fish, which was now only a head and a tail connected by exposed bones. "I told you so," he said, grinning at Engel. "Still kicking."

Bruce was not surprised when the next course appeared, another gasping, carefully dissected fish. Catching Engel's expression, Ryu asked with a grin. "You okay, Maria? Do you want me to check if they can do you a burger or a plate of chips?"

"It's fine," she responded with a glare. "It's just that I'm not used to eating things that're still alive."

"Oh, never tried oysters then? You should always be able to see the reflex reaction when you drop some lemon juice on them. Alive right into your mouth."

While Ryu continued to bait Engel, Bruce and Michiko's conversation had drifted in the direction of work. She was obviously very curious to know what was going on, even if it was supposed to be *commercial*. Bruce explained that it was microbiological sampling—as was completely obvious in any case from the biohazard and GM microbe signs on their sample containers. As an area of obvious interest to the 1F waste team, however, Bruce focused on the potential role of bugs in setting redox conditions and influencing the production and consumption of gasses like hydrogen and methane. Without further steering, Michiko jumped on the possibility that microbial activity could explain some of the strange readings from her new probe. Bruce promised to send her any relevant data as soon as it was declassified, which seemed to remove her last reservations about their work.

A third fish had arrived and, although it was smaller than the others, even the Japanese seemed to have reached saturation. Everyone had to try a taste, but the fish was removed, still gasping, with most of its body uneaten.

After the usual melon and green tea, Ryu ordered a taxi and enquired about how they would like to spend the rest of the evening. Claiming jetlag and an early start, Bruce decided that the gaijin should call it a night, "....not that it stops you folk going somewhere for a drink or two." He winked at Ryu.

While waiting for the taxi, Ryu attempted half-heartedly to talk Bruce into a pub-crawl, evidently noting clear signals that Michiko would be happy to continue on with him as a twosome. While they clambered into the small car, Bruce and Engel thanked their hosts for a most interesting evening and waved as they set off back into Mito Plaza. "Dinnae dae anythin' a widnae," Ryu shouted as the door slid closed.

Back at the hotel, Bruce led the way to the lift and they went directly to Angela's room. The two scientists were sitting together on her narrow bed, wearing yukatas and drinking cognac out of small wine glasses. Engel headed straight for the minibar and selected a can of Asahi, a large Toblerone and a tin of cashew nuts.

"Have a nice meal?" Angela enquired with a smile.

Bruce also chose a beer and, after flicking off his sandals, joined Engel on the foot of the bed. He sipped his beer quietly while Engel described their dinner in gory detail, steadily working her way through the Toblerone as if the sweet, sticky chocolate was cleansing her mouth. "I thought you ninja types were tough," Eva teased after Engel finished the story of her ordeal.

"We just have to kill people, not eat them alive," she retorted. "It's weird, I've no problem eating animals—it's what they're for—but having fish alive, watching you while you eat its flesh, it's not pleasant." She gulped and then had a large swig of beer as if to wash away any trace of her dinner.

By comparison, the others had eaten a normal, if extremely expensive, Chinese meal in one of the restaurants within the Mito Plaza complex. In addition to Ito-san, two NRA directors and a vice-president from IRID had attended. Although starting very formally, the Japanese had relaxed after a few drinks, no doubt encouraged by the outrageous clothing that the two beautiful women wore.

After dinner, the ladies had gone to the basement lounge for a drink with Ito and Nakamoto, one of the NRA guys. Angela had been very amused to find out that their first names were Akira and Tetsuo, yet neither had heard of the *Akira* manga. After one drink, Angela managed to organize their escape from the red-faced pair of Japanese salarymen, with excuses of tiredness and a slight fever that could indicate some bug picked up during their travels. She noticed, however, that a pair of Japanese hostesses had taken their places before they had even left the bar.

Bruce proposed an early night as he was really feeling a bit jet-lagged. Although a range of bio-clock resetters was available, he tended to avoid using these unless he knew he was going to be in one place for a while. Engel was already setting up a second round for the other women, so Bruce shrugged and kissed his goodnights, before heading off for his room, having agreed six fifteen for breakfast.

He was already sound asleep when he was awoken by a small body squeezing into the narrow bed with him. He passively allowed Engel to rearrange his body to suit her desired sleeping position, while her words gradually penetrated his drowsy state. Eva hadn't mentioned it to Angela, but she thought that she had glimpsed the two Japanese from *Bottoms Up*, who had again appeared in the Shamrock. The pair had been in a dim booth in a corner of the hotel bar, so it could have just been paranoia on Eva's part, but Engel was clearly worried.

When his diminutive partner drifted off, sleep was no longer an option for Bruce. *Fuck! No matter what we do, we can't shake these bastards. In fact, we may have led them straight to their goal, revealing what the purpose of this road-trip is. If that's the case, we are walking around with targets on our backs. Angela could be of value to them, but the rest of us are just annoyances, better taken out of the picture as soon as possible. I'd just*

drop everything and hit the road now, if not for the fact that, if it wasn't our tails in the bar, this would be the strange behavior that would attract attention. Hung if we do, hung if we don't. I just don't have the information needed to make the life and death decisions that we face.
It's like blindfold knife-fighting, one false move and things go horribly wrong.

Extremophile

Day 8 ...oot frae the East ther kem a wee hard man

Bruce was awoken by Engel slipping out of the bed, but she had already disappeared into her own room before he had time to rub his eyes and note that it was five forty-five. He sighed when he became aware of his usual early-morning hard-on. *Caused by pressure on the bladder,* he tried to convince himself while he headed for the bathroom.

He eased himself into the small shower, observing that urination did not seem to have solved the problem. Setting a soapy spray, he rinsed himself, concentrating subconsciously on his erect penis. In the middle of a long soapy caress, the shower door slammed open.

"B'Jesus, but you're a sad auld beast. My beauteous body available all night and nary a grope, not the one. Leave you to yourself for five minutes and you're wankin' in the shower. Shame on you."

"Fuck," he exclaimed involuntarily, feeling blood warm his cheeks. "Don't you ever knock when entering a strange man's shower? Where's your bloody manners? You never know, I could have been in here with someone else," he finished, somewhat lamely.

"Strange man? Fuckin' perv I'd call you," she responded while she squeezed herself in with him. "In fact, a perv with a wild imagination." Engel was really getting into the swing of things as she slapped his hands away and took control of his engorged member. "Let's face it, nae bitch'd touch your wee skinny prick with a fuckin' barge pole unless they're gettin' paid fer it. Ma bonus better be fuckin' huge ta compensate me fer this, but I suppose that if ye don't get yer end away, you'll be even more fuckin' useless than usual." She really had Ryu's gutter Glaswegian down pat.

Not more than sixty seconds later the door slammed open again and he was pushed out of the shower. As the door shut, Engel got in a last gibe. "...and no staying power. I'd be better off with Eva...or even the old fat one...if I wanted some sexual gratification."

Bruce considered going through to Engel's room to clean up, but finally decided that a towel would suffice. He was already dressed when Engel strutted through the room, unselfconsciously scratching her bottom. Trying to avoid staring, he turned away and called up a weather satellite feed, noting that the worst of the typhoon should have passed by midday, which was perfect timing for their planned travel.

Smooth flesh rubbed against the back of his thigh. "Action replay? We've still got a couple of minutes before breakfast."

"Actually that might be possible, if I close my eyes and think of Angela, like I did last time." Bruce threw himself forward in a breakfall, which took him well clear of a kick that would have caved-in his ribcage.

"See you in Angela's room, but don't rush," he finished to her retreating back while she stomped out of his room.

Bruce entered Angela's room just as she was in the process of opening a bottle of champagne. "Isn't it a bit premature to celebrate now?" he asked in surprise.

"Don't be silly, Bruce, it's for Maria's birthday. Don't you remember?"

Actually, he had completely forgotten, but said nothing as four glasses were poured, just in time for Engel's arrival.

Engel looked confused when she was greeted by a chorus of *Happy Birthday* and had a glass of champagne pressed into her hand. He bent to kiss Engel after the other women had fussed over her. *My God, I think she's blushing. Who'd have thunk it possible?*

Over breakfast, logistical details for the day were finalized. Angela and Eva would take the 10am shinkansen to Tokyo and transfer there onto the NEX to Narita airport. Ryu would pick up Engel and Bruce for the final sampling session. After that, he would run them directly to Narita, taking Engel directly to the airport after dropping Bruce off in the city, where he would pick up a taxi.

Angela was clearly unhappy about Bruce's smuggling arrangements. However, she couldn't suggest any better option. Just before he left her room, she crushed him in a hug. "Look after yourself." Over her shoulder Bruce could see Eva, who winked and blew him a kiss.

Bruce and Engel packed their luggage, checked out and were waiting for Ryu when he drew up five minutes early. The tall Japanese was even more manic than usual. "Brilliant night, last night, eh, Carruthers? You cannae eat any better than that. And the fish wisnae bad neither." He leered theatrically.

Without any encouragement, Ryu maintained a

flow of insinuation, double entendre and lavatorial humor the entire way to 1F, oscillating randomly between mid-Atlantic English and exaggerated Glaswegian.

Michiko was awaiting them in the vault entrance car park and greeted them all warmly, although with some embarrassment in Ryu's case, suggesting that not all of his previous claims were completely unfounded.

All formal procedures had been dropped, so Aoki-san was able to take them directly to the hot cell, where the sampling from the final probe proceeded smoothly and was completed within less than an hour.

The sample containers were then remotely transferred through a decontamination system to the upper *pink-zone* laboratories, where final checking of surface contamination took place. The six cylindrical water sample containers caused no problems. The small flat-pack for the filter samples needed special attention, however, as the non-standard geometry caused difficulties for the automated systems.

As a final stage, the containers were transferred through a chamber in which a sealing layer of diamond-like carbon was vapor-deposited over all surfaces prior to transfer to the green-zone release area, where they would be placed in the coolbox carriers.

Back in the car park, Michiko helped them load the transfer containers into the van and waved goodbye as they drove off. "Another heart broken," Ryu commented with attempted bravado while they drove off, but both his passengers noticed his shy wave before the door closed.

"You big soft shite, well I guess it'll be wedding bells now." Bruce grinned.

"Can I be bridesmaid?" Engel chipped in. "The poor girl is clearly both blind and mentally challenged, and I'm very good with such hopeless cases." She was clearly set on revenge for Ryu's special dinner.

The barrage of slagging continued for most of the trip to Narita, Ryu fighting back with speculations about the relationship between Bruce and Engel. While they were en route, Bruce scrambled into the back of the van, unpacked his shoulder bag, and fit the slim sample pack into a compartment in the base of the bag. He repacked the bag with only light items of clothing, taking some clothes from Engel's backpack to ensure that it appeared filled to bursting point. Residual heavier objects like his laptop, he then shoved into Engel's bag.

He then hefted the two bags. His was heavier, but its weight wasn't so much more than Engel's and didn't seem excessive, given its well-stuffed appearance. Bruce felt distinctly naked without his laptop, but at least he had a small palmtop, which fit into a pouch that he clipped to his belt.

Back in the front, Bruce was amused to find that, in his absence, Ryu had changed from slagging Engel to chatting her up. Shortly later, they entered the Narita City dome, and Bruce was dropped off by one of the main railway station entrances. Ryu warned him that he should get a taxi as soon as possible because the area had a bad reputation, but was prevented from going into more detail by Engel who ran her hand up his thigh and suggested that they were wasting time that could be spent elsewhere. Ryu finished his goodbyes with alacrity, his face sporting a huge grin before the van shot off towards the airport.

Bruce shouldered the bag and strolled off jauntily in the direction of the 'U-city' hotel, where he intended to pick up a taxi. Things had gone so well that he took little notice of the run-down appearance of his surroundings. Only when three young Japanese stepped out of an alleyway and stood across the pavement, blocking his passage, did the feeling of wrongness fully crystallize. His ebullient mood evaporated instantly when he realized that there was nobody else in sight, he was carrying a load of extremely sensitive contraband, and that his combat pharms were in a side pocket of his bag. *Fuck! Not a good time to start rooting through my luggage. After all the worrying of the last couple of days, I relax for ten seconds and this happens.* "Fuck!" He stepped into the street to avoid the youths.

The three teenagers spread out farther to block his path and started swearing at him in Japanese, the tenor being obvious even though the only word he was able to make out was *gaijin*. Bruce felt himself going cold as he assessed the odds. The three were in their late teens, maybe early twenties at the oldest. For all their apparent hatred of foreigners, they were dressed like US ghetto street-shit and looked like they pumped iron rather than working out in a dojo. The Yank-thug theme was confirmed when they drew out what appeared to be matching flick-knifes. *I haven't seen one of those since West Side Story*, was Bruce's last conscious thought before the yob in the middle lunged forward with a blade aimed at his gut.

The guy was very slow, even for Bruce's unenhanced reflexes. Diverting the knife with his right hand, he turned his assailant round and punched him hard in the kidney. The punch should have dropped the small Japanese. Instead, it was like hitting a leather punch-bag and evoked only a grunt. *Not muscles from pumping iron*, Bruce now recognized with a groan, *chemically induced muscle bulk and body panzering.*

I could be in deep shit here.

Bruce slipped off his shoulder bag. To his dismay, before he could attempt to get his pharm pouch, attacks came from both sides. These were even slower than the first. That, paradoxically, made them more difficult to handle, as there was not enough momentum for him to use against his assailants. Twisting around the attacker to his right, he kicked him on the side of his knee with all the force he could muster and was rewarded by a satisfying crack and a scream of pain before the boy toppled forward. Although now shielded from the blade to his left, the move opened Bruce to his first opponent, who was already slashing towards his face.

Bruce's duck was almost enough, but the tip of the blade nicked his ear. He could immediately feel the flow of blood down his neck, although there was little sensation of pain. *Shit, these knifes may look like antiques, but they're fucking sharp.*

The two standing youths moved towards him.

He backed off a couple of steps. *That's it, no more Mister Niceguy.* Selecting the taller lad as the most confident, Bruce moved towards him, causing his eyes to open wide in surprise and his buddy to hesitate noticeably.

"Ya fuckin' wee shite!" Bruce yelled at the top of his voice while he lunged forward, further confusing his attacker. Grabbing the knife-hand by the wrist, he jammed two straight fingers into the boy's eyes. One finger only scraped against his eyebrow, but the other penetrated his eyeball with a sickening squelch. The resultant high-pitched scream was a lot louder than Bruce's original challenge had offered.

Unfortunately, in some kind of reflex, the blinded kid managed to grab a hold of Bruce's gory hand, which left him open to the third attacker. Even while he wrenched free and twisted round to use the screaming kid as a shield, he felt warm moisture soaking his side.

Continuing the turn around the outside of the dripping blade, Bruce captured his assailant's wrist with his left hand and pulled the young thug forward. He then reversed the direction of his turn and used his right hand to crush on a wristlock, which slammed his attacker onto his back, the knife clattering as it bounced along the street.

Extremophile

The mugger's shout of pain choked off as Bruce stomped on his larynx with all his weight and then kicked his nose, causing a torrent of blood that transformed the choking into a more terminal-sounding gurgling noise.

Stepping round the taller boy, who was now crying with his hands over his bleeding face, Bruce noted that the first downed attacker was trying to crawl away, dragging Bruce's shoulder bag with him. Although the boy abandoned the bag and rolled into a fetal position on his approach, Bruce kicked him hard three times on the exposed back of his head, with a final stomp on his cheek for good luck.

Catching his breath, Bruce now noticed that the commotion had brought several faces to room windows and that a couple of security guards were emerging from the hotel, only a couple of hundred meters distant.

Deciding discretion was the better part of valor, Bruce grabbed his bag and slipped into the dark alleyway from which his assailants had emerged and hurried away from the scene, very conscious of the feeling of blood running down his right leg and the left side of his neck. He was aware of a confused feeling—partially relieved that he had escaped from a very tricky situation but mainly seriously pissed-off that things had become complicated so close to getting out of Japan. There was no way that he could accept that this attack was simple bad luck. Somehow the bad guys were not only still on his tail, but seemed to have a paranormal ability to predict all his moves in advance.

He gradually looped his way back to the station, sticking to the edges of the smallest streets and alleyways. As he turned one corner, Bruce almost bumped into a young Japanese who could have been a clone of any member of the group who attacked him. Before he could prepare himself for another round of street fighting, the young man hurried off, evidently not keen to mess with this blood-soaked foreigner.

A great thing about Japanese railway stations is that they have toilets everywhere. I just need to get into one before I attract any more attention.

He used his handkerchief to wipe away the worst of the blood from his face before making a dash for the station entrance on the first occasion that nobody was in sight. Thirty seconds later he rushed into a toilet, startling a middle-aged man who was busy brushing his teeth at a sink. One glance at Bruce and he grabbed up his toiletries and scurried out.

Bruce used a credit chip to extract five packets of

tissues from a dispensing machine and splashed water over his face to check the damage to his ear. A very clean cut halfway through the lobe: completely trivial but bleeding heavily. With his first aid kit, he could seal it up in an instant but, unfortunately, that was one of the pieces of his luggage now in Engel's bag.

Looking round the toilet, nothing useful was evident: water, soap, tissues, condoms. *That's it*, with a flash of inspiration Bruce used the chip again to obtain a packet of three condoms—fruit flavored, if the picture on the dispenser meant anything. Wiping as much blood as possible away with a wad of tissues, he rubbed his ear with the lubricating fluid of one of the condoms. Almost miraculously, the bleeding stopped as the coagulants within the cocktail of spermicides, antibiotics and other good stuff kicked in.

Cleaning the cut left the earlobe a bit of a disfigured mess, but at least, it wouldn't call particular notice to him. Hearing someone approach, Bruce chucked tissues into a bin and scuttled into one of the cubicles, glad that it had a European style full door rather than one of the stupid American knee-to-neck jobs.

Bruce latched the door and struggled in the

limited space to strip off his blood-soaked shirt and trousers. A five-centimeter gash in his side was hanging open and pouring blood, a flow evidently increased by the action of peeling off the shirt. Taking out his Swiss army knife, which sat in the belt-pouch with his palmtop, he carved up the shirt and rinsed the pieces in the, thankfully clean, toilet bowl. Rubbing two condoms' worth of lubricant onto a folded pad of material, he pressed it hard against the wound and used several long strips to bind it tightly against his side. Delving into his bag, he sacrificed another shirt and put another pad over the already darkening cover of his wound, again binding this tightly in place with another couple of long strips of cloth.

The rinsed trousers were used to wipe down his lower body, necessitating several flushes to remove bright red water. One of Engel's dresses was then used to dry his body, wipe off his sandals, and remove spots of blood from his bag.

Dressing in clean shorts, a blue shirt and his light suit jacket, Bruce waited until the toilet was silent and then emerged, throwing the pile of damp, soiled clothing into a bin. Although feeling as if he was a walking neon sign, he attracted no more attention than any other gaijin would do as he worked his way to the station taxi rank.

"Airport, JAL international, please." Bruce spoke into a grill in the smoked glass partition, the driverless taxi accepting his request without response. He was deposited at the appropriate terminal building fifteen minutes later. Before checking in, Bruce purchased some quickly chosen shirts and crammed them into his bag to return it to its previously bulging appearance.

The first class check-in for JAL was at one edge of the terminal, evident from the pretentious red carpet that led from the exec limousine drop-off. Bruce slipped in behind a Japanese couple who were dressed in the very latest of designer clothes, obviously some kind of celebrities from the attention that they were receiving.

Baggage for check-in was collected by porters who put it through an x-ray / sniffer system for in-hold luggage, while passengers went through their own tunnel with hand luggage. The porter was evidently a bit surprised that such a small bag was being checked-in, but accepted it without comment. Bruce held his breath while the bag passed through the machine and felt his stomach turn over as the attendant on the receipt side waved him over. "The shoulder strap, it is best if you remove it," he pointed out.

Bruce removed the strap and crammed it in the top of the bag, keying the lock with his thumb. A porter then lifted the bag for him and waved him to a check-in desk. Check-in took only seconds and a hostess offered to guide him to the first class lounge. Bruce declined politely, claiming that he wanted to wander through the duty-free shopping area.

First class had a special emigration control that was almost invisible, although Bruce spotted the red-eye flash that indicated a retinal scanner at work. He passed the usual front-line duty-free shops, heading for a small pharmacy that specialized in designer drugs, many of which were either banned or not yet authorized outside Japan. Bruce purchased a couple of top line blood / body mass builders and, as if an afterthought, a small first aid kit.

Noting that he had only thirty minutes until his flight boarded, Bruce strode back to the first class lounge and, refusing the welcoming glass of champagne, headed straight for the well-equipped toilet. Locking himself in a top-range shower, he stripped off, placing his clothes in the instant fresher. When he removed the improvised bandages, the wound in his side started bleeding again, almost as heavily as before.

Extremophile

Holding the edges of the cut together, he applied first a regenerant cream and then a cut sealant to the wound. Finally he sprayed a layer of protectant over the ugly scar. A touch of sealant and a covering layer then made his ear look a bit more presentable.

Repairs completed, he showered, water running red for the first minute or so while he cleaned up the mess of crusted blood left after his rushed ministrations in the Narita station toilet. Dried in scented air and dressed in freshened clothes, Bruce felt fit to face the first class lounge. When he emerged from the shower, he noted that his flight was now boarding but, feeling a bit faint, took the opportunity to wash down a body-builder capsule with a bottle of Asahi, closely followed by a handful of bite-size sandwiches and a couple of pieces of sushi. He left the lounge aware of the surprised glances that his rather gross eating style had caused, but also feeling the pangs of hunger caused by the pharm. He remembered the warning from the package, *the use of such active tissue-building drugs is recommended only under medical supervision and with structured intravenous nutrition. Some chance.*

Settling into his enveloping first class seat, Bruce polished off two glasses each of champagne and orange juice before takeoff, which the hostess served as if this was a normal event. Once in the air, Bruce noted that there were only two other first-class guests in the compartment, passengers thus matching the number of hostesses serving them.

During the three-hour flight, Bruce chatted to the hostess who adopted him for the duration of the flight, a young Japanese named Susan, for some reason he was never able to work out. Explaining his rather odd behavior by a crisis business meeting that meant that he had not eaten for two days, Susan fussed over him, providing a continuous stream of food, wine and mineral water during the flight. If she noted that he managed to consume such a large volume of liquids and solids without once going to the toilet, she refrained from mentioning it.

Due to crossing the International Date Line, the supersonic flight arrived late in the day before it took off, something which the pilot felt necessary to comment on in detail, but which Bruce's palmtop had corrected for automatically due to its GPS link. On landing, the first class passengers were escorted to an arrivals lounge, where they completed immigration formalities and waited for their checked-in luggage.

A porter arrived with Bruce's single bag and guided him through exit formalities. They had actually passed through customs and were heading for exec transportation before Bruce remembered to worry about the consequences of being caught with smuggled radioactive materials. He mumbled something about meeting friends and took his bag from the porter, tipping him with an excessive handful of ecs.

Feeling woozy, Bruce settled into a seat opposite the main arrivals gate. The alcohol that he consumed should have been quickly broken down, but his hyperactive metabolism was tiring him. He considered dropping a wakeup pharm, but decided it would be best not to mix any more drugs at present.

He was shocked awake by a rough shake of his shoulder. "Missing us a lot, were you?" Engel peered at him, her face only inches away. "Maybe just been over-indulging in all the super first-class bevvy?"

Bruce blinked and shook his head, feeling momentarily disorientated. "Hi, Engel, you're looking like...shit. Where are the beautiful women?"

He didn't even attempt to dodge the slap, which stopped just before touching the side of his face. "What happened to your ear, Beast?"

Bruce thought he could detect an uncharacteristic trace of concern in her voice. "I'll tell you all about it later. Now we ought to get moving." He dragged himself to his feet. "Where're the others?"

"Angela's checking the jet. There should be a car waiting for us at the exec pickup point." Engel led the way.

Bruce dragged wearily behind her, exhaustion weighing him down. *I should be jumping with joy. We've actually gotten away with it. That last attack caught me out, but we're now safe in the arms of Angela's mega sponsor. Time to break out the Champagne...but maybe a snooze first.*

A small minibus was already waiting with Angela and Eva on board. As Bruce climbed in behind Engel, he received quizzical looks from the two women, but they said nothing while the bus drove the short distance from the international terminal to the small airstrip for internal private flights. The minibus passed through a well-lit security gate with minimum formality and took them directly to a small jet that was standing on the tarmac with engines warming up.

Two hostesses were standing by the boarding steps to take their luggage and help them board. Bruce kept a careful eye on his bag as it was stored in a locker at the front of the main compartment, which was set up with a row of four large leather seats facing forward on either side. As soon as they had belted-up, the cabin lights dimmed and the plane began to taxi onto the main runway. The hostesses took their seats at the rear of the cabin.

After takeoff, the hostesses bustled around, rotating the chairs so that they faced each other and offering drinks and menus. Conversation was kept carefully neutral during the meal, Bruce again using his crisis meeting excuse for the hostesses to explain eating two full dinners, while polishing off the best part of two bottles of red wine and a liter of mineral water.

Bruce excused himself to go to the toilet and was surprised to see Angela get up to follow him. At the back of the cabin she caught his shoulder and whispered, "You're on some kind of rebuilders and missing half an ear. What the hell happened?"

"A wee bit of a ruckus in Narita city, nothing critical," he answered lamely, noting that Eva had managed to talk the two hostesses into withdrawing to the cockpit and that Engel was stomping towards him.

"Your side is it?" Angela enquired, but Engel gave him no chance to answer as she pulled his shirt open.

"Nuthin', just a wee totey scratch," Engel commented dismissively, but Angela examined the damaged area in more detail.

Ian Mckinley

"There's been a bit of internal bleeding and there's inflammation around the scar. What kind of sealant did you use?"

Angela looked concerned, but Engel burst into laughter when Bruce briefly described his improvisation in the station toilet.

Without being asked, Eva tossed Angela a small pouch that she had extracted from her luggage. Angela then ripped off the sealant covering his wound, causing an intake of breath. *Both cuts were effectively painless, but that bloody hurt.* Bruce struggled to hide a groan.

Angela applied a strip of thin derm onto the scar and then re-covered the area with a sealant spray. Bruce was then allowed to escape into the toilet, while the three women started going on about how impossible it was to leave a man alone for five minutes without him getting into trouble.

When he returned to the cabin, Bruce was glad to see that the hostesses were now serving coffee. He slumped heavily into his seat, closed his eyes, and fell instantly asleep.

In his dreams he relived the fight in Narita several times, in each the feeling of foreboding building up to a more intense level. There was something that he was missing. Something that indicated the threat was far from over. But he just couldn't pin down what it was.

***

Angela was tapping his hand when Bruce gently drifted back to consciousness, aware of being hungry and extremely thirsty. A hostess offered him a glass of water without prompting. It was only after he had drunk it down that he realized that they were on the ground. "Smooth flight," he murmured.

Angela smiled. "The turbulence over the Cascades was terrible, but you snored your way through it all. Anyway, time to get off now."

Bruce staggered sleepily out of the plane and climbed down the steps towards the waiting stretched limo, beside which three very heavily built men in chauffeurs' uniforms were standing with their backs to the early-morning sun. As Bruce reached the bottom of the steps, he missed his footing and pitched forward before being caught by one of the men, who had moved at a speed seemingly incompatible with his bulk. Straightening himself up and thanking the big man, Bruce couldn't help catch a glimpse of the pistol in a quick-draw shoulder holster.

Bruce felt as if he had been hit by a bucketful of cold water: tiredness vanished and he felt his muscles tense. His mind raced as he stumbled towards the open door of the car, the vague concerns of his nightmares suddenly crystalizing. Halfway into the limo, he stopped and climbed back out. "Engel, did I give you your palmtop back? I think I left it somewhere on the plane."

Engel looked at him in momentary confusion, but quickly responded. "Oh, shit. No, I don't have it. Come on, I'll help you look for it."

Bruce quickly explained what they were doing to the hostesses standing at the bottom of the steps, but turned down their offer to help.

As Engel preceded him into the cabin, she turned to whisper. "What the fuck's this all about? You know I don't even have a palmtop with me."

"The gorilla who caught me at the bottom of the steps is packing a pistol and this is the US of A. I know that we're hot, but no Pharm is going to fuck about with handguns here. What the fuck do we do now? You're the fuckin' ninja, work your combat skills for me."

"Okay, I'm getting the picture. Do you think the bimbo hostesses are involved?"

"Not a clue but, when in doubt, assume the worst."

"Right, got it, get ready to move your fat arse. I'll

have to get Eva moving to be on the safe side." She slipped a slim pouch out of the waistband of her skirt and handed him a purple pill and a couple of small derms. "These'll make you less slow and help you take down the two wee girlies." She grinned ferally as she used a strap from the luggage rack to tie the door into the cockpit so that it couldn't be opened from the other side.

Winking at him, she started to shout, "Take your fuckin' hands off me, you bastard. Just don't fuckin' try it." She slapped him on the face, ripped her blouse open, and pulled it off one shoulder to reveal a pert breast, then turned and ran down the steps in a flurry of screamed abuse.

When Bruce emerged at the top of the steps, he was the center of all attention, except for one of the chauffeurs who was obviously more interested in Engel's chest. He saw Eva boiling out of the car, closely followed by Angela, when the drug cut in and motion seemed to slow down.

Engel ran towards her admirer with open arms as if seeking protection. The big man's startled look as he began to open his own arms turned to shock when Engel's armored foot sank into his groin. He had only started to buckle at the knees when Engel spun past him and her back roundhouse kick smashed the nose of the second man.

Bruce spotted Eva vaulting over the door of the limo onto its bonnet while he slid down the rails of the steps and slapped a derm against the neck of one of the hostesses. As he turned towards the second, she caught his arm and flipped him over her shoulder, slamming him onto the oily tarmac with a shock of pain as he felt his right shoulder dislocate with a distinct pop.

Momentarily immobilized by shock, Bruce saw the third man manage to get his gun out and snap off a shot at Engel before Eva's kick landed on the back of his head. Interest in other fights vanished as his heightened senses picked up the foot flashing towards his head, just in time for him to roll over and grab a shapely ankle with his good hand. One good pull and a wriggling form landed on top of him, driving the air out of his lungs and sending another shock of pain through his injured shoulder.

Scrabbling frantically, Bruce grabbed a handful of blouse and pulled the girl towards him, butting her hard on the side of the head. When he drew back his head to butt her a second time, she ripped herself loose, leaving her blouse in his hand.

Bruce rolled again with a grunt of pain to escape an expected kick, but was surprised when the small body slumped over him, motionless. While he lay panting, he noticed Engel standing over him. "If you'd spend more time hitting the girl instead of undressing her, you'd maybe get somewhere." She grinned, evidently unfazed by the danger of taking on armed opponents.

Bruce shoved the unconscious girl off his chest, aware that one finely shaped breast had slipped from her bra.

"Stop ogling." Engel kicked him lightly on the hip. "We've got to move it, sharpish."

As he climbed awkwardly to his feet, Engel noted his loosely hanging arm and probed it with gentle fingers. "Don't be a baby," she taunted, "it's only dislocated. Well, this is certainly going to hurt you more than it hurts me," she warned cheerfully before she took hold of his arm with one hand and slammed an open-handed blow against his shoulder.

His eyes filled with tears as the shoulder clicked into place. "Fuckin' hell!" he muttered while he cautiously moved his injured arm. "You don't have to fuckin' enjoy it. A bit of sympathy would be nice now and again..." His complaint died off as he noticed for the first time blood coursing down Engel's calf. "Are you okay?"

Engel looked confused but, following his eyes,

saw her wound. "Och, just a wee scratch. To tell the truth, I was enjoying myself so much that I never even noticed it." She lifted her leg effortlessly to examine it in more detail. "Small caliber hole, straight through without hitting anything significant. Lucky shot, anyway."

Looking past Engel, Bruce could see the three brick shithouses lying together in a pool of blood, although it wasn't clear how much contribution each was making to the mess on the tarmac. In contrast, the other hostess was slumped on the steps, sleeping peacefully with an enigmatic smile on her lips.

Eva had opened the driver's door of the limo and was rooting about inside. Angela was bent over one of the hulks and looked about to take the gun from his holster. "Move well away from that!" Bruce shouted, causing her to jump. "Get Engel into the car and check her leg. Eva, is the car drivable?"

"Engine's running and seems to use more power for the air conditioning and refrigerator than it does to move this brute," came a muffled voice from the car. "Put it into gear and we're off."

Just as Engel was about to get into the car, one of the bulky figures made the mistake of grunting. In a flash, Engel was beside him, pumping a blurring series of short jabs into his face and neck. Bruce grabbed the collar of her loosely flapping blouse and pulled her back towards the car.

"That was the cunt that fuckin' shot me." She glared at him. "Or, at least, it might have been," she finished with a grin.

"Clean her up," Bruce ordered, pushing his bloodthirsty partner towards Angela and slamming the door. He then climbed into the passenger seat beside Eva. "Right, let's get our asses out of here. Head out past the hanger and onto the main road towards Bend. I guess it's probably left."

The small airstrip appeared to be deserted, but Bruce noticed a couple of faces peering out of the door of a hanger. In any case, nobody seemed to want to investigate the fracas at the plane. The glass dividing partition slid down and Angela leaned forward from the cavernous passenger compartment. "Here, take this when you get a chance." She handed him one of her special clearup pills.

Once on the road, Bruce sent an anonymous text message to the Bend police that reported an incident with firearms at the Smith's Rocks field, having noted this name on the side of the hanger. About five minutes later a police gyroplane shot over them, heading in the direction of the airfield, to be followed ten minutes later by two ambulances. Bruce directed

Eva to a car hire firm at the edge of town, where she dropped him off and continued on as agreed, following signs to the Mount Bachelor ski area.

Bruce quickly organized formalities to hire a grossly over-priced gas-turbo, four-wheel drive SUV from the completely automatic agency. Within fifteen minutes he was following Eva towards Mount Bachelor.

The road was clear as far as the ski-lodge car park, although the snow piled at the side of the road became steadily deeper, being about two meters high around the lodge. Strangely, the air temperature was fifteen C, but there were still a large number of cars in the park, and the lifts were running. He stopped briefly in front of the lodge while the others piled in, throwing luggage into the back. Eva sat with him in the front and set up a back-road route to Portland on the nav screen while Bruce drove off.

Their route wound through spectacular scenery, the volcanoes of the Cascades covered by thick caps of snow, which were melting rapidly in the summer heat to give rise to raging torrents of blue-white water. The group paid little attention to the view, however, concentrating on analysis of their present situation and options for the future.

Engel had already explained the events leading

Extremophile

up to their fight at the airfield to the other women. It had been clear to Bruce that their reception party was not from any Pharm when he saw the handgun, banned in the US since 2027. Eva had not known the background to this legislation, which followed the 666—6th June 2026—attacks on lawyers throughout the States. The bizarre web-based coalition of right-wing, left-wing, anarchist and religious groups called HAL, Hate All Lawyers, was apparently well known to law enforcement groups, but considered to be harmless cranks. Indeed, it was acknowledged, many of the agents who investigated it were openly sympathetic to its stated aims.

The excesses of the legal profession in profiting from tragedies reached its peak in the aftermath to the series of terrorist attacks on the US in the first few years of the century. Several companies were driven to bankruptcy by obscene compensation claims, not only on behalf of the victims but also, in many cases, on behalf of the perpetrators. A Washington Post article in February 2026 revealed that, on average, more than ninety-five percent of the payouts ended up in the hands of the lawyers involved.

June 6th...the designated *shoot a lawyer day*...exceeded everyone's expectations. Major conventions in Las Vegas and New York were bombed, causing over a thousand deaths in these two cases alone. A further six hundred lawyers' offices and courts were attacked, and there were more than two thousand individual shootings. The final death toll was over three thousand lawyers and fifteen hundred bystanders, including twenty-eight congressmen, fifteen senators, three Supreme Court judges and four state governors.

Despite the horrific carnage, there was little public sympathy for the legal profession and, indeed, further shootings of lawyers continued at a rate of about ten per day until emergency legislation was passed banning all handguns. This was enforceable only by setting draconian penalties for even possession of a gun, imposed not only on the individual involved but also on any organization encouraging or authorizing staff to carry guns.

The net result was that the US was not only effectively a gun-free society, but also had a percentage of lawyers in the population lower than that of any industrialized country. Few of the original planners of HAL were identified. It was suggested by many that they should be rewarded rather than punished. The resultant topic was a can of worms that no politician was willing to open.

Whether the aircrew was involved or not was

unclear, but the team agreed that there must be a leak somewhere in Angela's support team. The fact the incidents in Basel and Bend being both associated by Pharm-coordinated travel was too much of a coincidence. It wasn't clear how the altercations in Shinjuku and Narita fitted into this picture, but a mole in the organization made a link somehow more believable.

Bruce had also now interpreted the warning in his dreams. It was the attacker in Narita who, in the middle of the mayhem, attempted to make off with his bag. Angela had arranged both transportation from Hawaii to Bend and a lab to be prepped for her to work in. Anyone accessing this information would know that they were carrying something valuable with them and, if they knew Bruce as well as they seemed to, would be able to work out that he would be the likely courier. *Everything's so bloody clear with the benefit of hindsight.* He groaned aloud before summarizing his analysis to the others.

Angela looked increasingly upset while she listened to his explanation. She was a little reassured when Bruce emphasized that nobody could have expected this to happen, but agreed that they would avoid all further contacts with her sponsor until they got back to Glasgow.

The main discussion focused on the two options for getting back on commercial flights—either a circuitous route, which would be hard for the opposition to pick up, or a direct route that would get them home as quickly as possible. Using Bruce's palmtop, Eva listed possibilities starting from Portland, assuming that they could drive to the airport by midday. By far the fastest option was a supersonic flight to London at twelve fifteen, which would land just after midnight, local time.

"If we can catch that flight, I'd recommend that we go for it," Bruce proposed. "It's certain that your Network could pick up anything we go for because they must have a good idea where we are now. The best idea is to get out of the States before they can mobilize teams to intercept us. The idiots with the handguns will have screwed things up, because they will now have cops, and probably the FBI, chasing after whoever sent out that crowd. On the other hand, the cops might also be after us by now. They must be very keen to find out who took down those heavies, especially if any of them snuff it."

Bruce then had to stop an extended squabble between Eva and Engel about how life-threatening the various injuries that they had inflicted would be. Not only was it wasting time, Angela was getting visibly upset by their blow-by-blow reconstruction of events.

"Well, if nobody has a better suggestion, we'll go for it," Bruce decided, setting the cruise control for eighteen percent above the speed limit, knowing that the automatic detectors in Oregon generally give twenty percent leeway. "Eva, set up to buy four first class tickets, but initiate the purchase only when we hit the Portland city limits. What's our ETA?"

Eva checked the route computer. "Should be twenty to, plus or minus five minutes. Won't that be a bit too tight?"

"It's doable. Set up a route directly to international exec drop-off. We'll simply abandon the car there. Make the ticket booking for hand luggage only and give them our arrival details. We'll be able to complete formalities in the lounge. I'll just have to risk that we can get the samples through security." Angela gave him a worried look.

During the rest of the trip, Engel and Eva worked through a range of options to get their group from London to Glasgow. Even if Portland went smoothly, it was almost certain that they'd have some kind of reception committee at the far end of their trip. Angela proposed getting a Pharm heavy team tooled up to meet them, but Bruce was loath to trust anything from that source. Before a final plan could be worked out, they were approaching Portland.

Bruce was glad to see the airport. His adrenaline surge had worn off a long time ago and he was feeling increasingly wasted: tired, hungry and conscious of being disheveled and unshaven. They had done their best to tidy up and repair the damage caused by the Smith Rocks fracas. Nevertheless, despite having changed his oil-stained shirt en route, a struggle given the limited range of movement of his right arm, Bruce felt completely backwards— hedgedragged.

The SUV screeched up to the terminal building at a quarter to, and the occupants piled out, clutching bags. Bruce threw the car access card at a startled black porter, followed by a hundred-ec piece, and shouted, "Hertz!" *If his grin had been any wider, the top of his head would have fallen off.* Bruce rushed past the smiling man with his companions following closely behind.

A hostess was waiting at the door to guide them to a little buggy that set off into a tunnel marked *official access only*, which took them through a maze of tunnels to a small private lounge at the departure gate. All emigration formalities were completed at the lounge, and their hand luggage was run though a small multi-analyzer. Bruce stopped breathing while his bag went through and the presence of depleted uranium was clearly indicated under the warning list appearing on its small screen. The next bag cycled through and Bruce exhaled noisily when he realized that nobody was actually paying any attention to the screen. There was probably an audible warning of anything appearing in a defined forbidden substance list, but DU was clearly an exotic that wasn't included therein.

The same hostess then led them to the plane. They appeared to be the last to board; all other first class passengers were already seated and enjoying drinks. The first class cabin was in the nose of the plane, and about half of the thirty or so seats were occupied. Angela and Eva were seated at the front portside window with Bruce and Engel two rows farther back.

Bruce slumped into the massive seat and gratefully accepted a glass of champagne, which he knocked back in two inelegant gulps. Without a word, Engel offered him her orange juice, which he polished off equally rapidly.

How long has this day lasted since getting up in the Mito Plaza?

He wearily tried to calculate it, taking into

account the time zone changes. *Something like twenty-four hours so far,* he estimated. *I'm completely shagged out and we're heading straight for a tooled-up reception committee. Given that they've picked up our trace when I've tried my best to hide it, they can't possibly have missed us here.*

Despite his worries, exhaustion got the better of him and he drifted off to sleep.

Day 9 ...rain, Scottish rain

Engel shook Bruce awake as they were overflying Iceland, with about an hour of flight time to go. Bruce peered blearily out the window. It was about 11pm UK time, but a very low sun shone over the continuous cloud cover below. "What's up?" he mumbled. His injured shoulder was throbbing. He attempted to stretch, but the pain stopped him from lifting his right arm above chest height.

"Better get some food down your neck." Engel pushed buttons to set his chair to an upright position. As a little table swung over, she helped the hostess pass him a loaded tray. "I ordered for you," she explained. "And you'd better take this as well." She handed him a small blue capsule.

Too tired to object, he swallowed the offered drug, washing it down with a glassful of mineral water. The effect was little short of miraculous; his eyes opened wide as a jolt like ten double-espressos shot through his body, bringing him immediately wide awake. "Jesus fuckin' Christ, what the hell was that?" he asked in amazement.

"Something of Angela's. We've all had a shot. It should be good for forty-eight hours unless you take the counter before then."

Bruce would have enquired further if a deep rumble from his stomach hadn't reminded him that he was starving. He polished off the soup, salad, steak and chips, and mousse-au-chocolat, accompanied by a half dozen bread rolls and a bottle of red wine, uncertain if it was supposed to be breakfast, lunch, or dinner. At some point during the meal he noticed that Engel was again a redhead. Apparently she and Eva had both removed their hair dye in the toilet just after takeoff, causing some amusement for the hostesses. Bruce didn't dare enquire if all of Eva's hair was now its original color.

The edge taken off his hunger, he slowed down over a final cheese platter, accompanied by fruit and crackers. While he ate, Engel outlined the options that she had worked over together with Eva. They had set up a diversion that would get them off the plane. The main problem was what to do afterwards, getting back to Glasgow without being intercepted en route.

Extremophile

The obvious option was a shuttle directly to Glasgow Docklands, but this would certainly be covered by their opposition at both ends. In this case, their chances of getting through without a well-armed support team seemed minimal. Train or hire car from London were also possibilities, but again seemed to offer too much potential for interception. Best chance was thus a flight to another Scottish airport, with a taxi or hire car to Glasgow Uni.

Bruce interrupted, struggling to speak despite a mouth half full of brie. "Back up a minute. If we arrive at the back of midnight, we'll have about five or six hours to hang about for the first shuttle. If we hire a car we could be home by then."

Engel disagreed. "Too easy to pick up. If the bad guys have CCTV scans on all leaving traffic, they could identify us then hook in spot satellite surveillance and arrange to intercept us anywhere they wanted."

"Yeh, but it's night and look at the weather." He called up a chart. "It'll be pissing down rain all the way. The big road-trains run the motorway from midnight till five. Get in tight behind one of them and we'll be completely invisible."

Engel looked like she was going to bring up more objections, but stopped and stared absentmindedly at the roof for a few moments. "You know, you're not totally useless after all. That might just work if we can get to a car without being picked up. It's just a pity you can't fight," she threw over her shoulder as she walked forward to have a palaver with Eva.

Bruce thought of reminding her of the result of their first run-in together, but decided that now was not the time to tease his volatile partner. He noted that they were starting their descent, just leaving time for a coffee and a few chocolates.

Engel returned to her seat in time to prepare for landing. "Your idea is good, but a hire car would be too tricky. We'll steal one instead." She smiled at his look of surprise. "It's okay, one of the things that I do. I'll need your palmtop, though, there's some kit I need to download."

Bruce handed over the computer from the pouch on his belt and watched as Engel worked her way into a heavily shielded comm link, before downloading encrypted data from a secure site. Even using all the free number-crunching capacity available on the plane, decrypting the data and implementing the routines took until they had landed and taxied most of the way to their dock.

The plane had just stopped moving when a very

worried-looking hostess rushed up and told Engel that they should leave the plane first as the medi-team were waiting. Bruce looked confused but, following a wink from Engel, unbuckled and stood up without saying anything. When he stood up, he could see Angela walking up the aisle towards him, face ashen and leaning heavily on Eva. With a gasp, he pushed past Engel and put his arm round the tall woman, who was racked by bouts of trembling while sweat poured down her face. Concerned-looking hostesses guided them to the exit, but were careful to avoid any contact with the group.

Engel stepped forward to pick up their few items of luggage, handing Bruce his bag as he passed her. Emerging from the docking tunnel, a buggy with a driver in a full isolation suit awaited them in an otherwise empty corridor. As soon as they mounted, the buggy shot off into a tunnel labeled *no access* and, after a few twists and turns, into an alcove identified as *contagion control*, where an ambulance and two similarly suited figures waited.

The buggy drew to a stop and the two other medics approached. Bruce saw Engel do something with his palmtop before she tossed it to him. She then ripped open the neck of the driver's suit and slapped a dermal patch against his cheek. Simultaneously, Eva erupted towards the other two suits, kicking one in the chest while ripping the helmet off the second and slapping a derm on his neck. Together Engel and Eva descended on the figure that had fallen on its back and ripped the front of the suit open, revealing an incongruent black silk bra and knickers. The doctor's squirming body relaxed after Eva slapped a derm on her belly.

Bruce turned his attention back to Angela, seeing her lift a pill to her mouth with a shaking hand. After she swallowed, she relaxed against his shoulder with a sigh and closed her eyes.

"What the fuck was that all about?" he started to ask before Eva tugged at his elbow.

"Move it now, but keep a good hold of the prof. She'll be okay but'll be a bit shaky for the next little while. Follow Maria. I'll take the rear."

Bruce pulled the large woman from the buggy with his left hand and supported her in a fast walk behind Engel. About fifty meters along the ambulance access road, Engel turned left following signs for *maintenance*. After about another hundred meters she turned left again and dropped down a flight of steps towards staff parking. A moving walkway took them into a large hall where, for the first time, they could see other people moving about—most of them clad in overalls. Ignoring some suspicious glances, they transferred onto the walkway towards *VIP long-term parking* and, five minutes later, approached a gateway manned by a bored-looking guard.

Engel turned to Bruce and held out her hand. Wordlessly, he handed over his palmtop and watched Engel initiate some hackware before walking confidently towards the guard and flooring him with a kick to the side of the head. Before the startled man could get his breath, the knockout derm had taken him out of action.

The gate led into a massive underground garage, which appeared to be about half full. Engel led them past a couple of dozen cars before selecting an extremely expensive-looking gas-turbo limousine. "You drive, I'll hack," she told Bruce as the doors opened automatically.

Bruce followed the route indicated by Engel, which emerged into pouring rain two minutes later. Another two minutes brought them onto the motorway that, even at this late hour, was packed with heavy traffic. Ignoring the two express lanes restricted to private care, Bruce directed the limo into the space between two mammoth eight-unit road trains and set the autopilot.

Relaxing somewhat, he turned round to check on

Angela, who now looked almost back to normal. "That was a pretty slick move, Engel, but maybe you could tell me in advance when you're planning stunts like that."

"Sorry, Beast," Engel responded, sounding not in the least repentant. "I reckoned you needed as much beauty sleep as possible. After we had set up things, I somehow never got round to telling you. I started to, and then you came up with the car idea, so it's really all your own fault."

Bruce decided not to argue the logic of this last statement. "So, what was up with Angela?"

"Mutually incompatible accelerators, enhancers and blockers: guaranteed to cause a serious hypo," Angela answered. "The symptoms are very similar to the latest plague reported in China, so when I told the hostess that a couple of the people we met in Hong Kong looked a bit off-color, she added two and two to make five. One universal neutralizer has now taken care of the problem but knocked out my wake-up potion as well. I feel okay, but am starting to fade fast. A few hours of sleep and I'll be right as rain, though."

Engel offered her hands to him, palms upwards. "Here, help me get these off," indicating the small blades taped to her index fingers.

Thinking back, Bruce remembered how the girls

had ripped through the medics' isolation suits. "Smart girl," he commented absently while he pried the tape off, being very careful to avoid contact with the scalpel-sharp blades. As soon as he had finished, Engel twisted round to help strip the knives from Eva's fingers.

The rest of the trip to Glasgow was a complete anticlimax. Angela slept, snoring loudly, while the girls searched all possible sources for indications that they had been picked up. Bruce was left to monitor the autopilot, occasionally over-riding it to move in behind faster moving juggernauts. *How on earth did anyone ever drive manually in conditions like this? I can't see a bloody thing, which I hope means nobody else can see us.*

***

It was five thirty when they entered Glasgow, almost fully light but still raining heavily. Eva's retinal print got them through the unmanned entrance to the university staff garage. Bruce then asked Eva to wake Angela so she could authorize their entry into the secure area of Uni compound. The nuclear bioengineering department had a separate underground parking area with its own security scan. Angela over-rode the authorization request and they were admitted to the empty parking bay surrounding the NB access lift.

"Bloody hell, we made it." Bruce stepped out of the cab and stretched with a groan. Angela looked a bit grey and extremely tired when she staggered out and put her arm over his shoulder. By contrast, the two girls were in an ebullient mood and were chatting merrily while they unloaded luggage.

Bruce shouldered his bag, following Angela to the lift. The girls bounced in, Eva ordering the lift to the twenty-third floor. At this stop, she got out with the flat-pack taken from Bruce's bag, while the others went on up to the twenty-eighth, directly to Angela's suite.

Angela was walking like a zombie as Bruce directed her into her bedroom. "Straight to bed with you," he suggested.

"No way," she responded weakly. "A shower first. I stink."

She threw off the shirt she was wearing, *one of mine,* Bruce noticed absently, and almost toppled over as struggled to peel off the tube she was wearing under it.

Bruce slipped an arm round her waist to provide support and was rewarded by an armpit thrust against his nose when she staggered again with the dress halfway over her head. No doubt about it, very musky although really not unpleasant.

Engel crashed into the bedroom at that point. "Christ, I can't leave you alone for five minutes. Stop sniffing the poor woman and help her out of her clothes."

Angela even managed a little smile when she finally got the dress free and hurled it into a corner.

Engel then stripped off her own clothes, dropping them in a little pile on the thick carpet. "Take those through to our room and throw them in the cycler," she commanded. "Dump your own smelly stuff while you're at it, then you can give me a hand in the shower."

Bruce meekly did as he was told, taking the opportunity to rub his aching shoulder with some pain-killing cream. This allowed him free movement of his right arm, although it still felt very strange when he lifted it above shoulder height.

When he padded back to Angela's bathroom, the two women were already in the shower. Opening the door, Bruce saw that Engel was standing on her toes, pressed against the larger woman and reaching upwards to massage her temples. Bruce had plenty of space to stand behind the brunette when he closed the door and started to wash her hair.

After about five minutes, during which he had moved on to massage the knotted muscles of her neck and upper back, Angela mumbled. "Mmm... I could put up with a lot of this, but I'm going to keel over if I don't get into bed within seconds."

Engel hit the blow-dry cycle and they then led the half-dozing woman to the massive bed. Engel bent to tuck the black silk sheets around the sleeping professor, whose eyes had closed as soon as her head touched the pillow, then kissed her gently on the lips. She turned and met Bruce's raised eyebrows with a glare. "Just keep it shut," she growled, taking his hand and pulling him into the living room.

She pushed him roughly onto a sofa, dropped onto his knees and curled up as his arms automatically encircled her. "Well then, I guess that's it," she murmured into his chest. "Job's done, just collect the dosh and fuck off."

Bruce squeezed the small form gently, still surprised at how petite she was. As he stroked the back of her neck with his thumb, he realized that he had showered with two women and now had one of them sitting naked on his lap without his usual embarrassing erection. *Either sexual exhaustion or a side effect of the stimulant drug,* he guessed.

They were sitting in the same position when Eva

bounded into the room about ten minutes later. "Good Grief. Can't you folk cavort in the privacy of your bedroom rather than smooching in the buff in the living room?"

Engel refused to rise to the bait. Sitting up, she extended a hand to the tall blonde. "C'm'ere, give us a hug." She pulled Eva to kneel beside them on the couch. Bruce opened his arms to enclose the two embracing women and squeezed them against his chest as his head sank back with eyes closed.

The girls were whispering something that he couldn't quite catch. Ignoring this distraction, Bruce replayed the last few days. *I first encounter Engel on a Wednesday evening and met Angela and Eva on Thursday. By Friday we're already off to Switzerland and then arrived in Hong Kong on Saturday. Sunday and Monday we spent in Tokyo and then Tuesday night in Tokai. A double day on Wednesday because we crossed the international dateline to the USA and now it's Thursday again...only a week since I first saw this room. It's hard to believe.*

He looked over the two heads at *House of Stairs*, feeling that he could sympathize with the strange rolling lizards which made their way through the 3D illusion. *Could it be that the job is really now done? I go round the world in eight days and then it's back to the real world, contracting out of Hasliberg.* He examined

Escher's picture more closely. *No, that doesn't seem right. Get into something like this and there's no exit. If I leave one door, I enter another on the back face of the stairway.*

What had Engel called me? A big soft dod of shite or something similar. Well, the Valkyrie doesn't look much tougher at the present moment, nuzzling Eva's ear with a distinct trace of a tear in her eye. He crushed them both in a bear hug. "Hey Maria, don't you think we should let Blondie shower, she's really smelly."

That certainly cleared up the morose mood, he thought as the two outraged girls leapt up and attacked him from both sides. His duck under a slap from Eva took him straight into a kick from Engel, evidently pulled as it made contact as a mere hard nudge.

Engel smiled at him briefly, clearly glad for the excuse to escape from their clinch, stopping Eva from repeating her attack. "Don't bother with him, he's only a poor old crippled bastard who dotes on me and is jealous when I pay attention to anyone else. Apart from that, it's true, you really are smelly."

A flashing kick towards Engel's face was blocked by an armored elbow, producing the sound of a plank breaking.

"Ouch," the tall blonde exclaimed. "That hurt."

Engel was beside her immediately, putting an arm round her waist. "Sorry, I didn't mean it. It was just a reflex. I'll kiss it better, honest."

"Even if it's smelly?"

"Especially if it's smelly. Smelly bits are my specialty." Her free hand ran up Eva's thigh. "But, anyway, the idea of a shower isn't bad, is it?" She stood on tiptoe to nibble the taller woman's earlobe.

As Engel pushed Eva towards the smaller bedroom, she caught hold of Bruce's hand. "Come on, Beast, you can make yourself useful by washing our backs." The small redhead stared into his eyes with a pleading look that initially confused him. Then realization dawned, *Engel was afraid to be alone with Eva. Their relationship was getting too strong for her. Well, playing chaperone in the shower for a beautiful lesbian and an AC/DC nymphet, that's an offer I don't get every day. Or even twice in a lifetime.* He bounced to his feet. *Never refuse a temptation that may never come your way again.*

Bruce slipped into the shower after the two girls and started to rub suds on Eva's back while Engel got to work on her front. Somewhat later, as the small redhead dropped to her knees to move her ministrations lower down, the lithe blonde's breathing began to deepen and her body pressed against his. Feeling his growing reaction to the situation, he was able to conclude that neither exhaustion nor drugs could prevent arousal in such a situation.

After Eva's extended and extremely physical orgasm, during which her head had slammed several times against his injured shoulder, she pulled Engel to her feet and draped herself round the smaller woman. Bruce continued the back massage until Engel looked up. "Get your willy out of this poor girl's crack. It's my turn for the back wash."

Bruce meekly squeezed round behind Engel and started massaging her neck and shoulders while he looked over her head directly into Eva's eyes. The tall blond who was, at that moment, rubbing soap onto Engel's breasts, smiled mischievously at him. Locking his eyes, she started a running commentary in a deep whisper. "Now I'm rubbing Maria's hard nipples, nice. My left hand now slips down her side and strokes the inside of her thigh." He could feel his diminutive partner shiver in response.

"Now you need to take a hold of her right nipple," she instructed, glancing quickly down to check that he was doing what he was told. "And now squeeze it, hard." She stared into his eyes again. "I'm now rubbing her clit, slipping my fingers inside her," she informed him while a small, tight buttocks began to squirm against his groin.

A surprised "Ah!" broke the spell. Bruce glanced down to see that Engel had clenched her teeth on one of the nipples poking at head height in front of her. Without thought, he took Eva's other nipple between the thumb and forefinger of his free hand. *Although Eva had much larger breasts, the hard nipples of both women seem to be the same size.*

Well, Bruce thought as the movements of the tangled bodies began to get more frenzied, *I'll be lucky to last twenty seconds here.* He actually managed about thirty.

After some rather intimate cleaning up, Eva left the shower to use the toilet while Bruce and Engel laser-shaved. They emerged after the blow dry and entered the bedroom to find Eva already sitting on the bed, offering them a couple of green capsules.

"It's the counter for Angela's super-stimulant," she explained. "It'll knock you out for about twenty-four hours, but we've nothing else critical to do at present, and we're better getting it over and done with." She moved to the far left side of the bed and patted the space beside her. "Come on, now...unless you fancy anything else beforehand." She raised an eyebrow quizzically.

"I could manage another couple of rounds, but the poor old Beast is totally shagged," Engel replied as she slipped between the sheets and took one of the offered pills. "Get in," she commanded, holding the sheets for him and passing over one of the capsules. "And don't get your hopes up. You've only got one shag left in you and it's the only thing holding you together."

The two girls swallowed the drug together and were sleeping in each other's arms within minutes. Bruce held the capsule while he watched the sleeping forms. It seemed weird somehow, like some kind on suicide pact. He drew the sheets around the girls carefully and simply lay watching them for a quarter of an hour.

Now we really are safe and sound. Nobody can possibly touch us here. How could they? He struggled to think of any credible threat before finally, with a mental shrug, he knocked back the pill and drifted into dreamless slumber.

Day 10 ...ticking like a time-bomb

Bruce slowly dragged himself awake, feeling more and more pains as he approached full consciousness. His head throbbed from the various inadvisable combinations of drugs that he had used over the past couple of days. His shoulder hurt, which was not helped by Engel, who had turned in her sleep and was now snoring against his armpit. His ribs ached and a burning sensation came from his side. Lifting the sheet, he peeled off sealant to look at the scar from the knife wound. Although a livid red, it looked reasonably healthy, the hot feeling probably resulting from the accelerated healing process. To complete his damage assessment, he rubbed his ear, noting the ridge from uneven sealing of the wound. *This kind of mutilation could be easily corrected with a bit of minor surgery, but it's probably not worth the bother.*

He slipped out from under Engel, noticing that

Eva was spooned against her back. Stepping out of bed he attempted to stretch, but groaned at the shock of pain when he tried to lift his right arm above chest height. He slumped into the bathroom and conducted a further inspection in front of the mirror: bruised knuckles, road-rash scrapes on his elbows and a chipped front tooth. He couldn't even remember the exact causes of these injuries. *However,* he acknowledged with a shrug, *it could certainly have been much worse.*

To hell with it. Shit, shower and shave and I'll feel much better. Rather to his surprise, he did indeed feel much better after his ablutions and even felt emboldened enough to put on judo trousers, with the thought of doing some gentle stretching exercises to try to loosen up his shoulder.

He entered the living room and was surprised to see Angela at the dining table, clad in a dark blue tube and studying some data presented by her palmtop, coffee cup in hand. The smell of coffee caused his stomach to growl, and he realized that he was famished.

Angela lifted her head to inspect him, beaming with good health. "Good morning, Bruce, you're looking very spruce on this fine morning."

Her observation about the morning certainly doesn't

reflect the weather. Rain lashed against the window and obscured the view over the university. "You're looking pretty good yourself. How're you feeling?"

"Never been better." She stood and stretched, straining the fabric over her breasts almost to the bursting point and causing the hem to ride up almost to her groin, revealing a flash of black pubes. She took his hand and bent forward to peck him on the cheek. "But you must be hungry, surely."

"Ah could eat a scabby-heided wean...as they say locally."

"I'm afraid weans, scabby-heided or otherwise, aren't on the menu, but I'll see what I can find." She smiled and stepped into the kitchen to prepare breakfast for him, starting with a mug of coffee and large glasses of milk and grapefruit juice. Steak, bacon, scrambled eggs, potato scones, black pudding and square sausage supported by fresh whole-meal bread sufficed to change his feeling of hunger to one of being stuffed to the gills.

Bruce sat back in his chair and patted his stomach contentedly. "That's what I call breakfast, or is it lunch?" realizing that he had no idea of how long he had been asleep.

"Call it brunch. You've been out for a bit more than twenty-four hours." A clock appeared in the corner of the display window, indicating that it was ten thirty-two. "The good news, though, is that the samples are en route from Sellafield and should be here sometime this afternoon."

"You're kidding. I wouldn't have expected them for at least a week. How on earth did they get here so quickly?"

"There's an accompanying e from Doctor Toyota." She threw the text on the window, blanking out the dismal rain.

Bruce, you are a truly jammy bastard. I arrived in Rokkasho two hours before a heavy lifter was leaving for BNF. It should have been away days ago, but was held up because of the foon. I knew you had pals above the clouds, but I didn't think they could influence the weather!

All the very best from stormy Japan,

Ryu

PS you owe me at least twenty pints of heavy for this malarkey.

PPS give that wee redhead a good shagging from me, she's a proper stoter.

PPPS if you don't want her, give her my address and post her off to Japan.

PPPPS if she doesn't like Japan, I'll move to Ireland — the Guinness will make up for the fact that they serve only dead fish.

"I assume all the PSs mean something to you," she said, raising a quizzical eyebrow.

"Ryu...well, he really is salt of the earth. I bet it wasn't trivial getting our package onto that flight. He's a brilliant guy. Tendency to waffle a bit though."

"I think he's really cute," Engel announced, causing Bruce to twist round in surprise, a move that reminded him of his bruised shoulder. "In fact, he also clearly has very good taste and I wonder if I shouldn't take up his offer, now that this contract is finished."

"Let's not count our chickens just yet," Angela said. "We haven't looked at any of the samples yet. Even if everything goes perfectly, you'll have to wait for a couple of weeks at least until we have enough prion extract. In any case, I bet you could do with some breakfast."

Engel was wearing the jacket that belonged to Bruce's judo trousers, which was much too large for her and made her look like some kind of abandoned waif. As she stood indecisively, Eva stepped up silently behind her, lifted the back of her jacket and slapped her bottom.

As the naked blonde moved back to defend herself from the flurry of blows aimed in her direction, Bruce registered that indeed all dye was now gone and Eva was again a true blonde. *Did I really miss that in the shower last night?*

The fight moved into the bedroom and seemed again to have transformed itself into another a tickling match.

Bruce and Angela were going over the list of individual samples in the different containers when the girls re-emerged, arm-in-arm in matching plain white T-shirts.

"I'll get breakfast," Eva announced, moving into the kitchen and starting to prepare stacks of buttermilk pancakes with bacon and eggs.

Bruce's overfilled stomach turned over as he watched the girls pour maple syrup over the pancake stacks and start carving into them with gusto. It might taste fine, but watching someone eat bacon covered by the mixture of egg yolk and syrup was disgusting.

After breakfast, Engel and Eva went directly into the dojo for a training session. *How do they do it?* Bruce was sure that he would throw up if he even walked quickly after eating as much as those two girls had packed away.

When the procedures for the sub-sample handling were worked out, Angela suggested that she have a look at his injuries. "I'm not a medical doctor," she admitted, "but I've done a fair bit of first aid training in my time."

The tall professor took his hand and led him towards the dojo. She completely ignored the girls, who had stripped off and were involved in some kind of floor exercise in which they were wriggling over the mats, trying to immobilize each other using joint locks. Bruce was considerably distracted by the thrashing, sweat-soaked limbs, but Angela pulled him to the far corner of the room, where a massage table stood at the end of the row of exercise machines.

"Drop your trousers and hop onto the table," she ordered, sounding more like a medical doctor than any he had encountered to date. He decided it was pointless to inform her that he didn't remember any wounds below the waist and simply did as he was told.

Lying first on his front, he felt Angela work systematically down his body, probing gently with professional fingers, applying creams and dermal patches and sometimes simply massaging areas of tense muscles. *A woman with hands to die for*. The pain eased out of his shoulder and he could feel his entire body slump with relaxation.

He turned over on her command and she worked down his front, spending a lot of time on his stab wound. She finished working down his legs, noting that he probably had one or two broken bones in his right foot. "Maybe caused by kicking something incorrectly," she guessed.

He remembered a strange sensation when kicking one of the kids in Narita, but decided that an explanation was not required.

"Well," she concluded, "you should now be fit for some mild exercise to loosen up. Some kata would probably be a good idea, but I wouldn't recommend iaido for a couple of days, until your shoulder heals a bit."

Without further ado, she peeled off her dress and walked naked onto the mat where she started some deep breathing exercises that evolved slowly into the graceful moves of Tai Chi. To Bruce, who associated Tai Chi with small, wizened Chinese men wearing pajamas, this was a bit of a revelation. He restricted himself to some gentle work on his joints so that he could watch the tall, large-breasted, wide-hipped woman slide sinuously through the formalized, slow-motion sequence that was a hybrid between dance and Kung-fu kata.

Bruce found himself holding his breath while she worked through some moves that involved slow motion kicks. Standing on one leg, her foot slowly and smoothly cut upwards to head height, held for a moment that seemed to completely defy gravity, then smoothly returned to the floor so that the technique could be repeated on the other side.

A sweaty arm slid round his waist, causing him to twitch in surprise. "You know, she's pretty good," Engel whispered. "...for an old, fat woman, that is." She grunted gently when she was elbowed in the ribs by Eva, who was standing in her other arm. "We're off for a shower. You can either join us or just stay ogling the old dear."

Bruce thought seriously about the offer, but remained behind when the girls padded out of the dojo. *What a contract. I seem to have spent more time in the shower than working. In fact, as I think about it, most of the rest of the time was eating, sleeping, or travelling. Although, I shouldn't forget the short, sharp bouts of getting beat-up.* He ran a finger along the scar in his side.

When Angela finished, her breathing was completely regular but she was bathed in sweat from head to toe. "Time for another shower." She smiled and took him by the hand.

Here we go again. Yet another shower.

She led him past her own bedroom, where the girls were noisily squabbling about something, towards the room he shared with Engel. During the shower, he restricted himself to massaging Angela's shoulders and back, lingering on her buttocks, an experience that was evidently pleasurable to both parties.

Angela returned to her own room to dress, while Bruce pulled on shorts and a light cotton shirt, slipping his feet into sandals. *There must be someone who cleans up this flat. I wonder what they make of the diverse items of clothing found scattered about the place.*

In the living room, the girls were sitting together on a sofa with the contents of several pharm pouches spread out in front of them. In addition to replacing material used during their trip, they were scathingly criticizing each other's choice of an optimum set. Bruce decided not to add his own pouch, an item he had been very proud of a mere week ago. *I should definitely get Angela to suggest some additions. She seems to have access to stuff I haven't even heard of...and gets it for free.* This thought warmed his Scottish heart.

The professor was sitting at the dining table, munching a large cheese sandwich. "I had breakfast ages ago," she explained after washing down a mouthful of food with a slurp of pale ale, directly from the bottle. "It's self-service." She pointed an elbow at the kitchen area.

Bruce helped himself to a bottle of Guinness,

which he poured carefully into a large glass. "How about the Gruesome Twosome, you pair want anything?"

"The cheese sandwich looks pretty good to me...and a glass of white wine," Engel responded. "And the same for my chubby friend," she added, catching Eva in a two-armed hug to prevent retaliation to this unfair jibe.

"And another beer for me," Angela added.

Demoted from back-washer to kitchen skivvy. Bruce shrugged, turning to collect the ordered drinks. While he prepared the sandwiches, he wondered if breakfast was long enough ago that he could have something to eat. He surreptitiously pinched the roll of fat at his waist. *No way.*

After finishing her lunch, Angela disappeared into her room and was soon followed by Eva. The pair reappeared a little later, wearing their labcoats. "Time for work. You two want to come along?"

Bruce jumped to his feet, grateful for something definite to do, dragging along an obviously reluctant Engel. He briefly popped into his bedroom to pick up his shoulder bag, which now again contained his analytical kit, together with the palmtop that slipped into the pouch on his belt.

The lift took them down to the twenty-third

floor, where Angela led the way along a corridor and through an airlock into a gleaming high tech lab that seemed to be completely automated. "The samples from Rokkasho should be here in about an hour," she reported. "Now we need to set up the protocols for the sub-sample work-ups."

Bruce and Engel sat on high stools while the other two women set up the handling programs for the automatic analysis and culturing systems. Bruce was fascinated. Even though he understood only a fraction of the detail of what was going on, he could follow most of the principles of the processes involved. Engel, however, was evidently bored and continually tried to drag Bruce into a discussion of their possible future after this work was completed, clearly something uppermost on her mind. Bruce's monosyllabic responses were not helping to improve her temper.

Just before Engel reached her breaking point, the sample containers from Sellafield arrived and were transported directly to the lab via an internal remote handling system. When extracted from the coolbox transport units, the cylindrical sample containers looked very small. Angela started to direct the waldos that would cycle them into a shielded glove box, but Bruce stepped forward to stop her.

"Call me a big, paranoid, old Hector, but could I check the sealing?" Catching Engel's quizzical look, he added for her benefit, "You break into cars and beat-up people. This is what I do."

Pulling the laptop from his bag, he hooked it up to a pencil-sized laser ablation/analysis unit and interfaced the micro-computer with the lab mainframe. Moving the probe around the seal, Bruce threw up an execsumm on a wall screen.

"Fuck, fuck, fuck," he mumbled while he scanned the results. Without further explanation, he moved onto the next sample container and repeated the process.

After he had checked all six containers, he turned to the mystified women. "They've all been opened and resealed."

"That's not supposed to be possible," Angela said with a frown. "These are approved transport containers for GM organisms. You can't open them without it being obvious from the tags."

"Actually, you aren't supposed to be able to open them surreptitiously without setting off the UV burster that sterilizes the contents. I don't know of any case where that's been done. However, with the right hackware, you can open them and then reseal with cloned tags as long as you're prepared to sacrifice the contents. This is what I think must have been done here."

"How can you possibly know that?" Angela enquired skeptically. "You haven't even opened one yet."

"I logged the C-isotope ratio of the DLC we used to seal the containers. You can see that on the bottom plot." He pointed at the screen. "Look at the sealing from all the containers. The C-12/13 ratios are identical, but different from my logged value."

"Instrument drift or some other kind of systematic error?"

"Extremely unlikely...almost impossible, I'd say. We could test for that anyway. Could you get me the flat-pack that I used for the filter samples?"

Eva rushed off and returned a couple of minutes later with the still unopened container. Bruce scanned it and projected the results beside the others. The isotope ratio was identical to that logged in Fukushima.

The three women hit him with a barrage of questions, but he ignored them all while he set up a search program. The results came up almost instantaneously.

"Okay, shut it, Engel. I don't know where the containers were opened, but I know where they were resealed and that's Sellafield. If you check the screen you'll see that I now have the isotope ratio of the diamond sealant used by BNF and it's identical to that on the containers."

"Maybe they just added a second coating, without opening the containers," Angela suggested, clearly unwilling to write off the samples.

"Nope, that doesn't work either. Look at the depth profile at the joint. It's constant all the way through. Some strange signature right at the depleted uranium interface though." He expanded the display to include the full heavy element mass spec.

"Fuckin' shit. Get out of here," he shouted, hustling the women towards the door. Torn between his laptop and the flatpack, he grabbed the latter with a sigh.

Bruce regarded it as an indication of what they had been through together that all three women moved as directed without any questions. Once in the corridor, he shouted an order to Angela. "Lead us out of the building as fast as possible." She immediately rushed towards a goods lift that opened at their approach.

"Basement!" Angela ordered and turned to Bruce for explanation as the lift dropped downwards.

"As you know, I'm completely paranoid and

probably completely wrong here. All the same, the signature of the bottom level of the sealant registered isotopically-pure plutonium 239. Maybe nothing, but I'd like to handle that container remotely..." The lift door opened and he led them out. "...from a distance of at least a kilometer."

"We can get to the carpark this way." Angela pointed. "But if you're suggesting what I think, then you're—"

Before she could complete the sentence, a deafening crash was accompanied by a shock wave that knocked them off their feet and threw the corridor into complete blackness.

Seconds later, emergency lighting kicked in and their eyes gradually adjusted to the lower levels of illumination. The reinforced concrete ceiling was cracked above them and, farther towards the exit, had partially collapsed. Water was pouring from a burst pipe behind them and, within the damaged building, something was burning, which was filling the corridor with acrid smoke.

Bruce pulled himself to his feet and propelled the dazed professor in front of him. "Come on, we've got to get out now. Move it."

Eva passed the staggering couple to lead the way, while Engel dropped back to help Bruce with

Angela. At the point where the ceiling had collapsed, they had to squeeze in darkness through the loose rubble on their stomachs, a narrow opening that required physical force to drive Angela through.

Eva had almost reached the door marked *carpark* when it burst open and she was confronted by a startled man holding a handgun. Stopping in place, he fell into classic marksman pose and shot the tall blonde full in the face.

Bruce stopped in shock and was hardly aware of the small form that shot past him in a dive, which took it over the falling body and straight into the gunman. As the man fell backwards, he hit someone else who was attempting to follow, but Bruce lost track of the action as Angela dropped to the side of the fallen girl.

Although grey with shock, the professor checked the horrifically smashed face of the girl in a strangely detached manner. "Back to the lift, there's a big first-aid kit somewhere near it. Get it fast," she commanded in a shaking voice, her tear-streaked face in weird contrast to her cool manner.

Bruce turned and sprinted along the tunnel, throwing himself recklessly through the roof-fall zone. He was panting heavily, choking on smoke, when he ripped the large red box from the wall by the lift and turned to race back, carrying its unwieldy bulk clutched to his chest. He was running so hard that he felt about to vomit, but didn't dare allow himself such a luxury.

A large block fell on his back while he pushed the first-aid kit though the collapse zone, but he ignored the pain completely and continued to crawl after it. Reaching Angela, he opened the box in front of her, trying not to look at the blood-soaked mess that had been Eva's beautiful face.

"You're going to have to help me now, lad," Angela instructed, her voice calm although her face looked more haggard than before, almost as if her full seventy-five years had suddenly caught up with her. "Lift her head a bit while I wrap this membrane round it."

Bruce did as instructed, aware of an awful gurgling sound from the wrecked throat while warm gore soaked his hands. Angela very carefully wrapped a protective membrane over the girl's entire head and then attached some kind of auto-respirator over what was left of her mouth and nose. After applying a couple of derms onto the side of her neck and an instrument package to Eva's chest, Angela sank back onto her heels. "Let's get moving," she commanded. "Here, this might help." She offered him a small pill before she slapped a derm on her own neck. "Tranquillizer," she answered his unspoken question. "I'm using an enhancer so that I can carry Eva. You need to clear a way for us out of here."

Bruce refused the pill, instead drawing together all his inner discipline to calm down his panicked breathing and shaking hands. At that moment Engel slid back through the carpark door, one hand and both feet bloody. Somebody else's blood, Bruce guessed from the way she moved. "Eva's in a really bad way," he explained briefly. "We need to get her out of here sharpish."

Engel's eyes widened as she caught sight of the blood-soaked body. Without comment, she lifted the gun lying beside the man crumpled in the doorway. His eyes flickered when she grabbed his hair and lifted his head. "Bastard! They're not going to rebuild you, you cunt!" He had just time for a momentary look of panic before Engel shot him between the eyes.

Without looking backwards, Engel led the way into the carpark. Bruce heard Angela's back crack as she carefully lifted the motionless body. Just then, Bruce noticed the flat-pack lying against the wall, where he must have dropped it when the shooting occurred. He lifted the heavy package and preceded Angela through the door.

The sound of a second shot echoing around the garage caused him to start, but he saw immediately that Engel had executed another large man who had been sprawled on the floor. She was now striding purposefully towards a very large black woman who was slumped halfway out of the door of a white electromobile. Superfluously, a siren was wailing and red lights flashed at the parking entrance. In the distance, some figures could be seen rushing about, but nobody appeared to be paying any attention to their corner of the basement.

A scream of pain brought his attention back to the car as Engel hauled the woman out of the car by her hair. By their appearance, Bruce guessed that both her arms were broken. The scream turned to a gurgle as Engel shoved the barrel of the gun into her mouth. The small killer hesitated in a sadistic manner to allow the black woman a moment of terror before the back of her head was blown off.

Bruce stepped over the fresh corpse and threw the flat-pack onto the front passenger seat. "Get this fuckin' thing going," he commanded while he opened the back door and helped Angela ease the body of the tall girl onto the back seat. As Angela knelt on the floor by the back seat to check the vital signs monitor, Bruce slammed the door closed and ran round to the passenger door.

Immediately he jumped in, the car moved forward, heading for the flashing lights. "Where to?" Engel asked in a quiet voice, looking lost behind the driver's console.

"Anywhere outside," Bruce responded grimly. "If you can get to the city central bypass tunnel, head west." He scrabbled with the nav system and finally managed to throw up a route onto the screen.

Once out of the NB parking, the rest of the warren of underground parking and service tunnels was in chaos. People, on foot and driving, were trying to evacuate while emergency services were trying to get in.

"Should we swap this for an ambulance?" Bruce turned to ask Angela. He was shocked as he caught her eyes and saw the look of pain and the tears coursing down her cheeks.

"Don't bother, just get clear," Angela answered in a voice that shook but was strangely distinct. "Have we got secure comms?" she added. "This has gone much too far."

Bruce handed over the palmtop from his belt pouch and watched while Angela logged onto a hyper-secure link, which blanked out her head in a sphere of holographic black light and covered her conversation with the total silence of anti-sound. After a couple of minutes, the sphere vanished for a second as Angela looked up at the route on their screen, but immediately rematerialized before Bruce could ask any questions.

They fought their way out of the Uni complex, eventually emerging into grey daylight and heavy rain. Even with the limited visibility, the change to the skyline was noticeable—at least the top ten stories of the NB tower were gone and most of the rest was engulfed in flame. Several of the surrounding buildings, which included the Hilton, were also damaged. The first emergency service aircraft were now arriving, dopplering overhead towards the disaster area.

They were already in the bypass tunnel, moving quickly through light traffic, when Angela finally emerged. Now there was an additional grim aspect to her appearance. "Head for Dumbarton, a medical veetol will pick us up there." The palmtop transmitted the route to the car's nav system.

"Can we depend on anything from your Pharm? It's dead certain now that the leak has got to be there. All our problems arose whenever anything was handled by your team," Bruce objected.

"Yes, I know." She sighed. "But now I've gone

over all my usual contacts, directly to the president."

Despite the seriousness of their position, Bruce could not help being impressed by this throwaway line. Presidents of major multinationals were more powerful than national presidents, prime ministers and other political figures. He had never before met anyone who had seen one of these legendary figures in real life, much less spoken to one.

"This just shouldn't have happened," Angela continued absently. "You know, the multi-nats are very like the Mafia families used to be. They're always fighting in-house and with each other, but with certain rules. Mafia hits were never carried out in churches. The Pharms don't hit production or R&D facilities. Nuking a research lab in a Uni is doubly taboo. We just keep our heads down and get Eva some help. It's a scrap between the big boys now."

"But our big problem is the mole in your Pharm who—"

"Was a problem," she interjected. "Our incidents are enough to build up an unambiguous profile of the mole. A certain director of internal security services has just had a heart attack...or at least will have one, after an interrogation session that I have been assured will be long and excruciatingly painful. A group of her underlings are being checked out. Some will be demoted and any with direct involvement will end up in an unfortunate plane crash."

She sighed again and closed her eyes, continuing quietly. "There seem to be clear links to the governments of India and a couple of richer African countries, supported by one of our major fine chemical competitors. Once these links are confirmed, punitive retaliation will be initiated."

As if exhausted, she turned to the form beside her and started mumbling something into the ear of the unconscious girl.

Bruce turned to Engel, who was driving manually at the maximum speed possible with white-lipped concentration. "ETA?" he asked.

Rain now lashed against the windscreen as they left the tunnels. "We should be at..." she peered at the screen, "...Levengrove park in about ten, twelve minutes."

They drove the rest of the way in silence, Bruce peering through the rain at the various abandoned buildings in the Clyde flood plain. He recognized the island of Dumbarton Castle, looming out of the murk just before a raised highway passed over the levees surrounding the center of the town. Crossing the River Leven, they turned left up a hill to a car-park outside the gates of a rundown public garden.

Seconds after they drew to a halt, the car rocked in the downdraft of air as a heavy-duty veetol landed beside them in a blast of spray. A cargo ramp dropped immediately onto the wet tarmac and a half-dozen white-clad figures poured out. Bruce laid a restraining hand on Engel's arm, as she seemed ready to move into attack mode. "These are our guys," he reassured her loudly. "I hope," he muttered under his breath.

One of the medics was pushing a trolley covered by a transparent hood. When this hood was pulled back, Angela opened the rear door and helped two seriously large nurses move Eva's body onto the cart. Engel and Bruce emerged from the car, surprised to be confronted by concerned medics. Realizing that this was due to the fact that both of them were covered by significant quantities of dried blood, Bruce waved them back. "We're okay. Just do something for the girl on the stretcher."

Within seconds, which was nevertheless long enough to get everyone soaking wet, the party was on the plane and the ramp was closing. The trolley locked into an operating table structure and, by the time they took off, two doctors were already cutting the membrane off Eva's wrecked face.

Bruce felt Engel stiffen when she saw the full

extent of the damage to the blonde's head for the first time. Bruce put his arm round her small shoulders and led her to a bench out of the way of the bustling medics. He sat and pulled her onto his lap, crushing her against his chest. Between sobs that were wracking her diminutive body, Bruce could make out whispered curses and promises of the exquisite tortures she was going to inflict on all those responsible.

About a quarter of an hour later, Angela dragged herself over to join them and slipped under Bruce's offered arm. "She'll live, but she's in a very bad way. We don't know yet if there's any brain damage and one eye's really messed up. As for the rest, it's a really big rebuilding job." She pushed her head against Bruce's shoulder and began to cry.

Later, after her crying fit had passed, Angela stood up and wordlessly set off towards the toilet at the back of the cabin. When she closed the door, Bruce stroked Engel's head. "Angela's taking it really badly. Do you think we should try to get in contact with Eva's family or next of kin? It might help to spread the load."

Bleary blue eyes looked into his. "Angela is Eva's next of kin."

Confused, Bruce spluttered. "What? Is she an

orphan or something?"

"Don't be daft," she responded quietly as her eyes closed and she pressed her head against his chest. "Eva's Angela's daughter."

This revelation was the final shock for his already shaken system. "That can't be...I thought they were... You said they were..." he babbled.

"Just don't think about it. It was just a little game they played. As well, it helped to divert attention from a relationship between a boffin and a post doc that could have seemed too close. Eva told me ages ago."

Bruce was still trying to reorder his confused thoughts when Angela returned, looking a lot better, although still very drained. Silently he pulled her to him and crushed the two women together as they wrapped arms round each other.

Just under an hour later the veetol landed at a private hospital in Cornwall, and the stretcher, now enclosed in a cocoon of tubes and wires, was wheeled off first, surrounded by a phalanx of medics.

When Bruce rose to follow, he stubbed his toe and looked down to see the blood-encrusted flat-pack lying against his feet. Silently, he handed it to Angela, who crushed it to her chest while Engel steered her out of the plane.

Ian Mckinley

Epilogue ...Jesus Christ, I'm nearly forty

Bruce stood in front of the mirror, lit by the harsh early-morning July sunlight. He pinched a handful of love handle and sighed. *Well, it may be flab, but at least it's brown flab. A hairy beast, indeed*, he acknowledged, *and going grey to boot.* Head, chest and pubes were getting streaked with white. *No bloody wonder, considering what I've been through in the last while.*

A slap to his buttocks shocked him out of his reverie. "Stop staring at yourself, you sad old bugger. If you weren't so short-sighted due to self-abuse, you'd realize what a sorry fuckin' sight you are."

Engel was wearing only a microscopic tanga, her bronzed, tight little body a picture of health. As usual, she had Eva in tow, the tall blonde wearing a g-string that was, if anything, even skimpier. Eva was a lighter brown color and covered with freckles, but also looked in tremendous form.

Only when he looked closely could Bruce detect a strangeness of the taller girl's facial expressions, a discontinuity of skin texture between the upper and lower portions of her cheeks and maybe pick up a twitch as she spoke. Apparently the vision of her left eye was improving daily although, so far, black and white only.

After a week of intensive care in Cornwall, they had moved to a specialist clinic outside Geneva. In this case it was a door-to-door transportation service by exec veetol. The focus in Switzerland included top-end cosmetic rebuilding and the first stage was completed within a fortnight, with reconstruction concentrating on use of artificial materials. Samples of her skin, bone, teeth, nerve and other connective tissues were now being cultured and would be used for the second rebuilding phase scheduled for early August.

In the interim, the team plus private doctors and physiotherapists were now based at a Pharm marine biology research facility in Bermuda. Angela had a full extremophile lab set up to her specifications and had already started work on the samples from Bruce's flatpack. Although not immortal, Angela confirmed that they were further developed than the lab cultures she had been working on back in Glasgow and had high hopes that they could be forced to evolve into something useful within a year or two.

Engel flashed up a kick, which stopped exactly in contact with his Adam's apple. "Stop daydreaming, it's time for you to get your usual early-morning kicking. Get your flabby body into some kit and move your arse downstairs. The prof is there already."

With a feeling of foreboding, Bruce pulled on the proffered judo kit and slowly wandered after the girls. Engel was clearly getting bored and, as a result, their workout sessions were getting increasingly rough. *If she doesn't get something to distract her soon, I'm going to end up with serious injuries.*

To his surprise, the beautiful dojo was empty when he entered. He walked to the full-length window looking out over the partially drowned town of Hamilton. Bermuda had been a loser in the climate change stakes: the total area of the island above storm-surge high water being half of what it was at the end of the twentieth century. On the other hand, it was out of the path of the main hurricane alley, which ran through the southern Caribbean, the Gulf of Mexico and southeastern US, rendering many West Indian islands uninhabitable and destroying most of Florida.

Also on the positive side, Bermuda was a long-established e-commerce center with particularly strong links to Switzerland. Over a time when its population had been reduced by sixty percent, its GNP had increased five-fold. *A fine place to live if you were very rich and had invested in property on the top of hills.*

He turned as the three women entered, the girls still in tangas and Angela in her usual tube and labcoat. "Well, Bruce." The tall professor was back to her dominating original form. "The girls want to plan what we're going to do over the next few months. Your contracts have been successfully completed and there's nothing special for you to do here." She looked at Engel, who squirmed uncomfortably.

"With your bonuses, you're both well off and we'll honor the rest of our bargain, if and when I ever manage to get a working extract. Priority, of course, is Eva as I'm sure it would greatly help her recuperation."

Engel squeezed the taller girl protectively.

"The question is whether it would be worth trying to sample another site, to increase our chances. The girls want to go ahead with it as soon as Eva has undergone the next session of surgery. But I think that this would only work if you were prepared to coordinate things."

"Not that we really need you," Engel interrupted. "But we reckon it's better to use the useless bugger we know than try to train up somebody new."

"In any case," Angela continued, "the conditions and bonus on completion of a successful sampling run would be the same as before."

"Don't worry about that," Engel interjected again. "We'd do it for nothing, just for Eva's sake. Wouldn't we?" She glared in Bruce's direction, daring him to contradict her.

"Well, of course I'd do anything for your lovely daughter...or even for the wee, pain-in-the-arse redhead." He easily dodged a slow kick to his groin. "I've actually been thinking about Chernobyl over the last week or so. I think it may actually be doable."

"Excellent." Engel beamed. "We've got our extremophile sampling team back on the road. The only problem is that the Beast can't fight, so we're going to have to get him into shape fast."

Angela walked to the corner of the mat and leaned back with a smile while the two girls prowled towards their prey, making a point of waiting until he gulped down a pill. Nobody knew that she had swapped Bruce's usual SLOWDOWN for a new souped-up, multi-enhancement drug that she had offered to test.

This was really going to be fun to watch.

About the Author

Ian is a Scot living in Switzerland, working in the rather esoteric field of radioactive waste management. He assesses the safety of disposal sites a million years in the future and analyses how the Oklo reactors operated two billion years ago—which is often hard to distinguish from science fiction.

Ian's experience ensures sound backdrops to his hard science fiction. Adult action thrillers showcase the evolution of society in the face of major technological advances and a degrading natural environment. All extrapolations over the next century are credible, maybe frighteningly so, given their dystopian nature.

Previously published novels offer offbeat takes on the impact of the collapse of a future, even more ubiquitous, Internet and the emergence of artificial intelligence.

Enjoy more short stories and novels
from TWB Press

www.twbpress.com